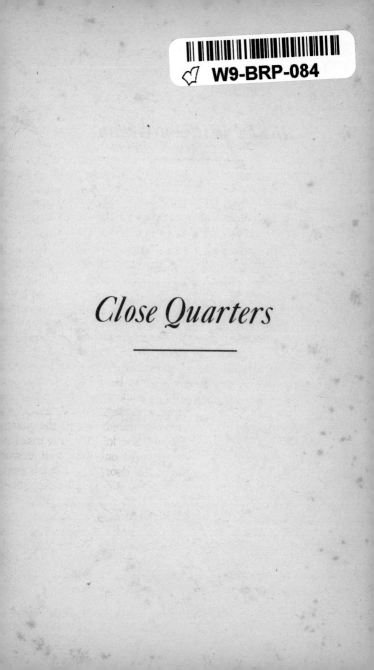

Close Quarters

Also by William Golding

Fiction

LORD OF THE FLIES

THE INHERITORS

PINCHER MARTIN

FREE FALL

THE SPIRE

THE PYRAMID

THE SCORPION GOD

DARKNESS VISIBLE

RITES OF PASSAGE

THE PAPER MEN

Essays

THE HOT GATES

A MOVING TARGET

Travel

AN EGYPTIAN JOURNAL

Play

THE BRASS BUTTERFLY

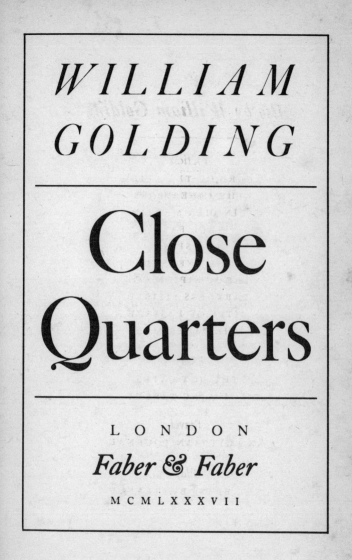

WILLIAM GOLDING

Close Quarters

LONDON

Faber & Faber

MCMLXXXVII

First published in 1987
by Faber and Faber Limited
3 Queen Square London WC1N 3AU
This continental paperback edition
first published in 1988

Printed in Great Britain by
Cox & Wyman Ltd, Reading, Berkshire
All rights reserved

British Library Cataloguing in Publication Data
Golding, William
Close quarters
I. Title
823'.914[F]   PR6013.035
ISBN 0-571-18090-6

Close Quarters

CLOSE QUARTERS

(1)

I signalized my birthday by giving myself a present since no one else seemed inclined to! I bought it, of course, from Mr Jones, the purser. As I emerged on deck with some relief from the fetor of the ship's bowels I met Charles Summers, my friend and the ship's first lieutenant. He laughed when he saw the manuscript book in my hand.

"The ship was aware, Edmund, that you had finished, that is, filled the book which was a present from your noble godfather."

"But how?"

"Oh, do not be surprised! Nothing can be hidden in a ship. But have you still more news for him?"

"This is not a continuation, but a new venture. When this is filled with an account of our voyage I mean to keep it for myself and no one else."

"There must be little of enough note for recording."

"On the contrary, sir, on the contrary!"

"More reasons for self-satisfaction?"

"And how am I to take that?"

"Why—elevate your nose as usual. Dear Edmund, if you only knew how maddeningly superior you can be—and now a writer into the bargain!"

I did not much care for his mixture of familiarity and amused irritation. For indeed I thought I had cured myself of a certain lofty demeanour, a consciousness of my own worth which had perhaps been too carelessly displayed in the earlier days of the voyage. It had gained me, among the common sea-men, the nickname of "Lord Talbot" though, of course, "mister" or "esquire" is all I am entitled to.

"I amuse myself. I pass the time. What else can a poor devil of a landsman do to occupy himself in a voyage from the top of the world to the bottom?"

"That is called folio size, is it not? You will need a great deal of adventure to fill it. The first one, for your godfather—"

"Colley, Wheeler, Captain Anderson—"

"And others. I wish sincerely that you will have much more difficulty in filling your second volume!"

"Your wish is granted here and now, for my head is empty. By the way—today is my birthday!"

He nodded gravely but said nothing and went on his way towards the forward part of our vessel. I sighed. I believe it has been the first time my birthday has gone unnoticed by all but myself! At home things would be different, with good wishes and presents. Here in this lumbering ship such modest entertainment, such pleasant customs go by the board.

I went to my "hutch" or cabin, that "little ease" which must serve me for sleep and privacy until we reach the Antipodes. I sat down in my canvas chair before my "writing-flap", my only desk, and cracked the folio open on it. The area was immense. If I bowed my head and peered at the blank surface—as I must, since so little light filters through the louvre in the door of my hutch—it seemed to spread in every direction until it was the whole of my world. I watched it, therefore, in the expectation that some material fit for permanence would appear—but nothing! It was only after a prolonged pause that I discovered my present stratagem and the full result of it in recording my own, surely temporary inadequacy. That unhappy shrimp of a man, Parson Colley, had nevertheless in his letter to his sister, as far as I could remember, unconsciously used the massive instrument of the English tongue with a dexterity which called up our ship and her people—I included—as if by magic! He had set her there, lolloping in the weather.

Yes, the weather, Edmund, the weather, you fool! Why do you not start with that? We have escaped from the *doldrums* at least. We were there too long for comfort. We have moved at last out of the fair weather of the equatorial regions and are now pushing south, the wind over our larboard bow so that there is once more a certain unsteadiness in the deck, a constant canting to the right to which I am now so accustomed I accept it and my limbs accept it as normal to living. The present weather is sharply defining our horizon for us in a dense blue which obeys Lord Byron's famous injunction and continues to roll on endlessly—such is the power of verse! I must try it some time. Sufficient and perhaps increasing wind (not, I seem to remember, included by his lordship) moves us slanting, or ought to but seems to have less effect on our vessel than it should. So much for the weather. Colley would have *integrated* it. But as far as I can see, it has no other effect than to cool our air slightly and set the ink in the well at a slight slant. Edmund, I adjure you! Be a writer!

But how?

There is an inevitable difference between this journal, meant for, for, I do not know for whom, and the first one meant for the eyes of a godfather who is less indulgent than I pretended. In that volume I had all my work done for me. By a remarkable series of strokes of fortune, Colley "willed himself to death" and "my servant" Wheeler drowned and the result was to fill my book! I cannot consult it, for it lies, all wrapped in brown paper, sewn in sailcloth, sealed and stowed away, in my bottom drawer. But I do remember writing towards the end of it that it had become some sort of a sea story. It was a journal that became a story by accident. There is no story to tell now.

Yesterday we saw a whale. Or rather we saw the plume of spray which rose where the creature was snorting, but the beast itself remained hidden. Lieutenant Deverel, that crony from whom to tell the truth I am anxious to detach myself, remarked that it looked for all the world like the strike of a cannon ball. At this Zenobia Brocklebank shrieked and besought him not to mention anything so frighteningly horrid, a display of proper female weakness—or the appearance of it—which enabled Deverel to move closer, take her unresisting hand and murmur some sort of comfort with a kind of echo of amatory matters in it. Miss Granham, our ex-governess, I remember, looked, if not daggers, penknives at least, and moved away to where her fiancé, Mr Prettiman, was extolling the social benefits of revolution to our marine artist, sodden Mr Brocklebank. All that on the poop under the eyes of Lieutenant Cumbershum who with young Mr Taylor had the watch! What else? This is small beer!

Yesterday there was part of a cable laid out in the waist, then wormed, parcelled and served for some mysterious operation of seamanship. It was the only thing to record but a damned dull sight.

What the devil! I need a hero whose career I may follow in volume two. Might it be our gloomy Captain Anderson? I do not think so. There is, for all his uniform, something indomitably unheroic about him. Charles Summers, my friend the first lieutenant? He is our Good Man and therefore only to be tragic if he falls from that small eminence which I do not expect or wish. The others, Mr Smiles, the remote sailing master, Mr Askew, the gunner, Mr Gibbs, the carpenter—why not our tradesman, Mr Jones, the purser? Oldmeadow, the Army officer with his file of greenclad men? I cudgel my brains, call Smollett and Fielding into the ring, ask their advice and find they have none for me.

I should perhaps tell the story of a young gentleman of much intelligence and more feeling than he was aware of who takes a voyage to the Antipodes where he is to assist the governor of the new colony with his undoubted talents for, for something or other. He, he—what? There is a woman in the fo'castle among the emigrants. Might not she be our heroine, a princess in disguise? Might not *he*, our hero, rescue her—but from what? Then there is Miss Brockle-bank of whom I do not desire to write and Mrs

Brocklebank with whom I am at present almost entirely unacquainted and who is far too young and
pretty to be tunbelly's wife.

Wanted! A hero for my new journal, a new heroine,
a new villain and some comic relief to ameliorate my
deep, deep boredom.

It will have to be Charles Summers after all. We at
least talk and do so with some regularity. Since as first
lieutenant he is generally in charge of the ship he
does not keep a watch. He seems to move about the
ship for something like eighteen hours in the twenty-
four and now knows the ship's company, let alone the
emigrants and the passengers individually by name.
I believe he also knows the fabric of the ship inch by
inch. His only break as far as I can see is for an
hour in the forenoon—perhaps from eleven to twelve
when he walks the deck like a man taking a constitu-
tional. Some of the passengers do likewise and I am
happy and really rather proud to say that Charles
commonly chooses me as his walking companion! A
pattern has settled into a custom. He and I walk
back and forth the length of the waist on the larboard
side of the ship, Mr Prettiman and his fiancée Miss
Granham do the same on the starboard side. By
common consent we do not walk as a group of four
but in two pairs. Thus just as they are turning to
come back from the break of the fo'castle so we are
turning to come back from the break of the aftercastle! As we move towards the midpoint the bulk
of the mainmast hides our two pairs from each other
so we do not have to raise our hats or incline the head
smilingly at each passing! Is that not trivially absurd?

Only the interposition of a lumpish column of wood
preserves us from having to employ all the actions
of landlubberly conduct!

I said as much to Charles the other forenoon and
he laughed.

"I had not considered the matter but I suppose it is
so; and a piece of neat observation!"

"The 'proper study of man' and most necessary to
one who intends to be a politician."

"You have your career charted?"

"Yes indeed. And more precisely than most men of
my years."

"You excite my curiosity."

"Why—I shall spend a few years—a very few
years—in the administration of the colony."

"May I be there to see!"

"Mark me, Mr Summers, in this century I am
convinced the civilized nations will more and more
take over the administration of the backward parts
of the world."

"And then?"

"Parliament. My godfather has what is commonly
called 'a rotten borough' in his pocket. It sends two
members to the house and the only electors are a
drunken shepherd and a cottager who spends the
weeks after an election in a state of indescribable
debauchery."

"Should you profit by such excess?"

"Well, there are difficulties. Our wretched estates
are heavily encumbered and since a seat in the house
is only tenable by a man of means I must pick up a
plum or two."

Charles laughed aloud, then stopped himself abruptly.

"I ought not to find that amusing, Edmund, but I do. A plum or two! And then?"

"Why—government! The cabinet!"

"What ambition!"

"You dislike that side of my character?"

Charles was silent for a while, then spoke heavily.

"I have no right to. I am just such a creature myself."

"You? Oh no!"

"In any event, I find you profoundly interesting. I hope sincerely that your career may prosper to your own satisfaction and the benefit of your friends. But does not the country begin to frown on 'rotten boroughs'? For is it not against reason and equity that a handful of English people should elect the assembly which will govern all?"

"Now there, Charles, I believe I may enlighten you! That apparent defect is the true genius of our system—"

"Oh no! It cannot be!"

"But, my dear fellow, Democracy is never and cannot be representation by everyone. What, sir, are we to give the vote to children, to men of no property? To the insane? To criminals in the common gaols? To women?"

"You had best not let Miss Granham hear you!"

"Indeed, I would not for the world denigrate that respectable lady. I concede the exception. Denigration? I would not dare!"

"Nor I!"

We laughed together. Then I resumed my explanation.

"In the best days of Greece voting was limited to a fraction of the population. Barbarians may elect their chieftains by acclaim and the thundering of swords on shields. But the more civilized a country is, the smaller is the number of people fitted to understand the complexities of its society! A civilized community will always find ways of healthfully limiting the electorate to a body of highly born, highly educated, sophisticated professional and hereditary electors who come from a level of society which was born to govern, expects to govern, and will always do so!"

But Charles was making quelling gestures with both hands. I believe my voice had indeed risen. He interrupted me.

"Edmund! Gently! I am not Parliament! You are orating. That time before Mr Prettiman vanished beyond the mainmast he was turning red in the face!"

I lowered my voice.

"I will moderate my voice but not my language. He is a theorist—if nothing worse! It is the common mistake of theorists to suppose a perfect scheme of government may be fitted over the poor, imperfect face of humanity! Not so, Mr Summers. There are circumstances in which only the imperfections of a contradictory and cumberous system such as ours will serve. Rotten boroughs for ever! But in the right hands, of course."

"Do I detect some of the elements of a projected maiden speech in the house?"

I felt a sudden warmth mantle my cheeks.

"How did you guess?"

Charles turned away for a moment and gave an admonition to a seaman who was idling with some twine, some grease, and a marlingspike. Then—

"But your personal life, Edmund—all that part which is not dedicated so straightforwardly to the service of your country?"

"Why—I suppose I shall live the way one lives! I shall have one day—may it be far off—to do something about the estates unless one of my young brothers can be induced to. I must own that my loftier flights into the future have seen me freeing the estates from their heavy load by"—here I did indeed laugh at the thought—"a gift from a grateful country! But you will think me a dreamer!"

Charles laughed too.

"There is no harm in that provided they are dreams of the future and not of the past!"

"My practical proposal, however, is no dream. At a suitable point in my career I shall marry—"

"Ah! I was wondering. May I ask if the young lady is already chosen?"

"How can that be? Do you think I propose to be Romeo to someone's Juliet? Give me ten years, then some lady perhaps ten or twelve years younger than myself, a young lady of family, wealthy, beautiful—"

"And at present in the nursery."

"Just so."

"I wish you joy."

I laughed.

"You shall dance at my wedding!"

CLOSE QUARTERS

There was a pause. Charles smiled no longer.
"I do not dance."

With a brief nod he went off, vanishing into the fo'castle. I turned to greet Mr Prettiman and his fiancée but saw them vanishing into the break of the quarterdeck. I returned to my hutch and sat before my writing-flap, thinking that this was a conversation I might retain in my journal. I thought, too, how likeable and intimate a friend Charles Summers had become.

All that was yesterday. What then this morning? Nothing has happened. I ate dull food, refused to drink since I drink too much, talked, or rather monosyllabled with Oldmeadow who cannot find employment for his men, *cut* Zenobia Brocklebank since she has made a habit of parleying with the common seamen—and found myself sitting once more in front of this vast white area with an empty head. Come to think of it I have one tedious matter to report. I have just walked again with Charles Summers on the deck. He said there was now more weight in the wind, to which I replied that I had not been able to detect any increase in our speed. He nodded.

"I know it," he said gravely. "There should be an increase but it is cancelled by the increase in our weed. We were rather too long for comfort in the doldrums."

I walked to the side and looked over the rail. The weed was visible, green hair. When we rolled there appeared further down a kind of darkness which suggested weed as long but of a different colour. Then we rolled back and the green locks spread on the surface again to be washed about then inclined all one way by our slight forward movement.

"Can you not get rid of the stuff?"

"If we were at anchor we might use the dragrope. We might lie up in some tidal creek, careen her and scrub her down."

"Are all ships as weedy in these waters?"

"Not the modern ships, up-to-date nineteenth-century vessels. They have coppered bottoms on which marine growths are slower to take hold."

"It is a great bore."

"So anxious to reach the Antipodes?"

"Time hangs heavy."

He smiled and went away. I reminded myself of my new employment, and came back to my hutch. There is this to be said about writing a journal which may well be read by no one but myself. I can decide that for myself! If I choose, I can be downright irresponsible! I do not have to look round me for witticisms which might entertain a godfather, or make sure that I present, as it were, my better profile like a bride sitting for her marriage portrait. I was, perhaps, too honest in the journal for my godfather and I have sometimes thought that instead of persuading him to think what a noble fellow I am, he may well have agreed with the literal meaning of my words and decided that I have shown myself unworthy of his patronage! The devil is in it if I can see a way out of that, for I cannot destroy my writing without destroying my godfather's present to me with all its

unnecessarily splendid binding. I have been a fool.
No. I have miscalculated.

Cumbershum and Deverel have urged Summers to
represent to Captain Anderson the advisability of
altering course towards the river Plate where we may
careen and rid us of weed. My informant was young
Mr Taylor, the more than ebullient midshipman who
sometimes attaches himself to me. Summers, however, will not do it. He knows that Anderson wishes
to make the whole voyage without visiting a port of
call. I have to own that Summers, good man though
he be and fine seaman though I am sure he is, does
not relish in any way differing from his captain. Mr
Taylor says that he refused them by pointing out
what this morning is unquestionably true—that the
wind has increased considerably and our speed is a
little increased in consequence. The wind is still on
the larboard bow, the horizon is a little dulled from
its former sharpness and we take spray aboard now
and then. All the ship's people and the passengers are
cheered by it. The ladies are positively glowing with
health and

(2)

It is necessary to suppose a space of some three days between that word with which SECTION ONE so inscrutably finishes and these I write today. I was interrupted. Ye gods, how my head aches, do I but turn my neck! There's no doubt I have had the devil of a thump, all unlooked for. I contrive to write in my bunk, for Phillips has given me a board to rest across my knees and done what he calls "chocking off" my back with an extra granite pillow or two. Fortunately, or unfortunately, I suppose I should say, the ship has little movement as far as I am concerned tho' the wind is pushing her back towards the doldrums, the devil take it all, twenty thousand times over! At this rate we shall reach the Antipodes when they are having their winter down there, a prospect I do not care for and neither do the seamen who have heard too much about the horrors of the Southern Ocean at that season! Summers came to visit me directly I was well enough to curse and told me with a painful smile that Captain Anderson refused the suggestion of the river Plate but had now conceded the possibility of calling at the Cape of Good Hope if we can get there.

"We are in some danger then?"

For a while he did not answer.

"A little. As ever. Do not, I beg of you—"

"Spread despondency among the other passengers."

He laughed at that.

"Come, you are better."

"If only I could make some connection between my tongue and the inside of my skull—do you know, Charles, I speak with the outside of myself?"

"It is the effect of concussion. You will be better presently. Only do not, I beg of you, perform any more acts of selfless heroism."

"You are roasting me."

"At all events, your head will not take any more cracks over it, let alone your spinal column."

"It is very true that I have a headache always on call, or on *tap* if you like and have only to move my neck so—ah, devil take it!"

He went away, and I set myself to the task of recording our adventure. I had been sitting at my writing-flap and idling with my pen, when the angle of the deck beneath my chair began to change. Since for days together we had made a dreary series of zigzags, or legs or beats or whatever the appropriate Tarpaulin is, I thought nothing of this at first. But then my posteriors (which have become a perfected seaman in their own right) felt the movement to be speedier than usual. Nor were there the usual concomitants of the operation such as boatswains' pipes, adjurations to the duty watch, leathery flapping of feet and the shivering of sails. There was instead a sudden and positive thunder from our canvas which ceased on the instant and with that cessation my perfected seaman informed me that our deck was tilting more and more rapidly, more urgently. I have become a writer; and my first movement was to jam

my pen in the holder and cork the ink bottle. By the
time I had done this I was dropped against my bunk
. . . there was noise enough now—shouts, whistles,
thumps and crashes—and screams from the next
hutch where my onetime inamorata, Zenobia, was
screaming in approximate unison with Mr Brocklebank's alleged wife. I scrambled up the deck, contrived to get my door open and went, spiderlike,
towards the daylight of the waist.

As they say in practically every travel book I have
ever read, what a sight now met my eyes, my blood
froze, my hair—and so on. The whole scene was
changed beyond recognition. What had been com-
paratively level planking was now sloped like the
pitch of a roof and increasing fast towards the per-
pendicular. I saw, with the kind of cool reason which
stemmed from my own helplessness, that we were
lost. We were going over, capsizing. All our sails were
bulging the wrong way, all the wrong ropes were taut
and all the right ones flogging like the ties of a rick
cover come apart in a gale. Our lee bulwarks were
nearing the sea. Then there came—not so much
from "up there" as "out there"—a slow grinding and
tearing and splintering. Somewhere forrard, the huge
beams that look so small and are called "topmasts"
swung sideways and hung down in a positive knitting
of ropes and torn canvas. On the windward bulwarks
there were a few men struggling now with ropes. One,
near the break of the fo'castle, I saw striking out with
an axe. Above me I saw what I still find difficult to
credit: the ship's wheel spun so that the two men

holding it were flipped away like raindrops, the one
farthest from me into the air and over the wheel to
land somewhere on the other side of it, the nearer
man flung down against the deck as if struck by
lightning. With the spinning of the wheel there came
a most dreadful thudding from the rudder. I saw
Captain Anderson himself let a rope go from a belaying pin and fling himself recklessly to haul on
another . . . I got there myself and hauled too. I
felt the rope move with our combined strength but—
as I am told—the rope he had flung loose was flailing
in that area, for I felt a terrible blow on the top of
my head and back. I will not subscribe to the common-
place of "From that moment I knew no more" but
certainly, what I did know was confused and hazy
enough. It seems to me that somehow I became en-
tangled on the deck with young Mr Willis. Apart
from the devil of a pain in my back and a loud singing
in my head I was almost comfortable. That was Mr
Willis, of course, on whom I was lying. In any other
circumstances I would not have chosen or endured
Mr Willis as a mattress, but as it was I felt a positive
anger at the ineffectual efforts the boy made to get out
from under me. Then someone pulled at him and in
a trice I had no pillow but a deck I now felt to be
level once more. I opened my eyes and stared up.
There were white clouds and blue sky. There was the
mizzenmast, its sails not furled but bunched up
against the yards. Further forrard, part of the mainmast still stood and with the lower sails also bunched
but with the topmast hanging down in the kind of

tangle for which seamen have a number of expressive
terms. The fore-topmast was down too, but that had
fallen free and lay partly outboard and partly on the
fo'castle across the capstan. I lay, waiting for my
various pains to subside. I could hear, but distantly,
Captain Anderson giving a continual stream of orders.
I have never understood him so little nor liked him so
well. His voice resounded with calmness and confidence. Then, believe it or not, there came a moment
among a whole volley or broadside of orders when he
paused and remarked in a more localized and conversational tone of voice: "Look to Mr Talbot there."
What a tribute! Phillips leaned over me but I was not
to be outdone in nobility.

"Let me be, fellow. There must be others in a far
worse case than I."

I am thankful to say that this had no effect on
Phillips, who was endeavouring to insert some rela-
tively soft material between my head and the deck.
I felt a little better for it. The scarlet pulsation behind
my forehead faded to pink.

"What the devil happened?"

There was a pause. Then—

"I can't say, sir. Directly we was on an even keel I
came to look for you immediate."

I flexed one leg then the other. They seemed un-
injured, as did my arms. The rope had done no more
than scorch my palms a trifle. It seemed that I had
got off from the catastrophe whatever it was with no
more than a sore head and a shaking.

"You should be looking to the ladies, Phillips."

He made no reply but inserted yet another fold of
material between my head and the deck. I opened
my eyes again. The hanging topmast was already being
lowered inch by inch. Sailors were crowded among
what was left of our rigging. I lifted my head painfully and was just in time to see the broken fore-
topmast brought inboard and freed from the capstan.
It was splintered and projected a yard or two over the
waist. Above me the gaff of the driver had been
lowered on its boom. I remembered the towering
sails that had bulged over me as she put her bulwarks
down till the sea foamed over them.

"What happened?"

"A ship full of fucking soldiers if you don't mind
me saying so, sir."

I felt a great disinclination to move my body and
did no more than raise my head further to look round.
The result was a stab of the most excruciating pain
which I have ever experienced—a kind of bright
dagger of it thrust through my head. I gave up any
further attempt and lay still. Summers and the captain
were speaking fluent Tarpaulin with much earnestness.
If the gudgeons were not too badly drawn—if she was
not too severely wrung. Experimentally I moved my
eyes so that I could see the two officers and found
the action not accompanied by much pain. I heard
what they said. Mr Talbot had most handsomely
endeavoured to help the captain at the maincourse
mizzen buntline until rendered unconscious by a flying sheet. Mr Summers would have expected no less
of me. Mr Summers begged to be allowed to con-

tinue his duties, which request was granted. I was
about to try sitting up when the captain spoke again.

"Mr Willis."

Mr Willis was standing by the abandoned wheel
which was turning gently, this way and that. I was
about to point out this awful neglect to the captain
when two seamen came bounding up the ladder and
laid hands on the wheel from either side.

"Mr Willis!"

Normally Mr Willis, one of our midshipmen, is of
a pale complexion. Either the blow to my head had
confused my eyes or Willis had in reality turned
bright green.

"How many times do I have to address you before
I get an answer?"

Poor young Willis got his lips together, then opened
them. His knees, I believe, were supporting each other.

"Sir."

"You were on watch."

"Sir, Mr, sir, he, Mr—"

"I know all about 'he', Mr Willis. You were on
watch."

Nothing emerged from Mr Willis's mouth but a
faint clucking. Captain Anderson's right arm swung
round and his palm struck the boy's face with a loud
crack! He seemed to leap into the air, travel sideways
and collapse.

"Get up, sir, when I am talking to you! Do you
see those topmasts, you damned young fool? Get up!
Have you any idea at all how much canvas has flogged
into ribbons, how much hemp there is now good for

nothing but stuffing fenders? By God, sir, when we have a mizzen masthead again you shall spend the rest of the commission there!"

"Sir, Mr, Mr—"

"Get him, Willis, do you hear? I want him standing in front of me and I want him *now*!"

I had not thought that so much anger and menace could be expressed in a single syllable. It was Captain Anderson's famous roar, an awful sound, and I felt that to lie still with my new reputation for valour was best. I kept my eyes closed and it was for this reason that I heard the following conversation though I saw neither party to it. There were stumbling steps, then Deverel's voice at once slurred and breathless.

"Damme, what's the boy done now, curse him!"

Anderson answered him angrily but in a low voice as if he did not wish the conversation to be overheard.

"Mr Deverel, you were on watch."

Deverel replied in as low a voice.

"There was young Willis—"

"Young Willis, by God, you fool!"

"I'll not—"

"You'll listen. There's a standing order against leaving a midshipman on watch at sea."

Deverel's voice rose to a sudden shout.

"Everyone does it! How else are the brats to learn?"

"So the officer of the watch can sneak off and swill himself into a wardroom stupor! I got on deck while she was still shivering and by God you weren't there! You come stumbling, you, you sot—"

"I'll not be called that by you or any man! I'll see you—"

Anderson raised his voice.

"Lieutenant Deverel. Your absence from the deck when you were on duty was criminal neglect. You may consider yourself under open arrest."

"Then sod you, Anderson, you sodding by-blow!"

There was a pause in which I did not dare even to breathe. Anderson spoke coldly.

"And, Mr Deverel, you are forbidden drink."

Phillips and Hawkins, the captain's servant, got me back to my bunk. I feigned as much unconsciousness as I could from policy. There must now be, I thought, a court-martial and I wanted to be no part of it as witness or anything else. I allowed myself to be revived with brandy, then grasped Phillips's sleeve to detain him.

"Phillips. Does my back bleed?"

"Not as I've seen, sir—"

"I was struck over the head and shoulders with a flying rope and rendered wholly unconscious. I feel cut to the very bone."

"Oh," said he, with great cheerfulness, "you was struck with a rope's end—what we call a starter, sir. It's what the last man down gets across his back or his bum, begging your pardon, sir. That don't hardly more than bruise, sir."

"What happened to us?"

"When, sir?"

"The accident, man, our broken masts—my aching head!"

So Phillips told me.

Taken aback. I was taken aback, thou wast, he, she or it was taken aback. I remember my mother telling her woman—"but when I heard what the creature wanted for a yard of the stuff, exquisite though it was, I declare to you, Forbes, I was quite taken aback!" That, from my dear mother who allowed me to travel on the Continent during the late peace but cautioned me against going too near the fence round the vessel! What a language is ours, how diverse, how direct in indirection, how completely, and, as it were, unconsciously metaphorical! I was reminded of my years of turning English verse into Latin or Greek and the necessity of finding some plain statement which would convey the sense of what the English poet had wrapped in the brilliant obscuration of figures! Of all human activities how we have chosen time and again to turn to our experience of the sea! To be three sheets in the wind, to sail too near the wind, to recognize someone by the cut of his jib, to be brought up all standing, to be adrift, to be on the rocks, to be half-seas over, to be sunk without trace—good Lord, we might fill a book with the effect on our language of the sea affair! Now here was metaphor come across at its origin. We, our ship, had been taken flat aback! Lying in my bunk I pictured it all. Deverel had nipped below for a dram, leaving the half-witted Willis in charge of the ship. Good God, as I thought of it my head throbbed anew. My country, said I to myself as I tried to attain to a state of good humour—my country might have suffered a notable deprivation. I might have drowned! So, with Willis on watch there had come a change, a confusion of the waves on the leeward bow, some foam, a squall, the water cuffed rapidly with two invisible hands that came even more rapidly nearer—those two fellows at the wheel would glance from the shivering leach of the main to the compass—glance round perhaps for Deverel and find only Willis with his mouth hanging open—would look for authority and find none—had they borne down on the wheel and brought her bows round to meet the squall they might fear flogging for it—so they did nothing because Willis did nothing and the squall struck into the wrong side of our sails which being sheeted home stopped her dead, then bore her back and down, sails bellied the wrong way, bulwarks forced down till the sea lipped over them, our rudder working in reverse!

So, while the crew laboured to undo the work which Deverel and Willis had achieved between them by a few seconds' inattention, I lay and waited for the throbbing in my head to cease which it partly did at length but only when I had got to sleep. The last thing I remember thinking before I slept was what a wealth of unexpected experience had come to me through that simple phrase "taken aback!"

CLOSE QUARTERS

(3)

But strangely, once in my bunk I felt myself compelled to stay there and that not just for an hour or
two but days and nights. Summers sometimes brought
me news of our state. We were now being borne back
with an awful inevitability into the doldrums again:
for if our vessel when fully rigged could make little
way against the wind, in her crippled state she was
helpless. Nor could we hope to set the same full sails
as before. We lacked the spars, said Summers. And
the reduction in sail area was more than equal to the
improvement made by the scrubbing he was now
able to give to that fringe of weed all round us at the
waterline. It was another of those metaphors perhaps,
a "set back". Three more days passed before I was
able to get up for more than the most necessary of
purposes. It was a tottering Edmund who at last made
his way into the waist. We were, I found at once,
back in a wilderness of heat, stillness and mist. Our
very bowsprit was out of sight and if I was able to
see the tops of our masts it was only because they
were now lower than before. The setting up of new
and temporary topmasts, as Summers assured me, was
a business which was taxing the resources of the ship
both in timber and muscle power. Meantime we were
helpless.

The fourth day, however, saw me more nearly recovered, and we soon had affairs that put all thought
of soreness out of my head. I was awakened by Phillips

and grunted him away even after I had heard him pour
the water into my canvas basin. The air was close and
seemed as humid and tepid as the water. As I rose
more nearly to the surface of awareness I sadly recalled the wettest and greyest days of winter—rain,
hail, snow, sleet—anything but this idling and crowded
monotony! I was, not to put too fine a point on it,
searching in my mind for any good reason why I
should get out of my bunk at all when I heard a distant cry. I could not distinguish the words but they
did not seem to come from the level of the deck.
Moreover, that cry was followed by a shouted hail
from nearly over my head, and another distant reply
to it. I heard a rumbling roar from the quarterdeck
which could only be Anderson himself, in his customary mood of belligerent admonition. Clearly there
was a change in our circumstances and it could only
be for the better. Wind, perhaps! I got myself out
of my bunk with some effort and I was already in
shirt and pantaloons when I heard a most extraordinary hubbub from the passengers all crowding
through the lobby. I had eased myself into my coat
when, with only the most cursory of taps, Deverel
flung the door of my hutch open. But this was no
longer the stiff and remote man consumed inwardly
by the fires of his own shame and resentment! His
eyes sparkled, his face, his whole bearing bespoke
pleasure and animation. I saw to my astonishment
that he held his scabbarded sword in his left hand.

"Talbot, old fellow! By God, Talbot! I have a way
out of my difficulties! Come with me!"

"I was about to go on deck. But what is it?"

"Why, man, did you not hear? A sail!"

"The devil! Let us hope she is one of ours!"

"Where is your spirit, man? They spied her royals and they are white as a lady's kerchief! She is an enemy, depend on it!"

"Summers promised us the French were quite beat down—"

"Oh, that! Why, did you expect a fleet action? But a single ship—Boney may have sent a flyer to intercept us—but Frog, damned Yankee, Dutchman is all one—a bloody battle pays all debts—lucky at women and war, that's your honourable John!"

"This may advance your career, Deverel, and I am happy for you—but as for me—the devil take all Frenchmen!"

Deverel had not waited for my last words and I must own they were not in the heroic vein. But freshly out of my bunk and hardly healed of a sore head—a man who could immediately act the hero at such a moment would be a veritable Nelson. However, I recollected myself and made my way into the waist. Our passengers were grouped, or I might say huddled, against the break of the poop. The emigrants were similarly huddled against the break of the fo'castle. The silence was complete in our universe which the mist reduced to no more than a portion of our ship. Summers stood on the poop with Cumbershum. Captain Anderson was leaning over the rail of the quarterdeck and listening to Cumbershum who was speaking in what for him were moderate tones.

"The man is a fool, sir, and cannot properly indicate a bearing. I have sent Mr Taylor aloft with instructions to say nothing but point at her if he should get a glimpse."

"She gave no indication of having seen us?"

"No, sir. But with two topmasts down there is some chance of us avoiding her."

"Avoiding her, Mr Cumbershum? I do not like that word 'avoiding'. I shall not avoid her, sir. If we should come together and she is an enemy, I shall fight."

"Of course, sir."

"Mr Summers—we have six great guns on either beam. Can we man them all with seasoned men?"

"No, sir. Hardly one side, in fact, not with the boats in the water at stem and stern and parties on deck to repel boarders. I am having the nets brought up now, sir. But for the rest—Mr Taylor is signalling."

Mr Taylor was visible above us in the mist. He clung to a quite indescribable jumble at the top of the mainmast. Captain Anderson peered into the binnacle.

"Southeast by east a half south."

"With respect, sir, from here Mr Taylor appears to be pointing southeast by east dead."

"Boats in the water, Mr Summers. Then bring her round. I think we might prolong our period of preparation by towing away nor'west by west."

"Debatable, sir."

"The merest cat's paw could throw all. No, Mr Summers. Bring her round."

"Aye aye, sir. Mr Deverel—"

The orders followed thick and fast. I could not follow the tenth of them. I heard the ladies instructed as to the way down to the orlop deck and told they must retire there immediately if so commanded. They seemed to be quite extraordinarily composed. Miss Granham looked capable of repelling boarders with her expression. Mr Prettiman, for an avowed Republican if not Jacobin, had an air of indignant truculence which might stem from sheer wonder as to what his attitude should be. Had I not been depressed and irritated by this possibly quick interruption and even termination of the career of Edmund Talbot, I should have liked to put the question to him. But there was no talk among us. We stood dumb, then by common consent drifted back to the passenger saloon where there was, I observed with interest, some slight consumption of wine before the meal as well as during it. I endeavoured to put off my own weakness and recurrent pain in order to raise the spirits of the company by declaring that since two ships in such an ocean would have difficulty in finding each other intentionally there was absolutely no prospect of us coming together by accident. But if we did, said I, why then we must fight; and I hereby lift my glass in a toast to victory! But never was there a sadder and less martial gathering! All that happened was that little Pike flung down his knife and fork and burst into tears.

"My children, oh, my children! Little Arabella! Poor Phoebe!"

His wife laid her hand on his shoulder to comfort him. I spoke to him bluffly, as man to man.

"Come, Pike, never fear, man! We are in this together and shall give a good account of ourselves! As for your little girls, be easy—they are far too young for the French!"

I must own that this last remark was unfortunate in its implication. Mrs Pike burst into noisy sobs. Zenobia and Mrs Brocklebank shrieked in unison. Miss Granham laid down her knife and fork and fixed me with eyes of stone.

"Mr Talbot," she said. "You have excelled yourself."

"I only mean—"

But Prettiman was speaking.

"Do not believe the stories that are so current concerning the behaviour of the French, sir. They are as civilized as we. We may expect to be treated with the same and indeed more generosity and liberality than we should treat them!"

"Are we to stand about and be herded like sheep? Mr Bowles, you have some experience in the law, I believe."

"A solicitor's clerk, sir."

"May we civilians not fight?"

"I had considered the matter. I believe we passengers may 'run up a gun', as it is called, which entails hauling on a rope. We could plead compulsion. But seen on deck with sword and pistol in hand and we are legally entitled to have our throats cut."

"You are matter-of-fact," said I. "You might even be called cold-blooded."

"There is a way out of it, sir. I have considered that too. Passengers could volunteer, be sworn in, be en-

tered on the ship's books, as it is called. I am not
certain what the situation would be over naval pay in
that event."

"A glass of wine with you, Mr Bowles! You show
us all where our duty lies."

Miss Granham was pleased to smile her Minerva's
moonlit smile on me.

"A noble resolve, Mr Talbot. I am sure I speak for
the ladies in saying that we are all much easier in our
minds for it."

There were noises of agreement and some laughter.
But then her fiancé, the comic Prettiman, cried out
above it with the passionate voice which often rises
from his involvement with the philosophy of government.

"No, no, no! With respect, Miss Granham—Mr
Talbot, how can you volunteer before you know what
enemy we face? Suppose that ship to be no cruel
emissary of a tyrant but one that has thrown off his
yoke and now serves the land of liberty itself? Suppose
she is from the United States of America?"

"What does that matter? We are at war with
America!"

There was a babble of argument.

"Will you volunteer, Mr Bowles?"

"On terms, Mr Talbot."

"I must own to finding the prospect of engaging
with a Yankee ship less exhilarating than battle with
the French. After all, the Yankees are our own men—
what the devil! That confounded rascal Paul Jones
had more British seamen in his ship than American!"

"And the Dutch?"

"Let them all come. We shall make a notable defence. You, Mr Bowles, will shed any blood provided the agreement is precise. Mr Prettiman will aid us against the French or Dutch or pirates or even slavers though he will spare any American who should be rash enough to come in his way."

There was, as I had hoped, renewed laughter at this. But it was interrupted from a most unexpected source. Little Pike leapt to his feet and positively bawled at me as if he had fallen into the hysterics.

"How can you joke so? What does it matter what ship is out there hidden in the mist except that she has guns and may shoot them at us? I will fight as well as any man here whatever his degree. But I will not fight for my country! I am leaving it! I will not fight for my ship or my king or my captain. But I will fight against any ship and any country in the world in defence of my, my family—"

He burst into noisy sobs which were only too audible in the silence which had fallen as he spoke. Miss Granham stretched out a hand to him, then took it back again. Mrs Pike pressed his hand against her cheek. He sat down and his sobs died away but slowly. I believe most people had their eyes fixed on their plates at this most un-English display of emotion. I thought it high time we came down from our flights of martial fancy and hysterics. Exhausted as I was, I felt it my duty to persevere.

"Come," said I. "Let us consider the situation. There may be a ship, her sails seen for a few seconds in the mist. Most likely she is not concerned with us. Most likely she has not seen us. After all, our topmasts are down. If she sees us—why, we are a Royal Navy ship of the line to all appearances, the most feared, the most fearful of all the engines of destruction in this modern century! Believe me, the chances of an engagement are remote. If I myself have seemed thoughtlessly exhilarated by the prospect of battle, I beg the pardon of those of our company who are responsible for more lives than their own. But depend upon it. A thousand to one we shall neither meet nor see that ship again."

"I fear it is not so."

I looked up, startled, my head again stabbed with a dagger of pain. Summers stood just inside the door, hat in hand.

"Ladies and gentlemen, for all Mr Talbot's laudable efforts to calm your natural apprehensions, I fear it is not so. That ship, whatever she is, is becalmed as we are. In a prolonged calm, I mean of days or even weeks, ships are drawn together by the mutual attraction of heavy objects when nothing holds them apart but a smooth and readily divided fluid. If the wind does not get up we shall be drawn together until we lie side by side."

Now the silence was deadly.

"Charles, I do not find this credible."

"It is true, nevertheless. Captain Anderson believes that you are better able to conduct yourselves with propriety if the plain facts are laid before you. We have as you know sighted, or rather glimpsed, a ship

which may or may not have sighted us. She may be
French, sent to intercept us—"

Brocklebank interrupted him.

"How the devil would they know?"

Summers looked at me.

"Depend upon it," said I, "their Ministry of Marine
will know as much about us as we do!"

"The French then," said Bowles. "Boney must have
designs of conquest on the Antipodes!"

"He's too busy in Russia for that," said I. "What
about the Yankees, Charles?"

"All we are sure of is that those white sails cannot
be British."

"What are we to do then? The gentlemen here have
engaged themselves to help you in what way they can."

Summers smiled.

"I expected no less and will provide you all with
suitable employment. Mr Askew, the gunner, is rigging some very pretty fireworks with quick match and
small parcels of gunpowder. Together with our few
great guns they may give the appearance of a full
broadside from the engaged side of our ship provided
the enemy sees us dimly through the mist. We must
hope that one thump will make him tow off, for we
must look ugly enough."

"But if she sees us only dimly through the mist?
And darkness is falling!"

"How will she know we are an enemy? She will burn
recognition lights and wait for our answer. If her lights
do not appear in our secret list we shall answer with
our broadside."

"And then?"

"One broadside and Captain Anderson can never be accused of giving up the ship without a fight."

"The devil he cannot!"

"Be easy, Edmund. We are a ship of His Majesty's Navy and shall do what we may."

He smiled round at everyone, put on his hat and withdrew. Little Pike, his sobs assuaged, positively snarled across the table at me.

"So much for your attempt at heartening us, Mr Talbot!"

"Summers has gone a better way about it. I have no sword. Have you a sword, Bowles?"

"I? Good God no, sir. The ship will have a supply, I don't doubt. They will be cutlasses perhaps."

"Mr Brocklebank, you are, forgive me, of a full habit. Will you descend with the ladies?"

"I have an inclination to remain on deck, sir. After all, though I have on numerous occasions depicted the war at sea, I have never before had an opportunity of taking notes in the midst of a battle. You will see me, sir, when the shot is flying, seated on my camp stool and observing with a trained eye whatever is worthy of notice. To take an example, I have often enquired of military men—I include naval in the term military— have often enquired precisely how a cannon ball in flight is visible to the naked eye. Obviously the more nearly the ball is flying directly towards the observer the more slowly it will appear to move. We could not be better situated for the observation. I only hope darkness is not too far advanced before we are engaged."

"On your reckoning, sir, the most accurate idea of

a cannon ball is to be formed by the man who has his head knocked off by it."

"If it comes, why it comes. 'Ripeness is all'—indeed if I may refer to my own case, overripeness is all. What is life, sir? A voyage where no one, despite all claims to the contrary—we know not what if you follow me—"

It was clear that Mr Brocklebank was approaching his customary state of inebriety. I stood up therefore and bowed to the company. The oddest thought had come to me. I might in actual fact be killed! I had only now realized it which may seem strange to anyone who has not been in a like case. Or say I had realized it and not realized it. But now the knowledge was—oppressive.

"I must ask the company to excuse me. I have letters to write."

(4)

It was a confusion of my mental state that led me to
say something as simple as that when in fact my abrupt
departure needed an elaborate explanation if I had
hoped to be understood. The truth was that all the
excitement attendant on our sighting of a strange ship
had made my head begin to ache even more than it
had previously from the blow with that flying sheet. I
had now foreseen a danger to my reputation and was
confusedly determined to forestall it. If this acute
discomfort in my skull was allowed to increase or even
remain as it was I would be in no state to face an
enemy! Imagine me, among the gentlemen volunteers
whining that I would like to take part in our defence
but was quite incapacitated by a migraine and must
join the ladies in the orlop! I got Phillips to bring me
something for an aching head and took it in my bunk
where to my astonishment I found it was yet more of
the purser's paregoric so that though mercifully I
stopped myself from swigging the lot when I found
what it was, my first sip was enough to put the ache in
my head about six inches outside it and up to the left
as I should judge. It produced in me too a desire and
ability to dwell with Fancy and in a few minutes I
found myself composing (but in my head and bunk)
letters to my mother and father and even to my young
brothers which I still think were pieces of prose with a
noble ring about them. But the most natural and at
the same time most dangerous effect of the drug was

(with an enemy hovering ever nearer us in the mist) to
send me fast asleep! I woke with a start from an unpleasant dream in which poor Colley in a supernatural
way only too familiar in that state had summoned the
enemy and was bringing it hourly nearer. I fell out of
my bunk rather than climbed out of it, my headache
subdued but my confusion complete. I rushed into
the waist. At first I thought the mist was enfolding us
more closely but then saw it was the swift approach of
the tropic night. Our ladies were grouped by the break
of the poop where I suppose they might most immediately descend to the orlop. They were staring
towards the larboard beam. Above them, on the
quarterdeck, some of Oldmeadow's soldiers were
mustered with the officer himself. Forrard, I could
make out in the gloom, parties mustered on the fo'-
castle. The emigrant women were gathered at its break.
All was deep silence.

Deverel came striding aft at the head of a group of
emigrants. His shoes made the only sound in the ship.
He was in a state of high if suppressed excitement. He
carried his scabbarded sword in his left hand. He was
shivering slightly.

"Why, Edmund! I thought you was mustered at the
guns!"

"Devil take it, I fell asleep."

He laughed aloud.

"That's cool! Well done, old fellow—but the others
are all gone down. Good luck to you!"

"To you too—"

"Oh, I—why just now I would give my right arm
for a bloody battle!"

CLOSE QUARTERS

He passed on, bounding up the ladder to the poop. I made my way down the contrary one to the cluttered gundeck.

Here at once a most unfortunate fact became plain. I was too tall for the gundeck. It had been designed for a company of dwarfs, miners perhaps, and I could not stand upright in it. I waited therefore to be directed. The gundeck was not much dimmer than the upper deck, for all the ports were open. Our six great guns were in position but their tackles not yet run up. There was a crowd round them but facing inboard where our commissioned gunner, Mr Askew, was pacing up and down as he addressed the company. He wore a belt with two pistols stuck in it.

"Now pay attention," he said, "particularly those what have never seen this done before. You have now seen the guns loaded and primed. Should we need to have a reload you will leave it to them that knows the business. You gentlemen and emigrants will lay your hands to such ropes as the captains of guns may direct and when he says 'Haul!' "—and here Mr Askew's voice rose to what can only be called a suppressed roar —"you will haul till your guts fall out. I want to see your guts strung out there and there and there and there and there and there! And you will be silent the first time you run up the guns because Mr Summers has directed us to be as quiet as little mice so as the Frogs don't know we are coming. So"—and his voice sank to a whisper—"when you have run the guns out silent you will pick your guts up, put 'em back, and stand waiting. If we should open fire you will see them gun trucks run back so fast you can't see 'em move! I have seen gun trucks there and I have seen gun trucks back there but I have never seen 'em halfway, gentlemen, they moves so quick. So you better not be lounging behind them or the Frogs when they come aboard of us will think you are what they calls *confiture*. Jam, gentlemen. Jam."

Little Pike put up his hand as if he were still at school.

"Won't the enemy be firing by then?"

"How do I know, sir, and what do we care? When fire is opened things is different, oh, you have no idea, sir, how different things is! It's very queer how different things is once a gun has been fired as they say in anger. So then you have the full permission of His Majesty the King, God bless him, to shout and yell and swear and shit yourselves and do what you like so long as it's noisy and you haul your guts in and out when told to."

"Good God."

Mr Askew resumed in a conversational tone.

"It's all flannel, of course. The Frogs don't scare so easy as you gentlemen may think. Howsomever we must play our game as long as we can. So if we have to fight and if any volunteer should feel that the other side of the ship is cooler like and just a little farther off from the enemy, these two little fire irons in my belt are loaded. So now, my heroes, run up them guns!"

The next few moments for me were complicated and infuriating. The man whom I supposed to be the captain of the nearest gun pointed to the end of a rope which projected behind Bowles who was the hindmost

of the four volunteers holding it. I had no sooner
crouched close when the captain of the gun roared
again, the volunteers leapt and Bowles struck me, cannoned into me so that I reeled two paces then fell, my
head once more striking the deck so concussively that
the whole world was obscured for a moment by a
brilliant display of lights. I struggled to get up and
heard, as far off, Mr Askew addressing me.

"Now, now, Mr Talbot, sir, where was you going?
Had we been in action I might have been forced to
put a pellet in your head, you come so close to the
mid-point."

The pain and the sense of having made myself a
common mock was too much to bear. I leapt to my
feet—and struck my head a second and even more
shattering blow on the underside of the upper deck.
This time I saw no lights and knew nothing until
through a dizzying sickness I heard roaring laughter
being shouted down by Mr Askew.

"Now then, you buggers, belay that and stand to!
That was a hard knock the poor gentleman took and
as stout a heart and head as there is in the ship I don't
doubt. God knows how much the beams is wounded
on their underside. Half the deck planking must be
started. Silence I said! How is it with you now, sir?"

I am sorry to say my only reply was a rehearsal of all
the imprecations I could muster. Blood was trickling
down my face. I sat up and the gunner held my arm.

"Easy does it, Mr Talbot. The gundeck is no place
for you. Why, with Billy Rogers and Mr Oldmeadow
you must be the three tallest men in the ship. You'll

do better on deck, sir, where the Frogs can get an eyeful of you all bloody and glaring. Keep low as you go, sir. Handsomely! A round of applause, my lads, for a gamecock of the afterguard!"

I did not know that fury could overcome dizziness and sickness so soon. I staggered up the ladder. The first person—by his voice—to notice me was Deverel.

"What the devil? Edmund old fellow! You are our first casualty!"

"I am too tall for the gundeck, God curse it! Where are the ladies?"

"Down in the orlop."

"Thank God for that at least. Deverel, give me a weapon—anything!"

"Have you not had enough? Where it isn't bloody, your face is corpse white."

"I am coming to. A weapon for the love of God! A meat axe—sledge hammer—anything. I will engage to carve and eat the first Frenchman I come across!"

Deverel laughed aloud, then caught himself up. He was shivering with excitement.

"Spoken like a true Briton! Will you board with me?"

"Anything."

"Mr Summers, sir, a weapon for my latest recruit!"

Someone put a cutlass in his free hand. He tossed it, caught the blade and presented the hilt to me.

"Here you are, sir. The plain seaman's guide to advancement. Can you use it?"

For answer I made the three sabre cuts then saluted him. He saluted back.

"Well enough, Edmund. But the point is queen, remember. Join the band of brothers!"

I followed him to the poop where Mr Brocklebank sat in the gloom on his camp stool, an unopened portfolio on his knees. His head was on his chest or perhaps I should say the upper part of his stomach. His hat was over his eyes. Above him on the quarterdeck the captain was now addressing Summers in a low and furious tone.

"Is this the silence I ordered, Mr Summers? Did I give you directions at the top of my voice? I command silence and am answered by a gale, a positive hurricane of laughter, orders shouted, conversations—is this a ship, sir, or a bedlam?"

"I am sorry for it, sir."

Old Rumbleguts subsided a little.

"Very well, sir. You may proceed with your duties."

Summers put his hat on and turned away. Captain Anderson went to the rail and peered down at the lighted binnacle.

"Mr Summers, she has drifted off half a point to the norrard."

Summers ran to the after rail and spoke down to the boat idling under our stern.

"Williams, bring her stern across half a point to starboard and roundly!"

He turned back. My eyes were full of water. I was still dazed and my head ached confoundedly. A settled rage had converted me from my, dare I say, usual calculating attitude to one of wishing for nothing so much as the opportunity to vent it on someone

physically! I glanced round and saw that the quarterdeck was full. Some of Oldmeadow's men knelt by
the larboard rail with muskets at the ready. I could
just see that the waist was lined with men holding
pikes to jab off any fool so thick-witted as to climb
into our netting. In fact the whole of the ship's length
on the larboard side was in a state of defence. I had
the ridiculous thought that perhaps the nameless ship
drifting inexorably towards us would after all approach
from our starboard and completely defenceless side so
that Captain Anderson would have to fire his great
guns at nothing if he wished to be credited with an
attempt at defence.

But Deverel was speaking or rather, since we were
so near the captain, muttering in my ear.

"Now, old fellow, you'll follow me close. You'll
have to scramble, d'you see? Wait till Oldmeadow's
men have fired though or you'll get lead through you.
Don't forget your boots."

"My boots, Jack?"

"Kick 'em in the balls, it's as good as anything.
Mind your own. Go low with the point! But it'll be all
over in seconds one way or another. Nobody goes on
fighting—that's only in books and the gazette."

"The devil."

"If you're alive after one minute you'll be a hero."

"The devil."

He turned from me as he spoke and whispered into
the crowding men.

"Are you all ready?"

The answer was a kind of muted growl and with it

there blew a thick waft of an aroma that came near to making me fall. It was rum and I made a mental note never to go into the commonest kind of danger without my hunting flask filled to the stopper. I was far, far too sober for this escapade, and the dullness of paregoric was fading.

"How d'you think it'll go, Jack?"

He breathed in my ear. "Death or victory."

I heard Summers speaking to the captain. "All is ready, sir."

"Very good, Mr Summers."

"Might I suggest that some heartening message should be passed among the various groups of men at their stations, sir?"

"Why, Mr Summers, they have had their rum!"

"Trafalgar, sir."

"Oh well, Mr Summers, if you think it proper, have them reminded of the unforgettable signal."

"Very good, sir."

"And, Mr Summers."

"Sir?"

"Remind them that with the way the war is going this may well be our last opportunity of prize money."

Mr Summers touched his hat. The men on the quarterdeck clearly being seized of his information, he stepped down the ladder and disappeared in the gloom. I heard a succession of noises, that same muted growl spreading from the waist and then forrard to the fo'castle. Heroics and rum! The thought of that combination made me a little less of a madman and more aware of the silly position I had got myself into. Dev-

erel, I knew, was the proper careless, dashing kind of
fellow for such an enterprise. Besides, he was driven
by the unquestionable fact that a gallant exploit would
get him out of his difficulties. Even Captain Anderson
would not be so mean-spirited as to proceed with the
trial and punishment of a young officer who had led a
desperate boarding party—but I, what had I to gain?
All I had was everything to lose!

Then all reflection was banished from my mind.
From out there in the darkness of the night and the
mist there came the sound of a kind of whispering and
multiplying creak. This was followed at once by a
series of dull thumps.

Deverel muttered in my ear. "She has run out her
guns!"

Silence again—and surely, a faint washing and
rippling and splashing, as if some heavy object was
being moved bodily sideways through the water, two
bodies, two ships, we and they— There had been in
Deverel's voice the fierce anticipation of a beast of
prey which hears its victim close! But I—all at once
I was vividly aware that out there in the darkness the
round muzzles of guns were pointed at me! I could
not breathe. Then instantly I was blinded by a brilliant flash, not the dagger in my head, but out there
in the darkness: and the flash was followed, no, surrounded, by the awful explosion of the gun—a kind of
wide roar with a needle-point of instantaneity in it.
The roar was like no peacetime salute. It rebounded
awesomely from the very sky in a brazen replication
which set me jerking and shuddering with excitement.

CLOSE QUARTERS

The cutlass fell from my hand and must have clattered on the deck though I heard nothing through the sound of blood beating in my head. I scrabbled after the hilt but my right hand was frozen and would not open to pick it up or close on the grip. I had to use both hands, then staggered up again.

Captain Anderson was speaking and apparently addressing the sky.

"Aloft there!"

Young Mr Willis answered from the rigging.

"All ready, sir. She missed us, sir."

"That was a signal gun, you young fool!"

"Signal gun," muttered Deverel, "that's just what the Frogs would do to make us show ourselves. There's still hope of a battle, my lads! Here she comes!"

Before my eyes the green after-image of the explosion was fading. I stared where Deverel was pointing with his sword. Like hills appearing through mists, or —but I cannot find a comparison. Like anything, the appearance of which is doubtful and gradual then suddenly and unquestionably *there*, the dark bulk of a huge vessel came into view. She was broadside on to us. Good God, I thought, and my knees trembled for all I could do—she is the same rate as *L'Orient*, 120 guns!

Then high up in her rigging, sparks appeared. Directly after, the sparks took fire, became three dazzling lights, two white lights with a red light between them. The lights danced and glared and smoked and spilled down drops and sparks that joined their own reflections in the water. I heard Willis shouting some-

thing then above my head but outboard there was an
answering dazzle—two white lights and a blue one!
A cascade of drops fell before me like blazing rain. I
saw Deverel staring up from one set of lights to the
other. His mouth was open, his eyes wide, face gaunt
in the glare. Then with a shouted or perhaps screamed
stream of imprecations, he struck his sword inches
deep into our rail! Captain Anderson had been using
a speaking trumpet but I had not heard what he said.
A voice spoke from the other ship, a hollow voice
through a speaking trumpet so that it seemed the man
hung among the brilliant rain from all the lights.

"His Majesty's frigate *Alcyone*, Captain Sir Henry
Somerset, twenty-seven days out of Plymouth."

Deverel's sword remained fast in the rail. The poor
fellow himself stood by it, his face in his hands. The
isolated voice through the speaking trumpet went on.

"News, Captain Anderson, for you and your whole
ship's company. The war with the French is over.
Boney is beat and abdicated. He is to be King of
Elba. God save our gracious King and God save His
Most Christian Majesty, King Louis of France, the
eighteenth of that name!"

(5)

The roar that followed these words was almost as extraordinary as the sound of the cannon shot! I saw Captain Anderson swing round and aim his speaking trumpet down into the waist but he might as well have had no voice.

Our ship was all filled with moving, and, yes, capering figures. Here and there lights were appearing as by magic though the signal flares had dropped one by one into the sea. Men were carrying lanterns up into the rigging of our ship. Someone was drawing the screens from our great stern lanterns. For the first time in my experience the poop and quarterdeck were irradiated by the powerful light of their oil lamps. *Alcyone* was moving closer and strangely enough was becoming smaller as she came. I saw that she was much of our length, though somewhat lower in the water. Summers was standing on our fo'castle and his mouth was opening and shutting but no sound could be heard. There was a petty officer or boatswain or the like roaring his head off with commands about ropes and fenders while an anonymous voice—could it be Billy Rogers?—was shouting for three times three so that huzzahs resounded endlessly to be answered from the deck of *Alcyone*! Now she was so close that I could distinguish beards and bald heads, black, brown, white faces, eyes and open mouths and grins by the hundred. It *was* a bedlam, and I, with light and noise and news near enough as mad as the others!

Then I knew that this was no conceit and I was mad indeed. Before ever a gangway was securely in place between the two ships, a man climbed up cleverly from her bulwark to ours. He was, he must be an hallucination! For it was Wheeler, that sly servant who had been lost overboard and drowned many days before—Wheeler who knew so much and contrived so much. It was the man himself, his once pale face blotched with the wounds of too much salt and sun, those two puffs of white hair still standing out on either side of his baldness. Now he was speaking to Summers and now he was turning, walking towards the quarterdeck where I still stood.

"Wheeler! Curse it, you was drowned!"

A strong convulsion shook the man. He said nothing, however, but stared at the cutlass in my right hand.

"Drowned! What the devil!"

"Allow me, sir."

He took the cutlass out of my hand with a slight inclination of the head.

"But, Wheeler! This is—"

Once more, that convulsion.

"The life was too strong in me, sir. You are wounded, sir. I will bring water to your cabin."

I was suddenly aware that my feet had been stuck in the same place and position for an age. It seemed they were embedded in the deck. My right hand was creased with the imprint of a hilt. My head, I discovered, was in a fearful state of pain and confusion. I was suddenly aware of what a figure I must present before so many new people and I hurried away to make myself as neat as possible. Peering into my small mirror I saw my face was indeed bloody and my hair matted. Wheeler brought water.

"Wheeler! You are a ghost. You were drowned, I said!"

Wheeler turned from the canvas basin into which he had poured a can of cold water. His gaze reached my neck but came no further.

"Yes, sir. But only after three days, sir. I believe it was three days. But you are right, of course, sir. Then I drowned."

My hair prickled. His eyes rose now to meet mine. They never blinked.

"I drowned, sir. I did—and the life in me so strong!"

Really, it was disconcerting and disturbing to be talked at so. Besides, the man needed calming.

"Well, Wheeler, you are a lucky dog. You was picked up and there's an end to it. Tell Bates I shall no longer require his services."

Wheeler paused. He opened his mouth and for a moment I thought he had some more to say, but he closed it again, bowed slightly and withdrew. I stripped to my shirtsleeves and washed as much blood as possible from my face and hands. When I had done I collapsed in my canvas chair, exhausted. It was becoming evident that I must pass this strange time in a wounded state where all was like a dream. I tried to realize what the news meant and could not. The war —except for the brief and deceitful peace of the year '08—had been the only state I knew. Now the war was gone, the state changed and I could not fill emptiness with anything which had meaning. I tried to think of a Louis XVIII on the throne of France and could not. I tried to think of all the glories of the ancient regime—now surely to be called the modern regime!—and found that I could not believe they would ever come again; common sense, a *political awareness* would not suffer it! The state of the world was too changed by catastrophes—the state of France, the ruin of her great families, a generation exposed first to the seduction of an impossible liberty and equality, then to the hardships imposed by tyranny, poverty and the draining of her conscripted blood— it would be a sad world which our people were greeting so noisily, that was my unwilling thought. But my head still rang with noises of its own; and though no man could think of sleep at such a moment I did not know if my strength was sufficient for the ordeal of our rejoicing! I tried once more to realize the fact—a turning point in history, one of the world's great occasions, we stood on a watershed and so on—but it was no use. My head became the arena of confused images and thoughts. A full shot garland such as the one I had crouched by on the gundeck seemed emblem of all the millions of tons of old iron lying about in corners of the civilized world—now never to be used, rusting cannon which would do for rubbing posts, muskets and musket balls sold as curios, swords, my famous cutlass—there seemed in my head no end to iron and lead. Then the ships newly built but now never to be launched!

CLOSE QUARTERS

I must own to a most eccentric feeling in the circumstances. It was one of fear. For a moment the reality of the situation did at last penetrate to my confused awareness. The fear was not a gross, common fright such as had rooted my feet to the deck when I heard as I thought my first shot fired in anger, but wider, almost a universal fright at the prospect of peace! The peoples of Europe and our own country were now set free from the simple and understandable duty of fighting for their king and country. It was an extension of that liberty which had already turned ordered societies into pictures of chaos. I told myself that one of the "political branch" should welcome this since affairs were now no longer put to the mortal arbitrament of swords. It was the politician's turn, our turn, my turn! But the moment of realization had passed and my head was all confusion again. The fact is that, for a while, I believe I wept.

But I could hear our ladies laughing and chattering as they passed by my door and issued into the waist. I even heard Miss Granham exclaim in a high voice: "And the skirt quite, quite beyond cleaning or repair!" It was time I emerged. I went into the waist, which was now full of light and people busy rather than hysterical with rejoicing. Our two ships were now fastened together by cables and though *Alcyone* was lower than we, it was no more than by the height of a deck. The whole area of our little world had expanded. There were so many new people! Good God, the Emperor of China had no more crowded and confused a country! But our "tumblehome" and theirs kept the people a few feet apart. Our officers were in a state of grave displeasure with the people: and the petty officers for the first time in my experience were using their "starters" in earnest. It was, of course, the prospect of a release from the discipline of the service coupled with those minutes of complete indiscipline which had done the damage! I reminded myself, selfishly enough I fear, that we could now hang up our arms and let common sense take charge. I climbed to the poop and then to the quarterdeck. Captain Anderson was standing by the larboard rail, hat in hand. Sir Henry Somerset, a gentleman of a full habit and a somewhat florid complexion, was perched in the mizzen shrouds of *Alcyone* so that he and our captain were at an equal height. Sir Henry had one foot on each of two rungs, sat on the third, held the fourth with his right hand and his hat in the left. He was speaking.

"—bound for India with utmost dispatch and may arrive there with the news just in time to prevent a very pretty battle! Devil take it, sir, if I succeed I shall be the most unpopular man east of Suez!"

"What of the Navy, sir?"

"Oh, Lord, sir, not a day passes but the order comes down to lay up another dozen ships or so. The streets are full of seamen waiting to be paid and begging. I never knew we had so many rascals in our ships! We are well out of it together, sir. But that's peace for you, curse it. Who is this gentleman?"

Captain Anderson, his hand on the rail where Deverel's sword had almost divided it, introduced me. He mentioned my godfather and his brother and my

prospective employment. Sir Henry was affable. He
hoped to further our acquaintance and to present me
to Lady Somerset. Captain Anderson interrupted our
exchange of courtesies with his customary lack of
savoir-faire. He hoped until we got a wind to have the
pleasure of Sir Henry and Lady Somerset's company.
But now the people, or his people at least, should be
brought up smartly with a round turn and a couple of
half-hitches. Meanwhile—

Sir Henry agreed, letting himself down the shrouds
with the casual dexterity of an old seaman, and went
to address an officer on his deck.

Captain Anderson vented his roar. "Mr Summers!"

Poor Summers came running aft like a midshipman.
In the glare of the lights from both ships I could see
that his usually composed face was flushed and sweating. He thrust this man and that out of the way in his
attempt to obey the captain's summons. I thought it
undignified and unworthy of him.

"Mr Summers, the men are breaking ship!"

"I know it, sir, and am doing my best."

"You had best do better! Look at that—and that!
Devil take it, man—we shall be robbed like a hen
roost!"

"Their rejoicing, sir—"

"Rejoicing? This is plunder! You may say the last
man out of *Alcyone* shall be strapped with a dozen and
I promise the like from Sir Henry!"

Summers saluted and ran off again. Anderson aimed
a grimace at me with a bit of tooth in the middle, then
set himself to stump up and down the larboard side of

the quarterdeck, hands behind his back, sour face staring this way and that. Once he stopped by the forrard rail and roared again. Summers answered him from the fo'castle but, unlike the captain, used a speaking trumpet.

"Mr Askew has taken in the packets of powder, sir, and had the quick match stowed. He is now drawing the shot."

Captain Anderson nodded and resumed his un-accustomedly swift stumping up and down. He ignored me and I thought it best to withdraw. By the time I got to the waist I understood some at least of our moody captain's concern. There was too free laughter among the people. It was evident that some of them by means unknown to me, or I think to their officers, had obtained strong drink. The operation of Newton's laws, if that is what it was—what else?—in bringing two ships together that had not intended the encounter was setting the Rigid Navy—my private phrase for the Royal Navy—some problems which were not in the book. For I saw a bottle fly from one ship to the other and disappear among a group of men who were engaged in securing the bridge, or should I say gangway, between the two ships; and though I watched as closely as my ringing head would allow I never saw it emerge from them. It vanished as completely and mysteriously as the cards in the hands of a stage magician. I could not but think that the gangway made the unlawful interchange of our crews even easier than before. But the confusion continued and the way was opened across the gap for social inter-

course and thievery. My restlessness seemed endless.
For all my buzzing head and the weariness of my limbs
I could not endure the thought of my bunk. What,
sleep when this hollow space in the hot mists of the
tropics was lighted brilliantly as a fairground and as
noisy? I remember that in my dazed state I felt it
necessary to *do something*, but could not think *what
to do*. I thought of drink and ducked into the lobby
by my hutch but was almost knocked sprawling by a
young fellow who rushed out. Phillips and Wheeler
and another man came after him but gave up when
they saw me. It did seem to me that a faint aroma, not
of rum but of brandy, emanated from Phillips's person.
He addressed me breathlessly.

"That bugger was an *Alcyone*, sir. You best keep all
locked."

I nodded to him and went immediately to the passenger saloon. Here, who should be present but little
Pike, his tears all dried and his chest out like the breast
of a pouter pigeon! He trusted at once that I had recovered from my injury, though he believed I looked
sadly. He left me no time to reply, however. I had
noticed in him normally a marked modesty in the
presence of other men, but now there was no quelling
him.

"Only think, Mr Talbot, I have served at the guns!
Then I stood by the tackle while the charge was
drawn."

"My congratulations."

"Oh, it was nothing, of course. All the same—Mr
Askew remarked before he dismissed us that a few days

CLOSE QUARTERS

of gun drill and he would have turned us out as prime gunners!"

"He did?"

"Why, he said we would be fit to fight all the Frogs in the world let alone the damned Yankees!"

"That was gratifying. Yes, the brandy, Bates. Bates—would you consult Wheeler about leaving a bottle of brandy and a glass in my cabin?"

"Very good, sir."

"A glass of brandy for Mr Pike here."

"Oh no, sir, I could not! I am unaccustomed to brandy, Mr Talbot. It burns my mouth. Ale, if you please, sir."

"You hear, Bates? That will be all."

"Aye aye, sir."

"I was very sorry to see you struck down, Mr Talbot. At the time when you hit your head on the ceiling—I mean the deckhead, as we ought to call it—I had to laugh it seemed so comical though of course it must have been very painful."

"It is."

"But we were so, what shall I say, strung taut as a violin string and the least thing set us off like it used to be in the office, for we were sometimes in the utmost distress not to laugh at Mr Wilkins—and when Mr Askew said you had come so close to the mid-point that—well—"

"I remember, Mr Pike."

"Call me Dick, sir, will you not, though in the office I was called Dicky or even Dickybird—"

"Mr Pike!"

"Sir?"

"I wish to forget the whole lamentable episode. I should be obliged therefore—"

"Oh, of course, sir, if you wish. Why, we were all comical it seemed to Mr Askew. Once I was standing there at the gun with my mouth open I suppose, though I was not conscious of it, but Mr Askew said, 'Now you, Mr Pike, sir, have you swallowed the tompion?' How the others laughed! A tompion, you know, Mr Talbot, is the plug at the end of the—"

"Yes, I do know. The ale is for Mr Pike, Bates."

"Well then, Mr Talbot, confusion to the—oh, we should not say that now, should we? A health to King Louis, then. Dear me, I shall be nigh on half seas over."

"You are still excited, sir."

"Well, I was and I am. It was exciting and it is exciting. Will you not allow me to buy you some brandy?"

"Not now. Presently perhaps."

"Only to think I have stood at a gun! I served at a gun on the, the larboard beam, it would be, would it not?"

"God knows, Mr Pike. The guns as I recollect were about half-way along the left-hand side of the ship as one looks forrard—towards the bow, the front end."

"Mr Pike."

It was Miss Granham. We rose to our feet.

"Mrs Pike asked me to be kind enough to say that she would value your assistance with the twins. They are so excited."

CLOSE QUARTERS

"Of course, ma'am!"

Pike dashed off, carrying his excitement where it might well not be appreciated. As far as I could see, his ale was untasted.

"Pray be seated, ma'am. Allow me. This cushion—"

"I had expected to find my, Mr Prettiman. Phillips was to cut his hair."

It was faintly comical to hear how she shied at the word fiancé. It was faintly human, dare I say, and unexpected.

"I will find him for you, ma'am."

"No, please, no indeed. Be seated, Mr Talbot—I insist—there! Good heavens, your head is wounded indeed! You do not look at all the thing!"

I laughed and winced.

"My skull now contains a large fragment of the ship's deck."

"It is a lacerated contusion."

"Pray, ma'am—"

"But there will be a surgeon aboard Sir Henry's ship, I believe."

"I have taken harder knocks at fisticuffs, ma'am. I beg you pay no attention to it."

"The episode was made to seem a little comical but now I see the result I rebuke myself for being amused by it."

"It seems I covered myself with blood but not glory."

"Not as far as the ladies are concerned, sir. Our initial amusement was soon lost in a positively tearful admiration. It would appear that you came from the guns, your face covered in blood, and immediately volunteered for the most perilous enterprise the mind of man can imagine."

This, of course, was my cutlass—also my two feet that had adhered so firmly to the place they found themselves in when the signal gun went off in the fog! I wondered for a moment in what way to accept the unexpected tribute to my courage. Perhaps it was the equally unexpected and faintly human look in Miss Granham's severe face which determined me in this instance to tell the truth.

"Indeed, ma'am, it was only partly so," said I, laughing again. "For looking back I see that when the comical fellow staggered up from the guns he was so abroad in his wits that they volunteered him before he knew what he was doing!"

Miss Granham looked on me kindly! This lady I had thought composed of vinegar, gunpowder, salt and pepper looked on me kindly.

"I understand you, Mr Talbot, and my admiration is in no way lessened. As a lady, I must thank you for your protection."

"Oh, Lord, ma'am, say no more—any gentleman— and Englishman—indeed—good God! But it must have been distressing for you down in the orlop!"

"It was distressing," she said simply, "not because of danger but because it was disgusting."

The door sprang open and little Mrs Brocklebank fairly bounced in.

"Letitia—Mr Talbot—our play! The party!"

"I had forgotten."

"A play, ma'am? Party?"

"We are quite unready," said Miss Granham, with some return to her customary bleakness. "The weather will not hold for it."

"Oh fudge! We may do it immediately as the Italians do, we might do it tonight—"

"It is already 'tonight'."

"Tomorrow then."

"My dear Mrs Brocklebank—"

"Down in that horrid place you was pleased to call me 'Celia' as I asked and even held my hand, Mr Talbot, for I am the greatest coward imaginable and what with the odours and the darkness and the rumbling and the, the—I was within an ace of swooning away."

"I will continue to address you as 'Celia' if you wish," said Miss Granham distantly, "though what difference—"

"Well then that is settled. But the most exciting thing—our captains are agreed that if the weather, I will not repeat how Sir Henry described it but if we are held for another twenty-four hours without wind—what do you think, sir?"

"I cannot imagine, ma'am, except perhaps they may agree that we shall all whistle for a wind together."

"Oh, get along with you, Mr Talbot, do, you will always be funning. You are just like Mr Brocklebank."

There must have been some instant expression in my face which showed the ladies how this comparison appealed to me. It set Miss Granham smiling and even impeded Mrs Brocklebank for a moment.

"I mean, sir, in the article of funning. Why, hardly a day passes but Mr Brocklebank makes a joke which has me positively screaming with laughter. Indeed I sometimes fear I am so noisy that I irritate the other passengers."

My head was singing and opening and shutting. The ladies were a long way away.

"You said that you had news for us, ma'am."

"Oh yes! Why, if we are still detained tomorrow they are agreed we may have a ball! Only think of it! The officers in full dress, and the little band from *Alcyone* to play for us—why, it will be a most elegant occasion!"

The confusion of my head merged with incredulity.

"Captain Anderson agreed to a ball? Surely not!"

"No, not at first, sir, he is said to have been most upright. But then Lady Somerset managed Sir Henry who visited Captain Anderson—but is it not remarkable—oh heavenly! More!"

"More, ma'am? What can be more heavenly than the opportunity—"

"This was unexpected . . . they say Sir Henry having gained Captain Anderson's agreement went on to assume that we had all had our boxes up on entering the tropics and was quite demolished when he found it was not so! Apparently all ships that carry passengers declare a day for airing and changing and arranging and—why, you will understand it all, Letitia, even if Mr Talbot does not! They say Captain Anderson had omitted this ceremony in sheer bad temper at being—what do you think he called it? I heard

from Miss Chumley who heard from Lady Somerset
who was told in the strictest confidence by Sir Henry
that Captain Anderson had described his anger at
being concerned to carry the emigrants, I suppose, as
being loaded with a cargo of pigs! But the upshot of
all is that we may have our trunks and boxes brought
up at dawn and the ball is to open at five o'clock
with dusk."

"If the weather holds. Suppose there is wind. We
cannot sail together and dance at the same time!"

"Lady Somerset declares there will not be a wind—
she feels there will not be! She is a sensitive. Sir Henry
declares that he relies on his 'little witch' to make the
weather behave. They are a charming and delightful
couple. It is said they will entertain some of us to
dinner or a luncheon."

A marked silence ensued. Neither Miss Granham
nor I seemed disposed to break it. Finally Mrs Brocklebank broke it herself.

"Lady Somerset has a fortepiano but declares she
is sadly out of practice. She presses Miss Chumley to
play, who does so delightfully."

"How do you know all this, ma'am?"

"And who," said Miss Granham, "is Miss
Chumley?"

"Miss Chumley is an orphan and Lady Somerset's
prodigy."

"Good God, ma'am," said I. "Can she be as finished a musician as that?"

"They are taking her with them to India where she
is to live with a distant relative, for she is quite without
fortune, except for her skill."

Have I reported that conversation in its right place?
I cannot remember. Certainly at some point I found
myself thinking—all this is absurd, cannot be happening—it is my head that is wrong. How did I get away?
I remember being pressed by Miss Granham to try
the effect of repose, but I walked instead past my
hutch and out into the waist, then up by way of the
stairs to the quarterdeck. I cannot tell how long I
stayed there staring at the invisible horizon and trying
to think! I have never known such a queer condition!
I understand now that it was the effect of excitement,
fear, and the repeated blows that had kept my head
ringing like a bell. At one point Wheeler appeared
and suggested that I should get some sleep but I
drove him off testily. I heard a muted roar from below
the deck and soon Bates came and begged me not
to walk the quarterdeck, for the captain's cot was just
below me and he turned into it. So away I drifted in
a kind of dream. Wheeler came to me.

"All the other ladies and gentlemen are turned in
long ago, sir, and fast asleep."

"Do you know, Wheeler, what I think about Mrs
Brocklebank?"

"You've had a thump, sir, they say. But don't
worry, sir. I'll stay near you."

"Is this a dagger which I see inside me, its handle—"

"Now come along and lie down, sir, I'll stay—"

"Keep your hands off me, man! Who has the
watch?"

"Mr Cumbershum, sir."

"We are safe enough then."

All this inconsequence! But Wheeler must have

persuaded or forced me into the lobby. I was surprised to find how the lobby had altered. For one thing, it was lighted by no less than two powerful oil-lamps! Trunks, boxes and bags were piled outside the cabins, my own among them, including, I noticed, the box that held the remainder of my travelling library. Wheeler got me into my chair and pulled off my boots.

"That reminds me. You are a careless fellow, Wheeler. How did you come to fall overboard?"

There was a long pause.

"Wheeler?"

"I slipped, sir. My brass rag blew out of my hand and caught in the main chains. I had to climb outboard for it. Then I slipped, sir, like I said."

It came to me in the confusion of my head that I knew the truth of the matter. His death had been convenient. He had informed on Billy Rogers and paid for it in the fearful currency of criminals. Yet so strange was my state that I merely nodded and let him continue with his work about me.

"You are a ghost, Wheeler."

"No, sir."

"Go and get some sleep."

"I'll stay with you, sir, you aren't fit to be left. I'll get my head down here on the deck."

I shouted at him, I think, and he went. As for me, I fell into my bunk.

CLOSE QUARTERS

(6)

THE GREAT DAY

Indeed I can call it no other. That day, from my rising to my strange setting, I could wish to go with me in every detail to my grave. I have little enough skill to preserve it. Words, words, words! I would give them all and live dumb for one moment of—no, I would not. I am absurd.

Only just now I was remembering Colley's long, unfinished letter. I cannot think that he supposed himself adept in description and narration, yet this very innocence, his suffering and his need for a friend if only a piece of paper, gave his writing a force which I can admire but not imitate.

Now, as I write this, my legs locked into the structure of the chair while the deck heaves and sidles—I wear my greatcoat even in my cabin.

But to return. I woke, sweatily in that humid heat. When I dressed myself it was only that the noise from the lobby was intense and would have kept me from sleep even if I had been capable of it. Moreover the calls of nature pay no attention to such trifles as a cracked head! So after I had dressed, I picked a careful way through the lobby to the privies on the starboard quarter. I mean on the right side at the back of the ship—and returning was like the exploration of a bazaar! There were not only bales and boxes, trunks and bags, but all our female passengers busy among them! They handled a mixed exhibition of stuff fit for

an Eastern market. Zenobia was there with little Mrs
Pike. Miss Granham rose from among a rainbow of
dresses and flashed her smile at me! I had intended to
plead my head as a reason for avoiding the ball, but
that smile, together with an archly kind look from Mrs
Brocklebank—I confess all this freely—changed my
mind for me. I told Wheeler to get out my tailed coat
and knee-breeches, together with the light suiting, the
material for which had been recommended to me by a
man who had done a tour in India. By the time I had
changed into this last, even the passenger saloon had
been turned into a milliner's shop. There was Miss
Granham, just where she had sat the day before and
looking, I will not say pretty, but indefinably excited
and good-humoured and handsome! She was wearing a
dress of dark blue silk and had a large and complicated
shawl of lighter blue crossed over her bosom. It seemed
more *oncoming* than was appropriate for a governess.
But then, good God, I remembered in time that she
was no longer a governess but the fiancée of a man who,
however outrageous his politics, was none the less of
considerable substance and unquestionably a gentleman. In short this was Miss Granham come out of her
chrysalis!

"Good morning, Miss Granham. Like it, you are
radiant."

"A pretty speech from our gallant defender. It would
be prettier if the sun shone."

"The mists are golden."

"That was almost poetical. How does your head,
sir?"

"I know now what is meant by 'heart of oak'. I appear to be roofed with it."

"Your own costume is admirably suited to the climate."

"I am dressed for comfort. But you ladies are going out of your way to delight us."

"You do not think highly of the nature of ladies, sir. The melancholy truth is we are prepared for a whole day of festivity. We dine in *Alcyone*'s wardroom. There is a ball to be given on our own deck, and an entertainment presented to us by our own seamen!"

"Good heavens!"

"I believe it may do some good in this, this—"

"Not entirely happy ship?"

"You have said it, sir, not I."

"But a ball!"

"Our neighbour has a band."

"But an entertainment presented by the seamen!"

"I hope it may be edifying but fear it will not."

"The ball at any rate—Miss Granham, may I claim your hand for a dance?"

"I am flattered but should we not wait? To tell you the truth I am not entirely informed of Mr Prettiman's views on such activities and until then—"

"Of course, ma'am. I say no more but will hope."

The door opened and in flew pretty Mrs Brocklebank. Her arms were full of some foaming material. In a second our ladies were deep in a discussion of such technical mysteriousness that I withdrew without interrupting them. If I defined our sailor's speech as "Tarpaulin", then I must define what our ladies were

saying (both speaking together) as perfect "Milliner".
It confirmed what I had felt when Pike had talked
about the "larboard beam". I saw my efforts to talk as
the seamen did as a crass affectation. I might as well
have talked of hems and gores and gussets! Let the rest
of the passengers make free with Tarpaulin. I myself
would stand out for a landsman's lingo! So farewell,
Falconer and his *Marine Dictionary*, without a twinge
of regret but indeed, with some relief.

I took my hat from my hutch and walked into the
waist. The sun was faintly visible in the mist and not
yet more than its own diameter above the horizon but
already the preparations for our extraordinary day of
festivities were well under weigh—I mean in process of
being completed. Perhaps "under weigh" is permissible
as a phrase which has lost its technical and precise
reference and become general? But the scene, though I
am persuaded I shall never forget it, must none the less
be described. At the height of our mainyard our ship
was roofed with awnings—either sails used for the purpose or awnings proper. Though as yet the swiftly rising
sun shone levelly under them, in later hours they
would provide a grateful shade. *Alcyone* had her awnings at the same level, though of course higher up the
masts. The effect was of two streets side by side—we
were a small township, or a village at least, a village out
here in this deserted wilderness. It was preposterous.
The wild almost mutinous behaviour of our sailors
when they heard the tidings of peace had subsided and
they worked everywhere in silence and with an apparent goodwill. It was the prospect of an entertainment.

Like small children they had entered the world of "let's pretend" and were, it seemed, satisfied there. Hand flags and larger bunting were being hung from the awnings. There were even flowers—not from the captain's cabin as I thought at first but most cleverly constructed from scraps of material. From *Alcyone* came the sounds of a small band at practice! Yet with all this, the ceaseless business of the ships went on— two men stood at our motionless wheel and two others stood at *Alcyone*'s. Our odd sailing master paced the quarterdeck, a spyglass under his arm, while a midshipman did the like aboard our neighbour! I had no doubt that above the awnings work still went on at the stumps of our decapitated masts and that somewhere in the fore or the main or the mizzen the lookout stared at the horizon, whence the sun was already drawing up mist. It was all so unexpected and quaint that I forgot the ringing of my head and came near to being myself once again. I now saw that our two streets were kept apart by those huge bundles of wood which are let down the sides of quays to prevent ships damaging themselves with rubbing on stone. The steep gangway formed an alley joining our two ocean streets. It was wide enough to be negotiated even by ladies. Two red marines were stationed at *Alcyone*'s end of the alley and two plainly disgruntled members of Oldmeadow's troop in green guarded ours. I went to the rail and looked over. I was in time to see a gunport close, or rather the last furtive inch of its closing! So that was one of the ways the people of both ships could communicate whether their officers wanted them to or no

—and, of course, across from mast to mast, yard to yard, the monkeys would swing as in a forest! Small chance of perfect discipline when ships lie together!

A midshipman from *Alcyone* came up the gangway, saluted and, after enquiring my name, offered me a white and slightly scented note. I unfolded it. Captain Sir Henry and Lady Somerset request the pleasure of the company of Mr Edmund FitzH. Talbot to dinner aboard *Alcyone*, twelve o'clock, wind and weather permitting. Dress informal, a verbal reply will suffice.

"I accept with pleasure, of course."

I returned to my hutch. I remember clearly telling myself that all this was not a dream nor a phantasy brought on by the wounding of my head. Yet with this extraordinary hamlet or village built a thousand miles from anywhere and wrapped now in a humid mist that seemed to invade my intellect as much as it drifted across our decks, what had gone before and what was to come seemed unimportant, trivial even, so that England at our back and the Antipodes before us were no more than engraved lines on a map. And Wheeler was back, intercepted by a frigate's course as improbably as that a thread thrown at the eye of a needle should go through it! *Here* was all. The two streets side by side—and *Alcyone*'s bell rang, to be echoed immediately by our own, so that it was four bells in the forenoon watch with the cry from her of "Up spirits" duplicated a few yards from me on our deck—the crowds that thronged those decks and the decks below them, the busy yet only half-understood business that was carried on twenty-four hours a day in both ships to

keep life supportable—the planking with its black and
sometimes bubbling seams—the very parallel lines of
them which sometimes would enforce a dreary and
sickening substantiality in which their movement was
malign—this was all that was real.

What bathos! I have tried to say what I mean and
cannot. This tropical nowhere was the whole world—
the whole *imaginable* world. This was a neck of history, the end of the greatest war, was the middle of the
longest journey, a . . . a nothing! An all, an astonishment, a cold factuality. I bend the English language in
an effort to say what I mean and fail.

"Edmund."

I swung around in my chair. Deverel was looking in
at the door. I must confess to finding his visit un-
welcome.

"What is it, Deverel? I am about to—"

"Good God! The man has his own supply of brandy!
A glass if you please for the bad boy of the school."

"Help yourself. But are not you—?"

"Forbidden the drink like the parson's son? Damn
him, it's peacetime and I'll not be shackled any longer.
If he does not let me out of arrest I'll snap my sword in
his face, go ashore and hey for the open road!"

"I don't know what you're talking about."

"Why, my good Edmund, what can he do? Obtain
for me the Lord High Admiral's Displeasure on Vel-
lum? Let him break me; it's no more than my sword
they break, a piece of damned cutlery I've no use for
now there's so much peace about!"

"A gentleman's sword—"

"A white man east of Suez may do well enough."

"We are not east of Suez."

Deverel emptied an extraordinary fraction of the tumbler of brandy down his throat. It made him gasp. Then—

"I cannot beg from the man. It would break me as well as my sword to do so. I must have my dignity."

"So must we all."

"This is my plan. You are to tell him what I propose."

"I tell him?"

"Who else? The rest are rabbits. Besides, what have you to lose?"

"The devil of a lot!"

"Tell him that I engage to cause no trouble till we make a port—"

"That's good."

"Wait. *There* I shall resign my commission."

"Or have it taken from you, Deverel."

"What's the odds? You're not drinking, Edmund, and you're cursed dull today. Tell him if you like that as soon as I've ceased to be an officer you'll bear him my challenge—"

"I?"

"Don't you see? Can you imagine old Rumble-guts faced with a challenge?"

"Yes."

"Why, when we thought *Alcyone* might be a Frog he was shivering like a tops'l."

"Are you serious?"

"Did you not see?"

"You underestimate the man."

"That's my affair. But you'll tell him?"

"Look—Deverel—Jack. This is madness."

"You'll tell him!"

I was silent for only the briefest moment in which I made up my mind.

"No."

"No? Just like that?"

"I am sorry."

"By God, you're not! I had thought better of you, Talbot!"

"Listen. Try to be sensible. Don't you understand that I cannot in any circumstances take to the captain what is neither more nor less than an open threat? If you were not in an overexcited state—"

"Do you think I'm drunk? Or in a blue funk?"

"Of course not. Calm down."

Deverel poured himself another drink, not as large as the first but large enough. The bottle and glass clattered together. It was essential to stop him getting really drunk. I allowed my hand to go out and take the glass from him.

"Thank you, old fellow."

For a moment I thought he was about to strike me. Then with an odd kind of laugh—

" 'Lord Talbot'. I must say you're a cool one."

"Was this for you? I'm sorry—"

"No, no. Have it."

"The first day of peace. So up spirits!"

I coughed mightily over it. Deverel watched in silence, then slowly seated himself on the further end of my bunk.

"Edmund—"

I looked at him over the glass.

"Edmund—what am I to do?"

Deverel was no longer looking fierce. It was strange but after all the devil-may-care actions of the past twenty-four hours it was as if a far less assured young man had appeared in the place of the one I knew. I saw now how although he was of more than average height he was of a slight build and lightly muscled. As for his face—I saw with astonishment that the forward-projecting sweep of his sidewhiskers was an attempt of which he was quite possibly unaware to compensate for a weak and slightly receding chin. Gentleman Jack, the honourable Dashing Jack! It was a paroxysm of rage and, yes, fright that had given his right arm the momentary strength to sink his blade so deeply in the rail. Comprehension became so complete that I felt as lost and frightened as ever he had been. It is a dreadful thing to know too much. I saw that had it not been for the support of his family name and an air which stemmed more from imitation than worth, he might have been an ostler, a footman, a gentleman's gentleman! It was confusing to look at this man whom I had once thought the most gentleman-like of the officers —which indeed—the question is such a confusion— which indeed he was! His negligence and intemperance had nothing to do with what I now saw and understood. His latest wild scheme, depending as it did on a physical cowardice in Captain Anderson for which there was less than no evidence, was phantasy. Anderson would treat a challenge from Deverel, civilian or no, with contempt and no one would blame him. Deverel must not be allowed to continue in it!

"Do, Mr Deverel—Jack? Let me think."

He sat back and slumped a little as if some strain had gone out of him. He seemed almost respectful as before a Thinker! But the truth was—

"Look, Deverel—"

"It was Jack just now, let alone when we were about to board."

"Aye! That was a moment we shall remember—eh? Jack, then. But look. I've had the devil of a clout or three clouts over the head—I'm really in no condition to think at all. It aches still."

"A glass—"

I made an involuntary and impatient gesture with my right hand.

"You know—I would like—I will—do what can be done. The first thing is for me to speak to Summers."

"Good God! The man's a Methodist!"

"Is he so? I know him deeply concerned with moral questions but had not thought—"

"Is that the best you can do?"

"It's the first step. I must know what the situation is, I mean in, in naval law. You are too personally involved and do not yet see the thing clearly."

"You were present!"

"In body, yes, but I was unconscious. The wits had been knocked out of me by a rope's end."

"And this is your offer of help?"

"The trouble with you, Deverel, is you want everything done at once."

"Thank you, *Mr* Talbot!"

"I am trying to help. You must not expect from me the instant action of a naval officer."

"By God, I do not!"

"Be easy again! You cannot go at this as if you was boarding an enemy. Haste will ruin all."

"What? With two post captains and half a dozen lieutenants senior to me in these ships? They can fix me with a court-martial as easy as kiss my arse! Devil take it and you!"

"Jack!"

The word was emollient. Strange again! Though he looked sullen and his breast heaved, nevertheless he spoke in a lower tone. "There is enough of them to fix up a court-martial here and now."

"When the wind may send us on our way at any moment? You know I am not instructed in naval matters but I would swear they cannot try you at sea. It is no longer wartime and not as if there was a mutiny. You have not offered the man violence! Besides, deuce take it, while the weather holds we are to have a ball and an entertainment and as if that was not enough I am to dine with Sir Henry! Confound it, man, can you not see that with the peace and abdication and this resolution of a great crisis in the affairs of the civilized world—"

Deverel jerked upright between his hands on the edge of the bunk.

"Dinner? Why, man, there's your opportunity! Anderson will be there, depend on it! A word with him in Sir Henry's hearing after the drinks have gone round—"

"He hardly drinks at all. Besides—"

All at once I was aware of how my wounded head was humming. No—singing!

"If you knew how my cursed head aches!"

"You'll do nothing then."

"I will find out how the land lies—if the expression means anything in this limbo of streaming water! There is much that may be done if we go about it carefully."

"You mean I must wait. Endure this humiliation from a man my father would not have at his table!"

"I will endeavour my best in your behalf, little though that best may be."

"There's no need to get your rag out!"

The cant expression amused me. I had indeed spoken with a degree of warmth. But somehow it made Deverel more likeable. He saw my involuntary smile, misinterpreted it and was about to fire up again, so that I spoke hurriedly and almost at random.

"I will lead the conversation to duelling if Anderson is there and try to find out what his reaction would be to a challenge."

"Why—he may have a positive horror of being shot at!"

I looked at him in sheer astonishment. Anderson, a post captain who by report had taken part in bloody engagements! Anderson who had *boarded* as a midshipman and later taken a fire ship into the Basque Roads under Cochrane! There was more here than I had foreseen. Deverel was now excited in a way that a single glass of my brandy could not account for. He was hectic and rubbing his hands and grinning! I tried to bring him down.

"What is more to the point, my dear sir, is that he may have the strength—what some people would call the strength of mind—to reject any challenge out of hand. There is a strong feeling about in the country that it is folly to set life itself at stake in a trivial matter. Not, of course, that your affair is trivial but others may think it so."

"They do, they do."

"I will sound him out."

"No more?"

"At the moment I *can* do no more."

"At the moment. It is a convenient phrase, sir."

I said nothing. Deverel eyed me critically. Then his expression changed to a veritable sneer. I spoke shortly.

"I repeat. I can do no more at the moment."

He said nothing for a while but looked towards the mirror above my canvas basin. Then—

"Like the others."

I made no comment. He went on.

"Oh, I know about Gentleman Jack and Dashing Jack, but do you not detect the sneer? Remember when Colley was slung overboard, Summers deliberately delayed telling me the driver should be afted until the rudder nigh on carried away? But I thought you who was a gentleman and not one of the cursed jumped-up lubbers, at least you would be on my side and not set out to ruin me—"

"You must be mad!"

He said nothing but after a few more moments stood up slowly. He looked at me sideways and began to smile unpleasantly, a kind of inward or withdrawn smile as of one who has infinite comprehension and wariness among enemies. He opened the cabin door, glanced quickly this way and that, then fairly darted out of sight. He left me in a state of great perplexity and confusion. The worst of it was I had committed myself to a degree of intimacy with the man and now felt little inclined to interfere with his punishment for what I could not but see as the just result of his neglect of duty. Above all I did not wish to injure in any way the degree of understanding and mutual tolerance which now existed between me and Captain Anderson. It was all most provoking. I had nothing to push me towards engaging in an advocacy in this instance and believed more and more, to use an abrupt phrase, that Deverel was simply not worth it.

I was called back to immediacy by the sound of the ship's bells. This was the very hour at which we were summoned to the feast! I glanced into the glass, settled my hair round my wound (hesitated for a moment—why go? why not turn in?). However, I settled my clothing and made my way through the new milliner's shop. As I did so I heard, among all the shuffling of naked feet, the sound of firm and familiar footsteps above my head. I followed the captain to the broad gangway down which he strode. He stood rigid at the bottom, his hat held across his chest. I, following close, had much ado to prevent myself from crashing into him. I had the wit, however, to seize a side rope with my left hand, snatch my hat off with my right, then stand nearly as rigid as the captain. The deck round the foot of the gangway was crowded and the ceremonial nearly as elaborate as that for Colley's funeral. Here were sideboys with white gloves, boatswains with calls,

marines with muskets, more marines with drums and
trumpets, some midshipmen, and a lieutenant or two
—and glittering at the end of the lane of ceremonial
stood Sir Henry Somerset, unkindly wearing full uniform, the ribbon of his order strained into creases
across the white splendour of his embonpoint! The
trumpets blared, the drums ruffled, the calls screeched,
our working parties stood to attention staring into the
mist. All this at a man's stepping from one plank to
another! The ceremony came to an end. Captain
Anderson was now properly aboard *Alcyone* and the
two crews might go about their business which I myself
thought astonishingly various and complex, in view of
the state of the weather, for from the gangway we
could hardly see either end of the ships. I stepped forward myself, to be greeted most affably by Sir Henry
who had not the privilege of knowing my godfather,
though he had, like all the world—and so on. He conducted us towards his own quarters, talking all the time
to our captain. Naval warfare is a lottery! Sir Henry is
large rather than impressive. His wealth showed everywhere. Any touches of moulding about the poop were
gilded. We walked to the ladder—no, I refuse to be
seduced—to the stairs, along a pathway of coir matting
laid lest our feet should be soiled by the melting seams.
There were canvas chimneys leading up from the
quarterdeck and secured to the mizzen rigging—devil
take it, I find my determination *not* to speak Tarpaulin
almost impossible to sustain!—in an attempt to replace
the fetor of a ship's interior with purer air. We reached
the quarterdeck and the end of the coir matting. I

looked down and began carefully and unsuccessfully
to avoid the seams when Sir Henry took notice of my
attempt.

"Do not trouble yourself, Mr Talbot, I beg. There
is nothing here to foul your feet."

Captain Anderson had stopped too and was looking
down.

"Splined, by God!"

It seemed my Tarpaulin was to increase just as I was
abandoning it.

"Splined, Sir Henry?"

Sir Henry waved a hand in a dismissive way.

"There was a cargo of rare woods among my prizes.
Very fortunate. It is ebony, you know."

"But *splined*, Sir Henry?"

"It means replacing the tar and oakum which is
commonly used, and makes such a damned mess of our
feet, by strips of hard wood. The narrow planks are
mahogany. I took up the idea from what I saw aboard
the royal yacht when I had the honour of being presented to His Royal Highness. Everything is Bristol
Fashion there, I can tell you! After you, Captain
Anderson, Mr Talbot."

"After you, sir."

"Pray, sir—"

We descended to the stateroom. The lady who came
towards us did not so much walk, or even float, as
swim. Lady Somerset had an immediate claim on any
gentleman's attention. She was a fine and most handsome woman and dressed in the height of fashion—
indeed her costume was more suitable, I thought, for

the evening than the middle of the day! Was this "informal dress"? On her bosom there glittered a positive appanage of sapphires which matched those at her ears and wrists. Sir Henry must have intercepted the jeweller to the Porte! Her gown was girt high under her bosom in what—but I have not yet learned to talk Milliner. Nor had I more than a moment to take in her appearance, for she was leaning towards me and moaning. I cannot by any other word describe the way in which having acknowledged Anderson's abrupt attention, abrupt nod down up—she broke from him, insinuated herself in my direction, gazed earnestly up into my eyes as if we were present at an occasion of most moving importance, then insinuated herself back to our captain and murmured in a deep contralto voice, "Such pleasure!" Since she appeared to be about to swoon at the thought of the pleasure, it was perhaps fitting that she should hold out a hand to each of us as if appealing for support. She was, however, a little too fragrant for my taste. Now I was lifting my hand towards hers when with a movement like that of weed in water she swung both hands in the other direction and moaned again.

"Dearest, valuable Janet!"

There was little doubt about the nature of valuable Janet. She held an embroidery frame in one hand with its material—the needle and thread still stuck in the pattern—together with a fan upside down: and in the other hand a book with one finger marking the page from which she had been reading. She held a cushion under her arm and, as if that load were not enough, a length of ribbon was clenched in her teeth. She appeared to me to be a female of extraordinary plainness. Busily sorting these new people according to what information I had, I at once put her in the compartment labelled "companion". As I did so she made a ducking curtsey, then bolted out of the stateroom.

"Miss Oates," murmured Lady Somerset, "a kinswoman."

"A distant kinswoman," amplified Sir Henry. "Lady Somerset will not be parted from her. It is her generous heart. She will keep her and how could I say no?"

"Dear Sir Henry, he refuses me nothing, but nothing!"

I was about to make the expected gallant reply when Sir Henry's face brightened and he spoke in a more energetic voice.

"Come in, Marion, come in! I was laying odds that you would be up and about!"

The lightning that struck the top of the mizzenmast ran down, and melted the conductor into white hot drops. The mast split and flinders shot every way into the mist. The deckhead burst open and the electrical fluid destroyed me. It surrounded the girl who stood before me with a white line of light.

(7)

"Captain Anderson, may I present you? Mr Talbot? Miss Chumley. You look delightfully, Marion, quite the belle—if it were not for, of course— This is Mr Edmund *FitzHenry* Talbot, my dear. Lady Talbot is a FitzHenry and Mr Talbot is proceeding—"

He must have continued to talk, I suppose. I came to as if from another concussion to find that the gentlemen were holding glasses and strangely there was one in my own hand. Since it is clear that I performed the act of taking a glass and continued to hold it in those first few moments of life I can only suppose that I had been talking as well but what my first words were I am quite unable to say. Oh, *thou*, Marion, rising from the meekest and deepest of curtsies, sum of all music, all poetry, distracted scraps of which with their newly irradiated meaning tumbled through my mind! But it was Sir Henry's words I heard when I first emerged from my destroyed state.

"Poor Marion has been positively prostrate! The slightest movement, good God, not just a lop but the least shudder at anchor, and up it all comes! Once she is in India, as I tell her, she must stay there for good, for the return journey would surely make an end of her!"

"*Alcyone* is lively then, Sir Henry?"

"So-so, Captain Anderson. She is long for her top hamper and 'utmost dispatch' is 'utmost dispatch', you know. How is your ship?"

"Steady as a rock, Sir Henry, and dead beat as a compass card. Why—even when that fool of a lieutenant allowed her to be taken aback she put her rail under for less than ten seconds by my reckoning and in a fresh breeze too!"

"Sir Henry, Captain Anderson, you are making the poor child quite pale! Come, Marion, the gentlemen will say no more about it. The floor is steady as a ballroom and I have seen you happy enough on that!"

"Why," said Captain Anderson, "I believe we are to hold a ball aboard my ship which is even steadier than this."

"*Alcyone*," moaned Lady Somerset, "*anything* is steadier than this beautiful, wild creature!"

I found my conscious voice at last.

"I am certain beyond a peradventure that Captain Anderson would offer his vessel as a refuge for the rest of your journey, Miss, Miss—Chumley!"

Miss Chumley smiled—Marion smiled! The corners of her mouth turned up—my very heart jumps at the memory—it is a sweet pleasure to try to record it. Yet even when Marion was not smiling nature had provided her with a mouth which made her look not merely good-humoured but as if she were enjoying a joke of such power it was a source of permanent pleasure. But I had no sooner begun to find that the only cure for staring impolitely at this mouth was to stare even more impolitely—and more helplessly—at the eyes above it, which ignores her little nose—says nothing of those eyebrows that implied astonishment which by reason of the smiling mouth meant that her

whole expression was lively and interested—oh, Lord!
The trouble is that since the days of Homer the
greatest of poets have exercised the utmost of their
art in the description of young women. There is no
eloquence, not a figure of speech from understatement
to hyperbole that has not been laid under contribu-
tion! Go outside the common rules of rhetoric—look
for an inspired absurdity, the positively insolent magic
of a Shakespeare or a Virgil—

I have got in a tangle and am going nowhere. How
was she dressed? It did not seem to matter at the time,
but now—

Her dress was white. Blue ribbon I *think* was
threaded through the neckline from shoulder to
shoulder and round the ruched sleeves just above the
elbows. Her earrings were silver flowers and a chain
of the same lay round her neck above the promise of
her bosom. She was slight, would always be slight,
always suggest, imply more than state—like the
greatest of poets!

But Captain Anderson was speaking—had spoken.
I recall the words I was not then conscious of hearing.

"No, no, Mr Talbot. We are not going to India
but Sydney Cove! Besides, our ship is full of emigrants,
passengers, cargo—"

"You see, my dear," said Sir Henry, laughing,
"there is no help for it! To India you must go and in
Alcyone too!"

"I cannot understand," said Lady Somerset, "why
there should be such an absolute requirement from
naval gentlemen of haste now that we have defeated
the French. Surely Captain Anderson—"

Both naval gentlemen laughed. Yes, Anderson laughed!

I found my voice again.

"Miss Chumley, if you will take passage with us I will abandon my cabin to you. I will sleep in the orlop or the bilges. I will guarantee to spend the nights pacing the deck on the side opposite to Captain Anderson—but come, sir—we *have* an empty cabin. I will move there instantly and Miss Chumley shall have mine!"

I believe all this was said in a sleepwalking voice. Men should be poets—I understand that now, Edmund, Edmund, thou scurvy politician!

Anderson was giving a brief account of Colley—how intemperate he had been and how at last after a shocking escapade he had succumbed to a *low fever*. But my determination to defend the memory of Mr Colley was a distant thing. My journal did that well enough and I put the thought aside. The lightning stroke, the *coup de foudre*, was all.

"The rumour went, Miss Chumley, that you was a prodigy which word I discounted but now I see it was no more than the truth."

"Prodigy, Mr Talbot?"

"Prodigy, Miss Chumley!"

Her answer was a peal of laughter silvery as the flowers round her neck.

"The word was wrongly reported to you, sir. Lady Somerset is sometimes kind enough to refer to me as her 'protégée'."

"For me, Miss Chumley, a prodigy, ever and always."

She still smiled but looked slightly puzzled—as well she might; for whatever the lightning had done to me, for her it had been no more than the experience of something—someone—unexpectedly and impossibly familiar; I mean familiar in the sense of recognized to be known, and perhaps also encroaching! Indeed, having guessed that this was so I immediately had proof of it.

"We have not met before, sir?"

"Indeed, Miss Chumley, I should remember if we had!"

"Of course. Then since we are unknown to each other—"

She paused, looking away, laughed uncertainly, then looked back and was silent. So was I; and we both examined the other's face with a serious intentness. I was the first to speak.

"We have—and have not!"

She glanced down and I saw that my left hand held her right one. I was not conscious of taking it and let go with a gesture of apology which she dismissed with a shake of the head.

I was aware of Sir Henry speaking by no means in the voice with which he had greeted Miss Chumley.

"Oh, come straight in, for heaven's sake, Janet! You need not be scared nor say anything, for you was only brought in to make up the numbers."

"Dearest Janet! There, if you please, between Captain Anderson and Sir Henry."

I drew back a chair for Lady Somerset who insinuated herself. Sir Henry did the same for Miss Chumley and I suppose Anderson did the same for the in-

valuable and unfortunate Janet. I could not but be
involved with my hostess for a while and made a sad
business of it, for most of my attention was on Sir
Henry who was telling Miss Chumley what a pity it
was that she could not sing in the entertainment and
let the people hear what was meant by real singing.
Fortunately Lady Somerset had the social perceptions
which seem natural to women of any race or clime.
For she turned away and engaged Anderson in a
trivial conversation which nevertheless must have
been a relief to him. He had been staring glumly and
silently at Janet whose eyes were deep in her plate.
Satisfied, I think, that Anderson was being looked
after, Sir Henry began to eat with an assiduity which
fully explained the rotundity of his person. Miss
Chumley was pushing a little food round her plate
with a fork but I did not see any of it touch her
mouth.

"You are not hungry?"

"No."

"Then neither am I."

"All the same, sir, you must trifle with your fork,
so. Is that not elegant?"

"It is charming. But, Miss Chumley, if you persist
in declining food you will become even more ethereal."

"You could not have said anything more flattering
to a young person, sir, nor held out a happier prospect!"

"For you perhaps; but for me the happiest prospect
would be—no, forgive me. I presume on—dare I say—
oh, indeed I must! An immediate sympathy, a
recognition—"

" 'We have—and have not'?"

"Oh, Miss Chumley! I am dazed—no—dazzled! Rescue me, for heaven's sake!"

"That is easily done, sir. If we are to entertain each other let me tell you quickly what you have in hand. I am an orphan, sir, learned my three R's, considerable French, some Italian and Geography at an establishment for the children of clergymen in Salisbury Close. I am also able to recite you the Kings of England, ending with 'George, the third of that name whom may God preserve'. I am, of course, pious, modest, clever with my detestable needle and can sing very nearly in tune."

"I beg you to eat at least a little, for all these accomplishments need to be sustained!"

The wondrous creature actually leaned a little towards me. Our heads came intoxicatingly close.

"Be easy, Mr Talbot. I am also a little devious and at the moment not at all hungry!"

"Miss Chumley, do not say it! Oh no! Biscuits in your cabin!"

The genuine and silvery laughter rang round the stateroom.

"Mr Talbot, I thought the secret would not disgust you!"

"You have bewitched me already. You must have done so before—when we last met, in—oh, Cathay, Tartary, Timbuctoo, where was it?"

Sir Henry interrupted his mastication for a moment.

"You have travelled, Talbot?"

"No, Sir Henry."

"Well I am sure Marion has not."

She laughed again.

"Mr Talbot and I are making up a fairy story, uncle.
You must none of you listen, for it is great nonsense."

"Nonsense, Miss Chumley? You cut me to the
quick."

Our heads drew together again.

"I would never do that, Mr Talbot. And fairy tales
are not nonsense to some."

I still cannot tell why tears came to my eyes! A
grown man, a sane, really rather calculating man, a
political creature to have water spring up behind his
eyelids so that he is hard put to it to keep them from
falling out down his face!

"Miss Chumley, you make me—inexpressibly happy.
I rejoice to be wholly defenceless."

There was a pause while I swallowed not food but
tears. Oh yes, it was my wounded head, my sleepless-
ness, it must have been—it could not have been what
I knew it was!

But she was murmuring.

"We go too fast. Forgive me, sir, I have said more
than I should and you too, I believe." Then looking
round: "We have silenced the table! Helen!"

But Lady Somerset, dear woman, came to my rescue.

"And what have we older ones to say that is more
important? Enjoy yourselves, my dears, while you
may!"

Anderson and Sir Henry talked. It was professional,
of course—who had been made post and so on. Lady
Helen smiled and nodded and, bless her, ignored
us.

So there I was, wishing with a sudden urgency that my wounds were real—not injuries but wounds! I wished I had led a forlorn hope and come back heroically wounded, wounded so severely that I must be nursed and by whom but this discovered angel? I desired with as much urgency as the other that I might have a uniform with which to dazzle her, or an order; and cursed inwardly the world that hangs ornaments on old men who no longer have a use for them! Yet I felt even in those first minutes that she was a girl of wit and understanding and not to be won by a confection of blue broadcloth and gold braid—oh, God, what have I said? She would not—

What did we talk about? I cannot now remember because our words meant little compared with the tides of feeling that swept through that strange drawing-room! At times I swear there was a living silence between us which was infinitely sweet. Like Lady Somerset we had become, I suppose, or I had become, by the power and influence of my feelings, a sensitive! I did really feel the very being of Marion beside me, a new thing in life, a new knowledge, means of it, awareness; and she I swear again was in the same way aware of me. The voices growled on in the stateroom but we were in a silver bubble of our own.

A bubble! I passed those blessed hours like a spend-thrift heir who thinks that money grows on trees and he need do nothing but bid his man of business wave a wand to make guineas fall instead of leaves. How I squandered those two hours which should rather have been divided into one hundred and twenty minutes, seven thousand two hundred seconds, each second, each instant to have been valued, savoured—no, that is too gross a word—every instant should have been prized—precious is a good word and so is enchantment. Like some knight in an old tale Edmund Fitz-Henry Talbot, with his whole career to make, spent those hours asleep on his shield in the ruined chapel of love! Forgive a young man, a young fool, his ardours and ecstasies! I understand now that the world will only give ear to them in the mouth of genius.

So what do I remember? Nothing clearly of that magic time but only its ending when we were brought out of it by hearing Anderson growl something about "the confounded ball".

"The ball—Miss Chumley, we are forgetting! There is to be a ball! A ball, do you hear? We shall dance the night away. You must promise me your hand for—oh, for what? For every dance of course, well if not, for some of them—most of them—for the longest dance—what is the longest dance? There will be a cotillion! *Yes!* And an allemande—shall we be allowed to dance the valse?"

"I do not think so, Mr Talbot. Lady Somerset as a devotee of Lord Byron cannot possibly countenance a valse, can you, Helen?"

"Lady Somerset, I implore you! Byron is a non-sensical fellow and if he will not allow the valse it is because he is lame and eating sour grapes!"

The argument became general, Marion agreeing with me and declaring (with Shakespeare *hors con-*

cours) that there was no poet in the English tongue
to equal Pope, Sir Henry declaring that most of what
was written was rubbish, Anderson grunting, Lady
Somerset quoting—"Roll on, thou deep and dark blue
Ocean—roll!"

"Helen! No! Do you desire to send me straight
back to my couch?"

The bubble had burst.

Lady Somerset broke off in the middle of "ten
thousand fleets".

"Sir Henry," I cried. "Should we not proceed in
company to the Cape at least? Captain Anderson will
tell you how hard put to it we were to make even a
show of defence!"

"I would do my best to oblige you, Mr Talbot, but
it is not in my power. Besides you need fear nothing,
for we are now good friends with the French!"

"I did not mean—"

Anderson turned to me.

"*Alcyone* is a flyer to have made such time out of
Plymouth. She would be hull down within hours."
Then turning to Sir Henry, "You must have judged
what she would carry to a hair, sir!"

"Why, as far as Gib, Captain Anderson, she was
positively snoring. I tell you, now and then I had to
take a look aloft! My first lieutenant would have the
main course off her at a catspaw. I have had to tell him;
Bellamy, I have said, this is a frigate, curse it, not a
damned company ship. How does your man?"

"Well enough. I have no complaints, Sir Henry, a
happy ship, you know. He knocked some sense into
the people while we were windbound at Spithead."

"Windbound, was it? You should have been with us back of Plymouth Sound, over across from Shit Creek. They took us out with a steam tug. Good God, I have never been so astonished in my life."

"The smoke," moaned Lady Somerset, "the smoke from that metal chimney. My coach cloak was soiled by it. Marion says her pillow was black."

"Helen!"

"You did, my dear. Cannot you remember what trouble we had with your scalp?"

"Come, Lady Somerset," I cried, "Miss Chumley is not a Red Indian! But what is a steam tug?"

"It is an extraordinary invention, Mr Talbot," said Sir Henry, "and I swear nothing but the inventive genius of our country could have brought it forth! It is a craft with a steam boiler, the force from which makes great paddle wheels rotate on either beam. It would throw up fountains of water were the wheels not cased."

"There is too much fire below," said Anderson. "I cannot like the things. If they should explode they might touch off a fleet like tinder."

"And if the paddles should carry away," said Sir Henry, "they have neither sail nor sweep. I tell you, Anderson, all the while I was in tow till we cast off on the starboard tack to pass east of the Eddystone I had anchors hanging fairly by the hawse with such a swing, crash and bangle we lost a man clean out of the heads on a fluke and the seat with him."

"They are building a larger one at Portsmouth," said Anderson. "They will be the ruin of real seamanship."

"They appear to have a limited application," said Miss Chumley. "Their appearance is quite horrid."

"They make a devil of a mess," said Sir Henry, "but there's no denying they towed us out against the wind in two hours when it would have taken all day kedging."

I gathered my wits.

"Might not a larger vessel operate on the High Seas?"

"I suppose it is possible, Mr Talbot, but there is not the necessity. Once given sea room a ship may do well enough for herself."

"Might we not have steam warships then, that paddle out of harbour and seek the enemy?"

Both naval gentlemen roared with laughter . . . indeed, I have never seen Captain Anderson so animated. For a few moments we heard nothing from them but an exchange of fragmentary Tarpaulin. At last Sir Henry wiped his eyes.

"A glass of wine with you, Mr Talbot, and when you come into government I beg you to accept any post but that of the Admiralty!"

Miss Chumley (and it was so *moving* to hear how she sprang to my defence) spoke up like a little heroine.

"But you have not answered Mr Talbot's question, uncle! I am sure he would make a splendid admiral or whatever it is!"

"Mr Talbot shall not be laughed at," said Lady Somerset, "and I am most anxious, Sir Henry, to hear what you have to say to him."

"Well, Lady Somerset," said Sir Henry, "it is the

first time I have heard you express an interest in the subject. I believed you was interested in nothing naval but yellow hair, heroics and poetry! Good God, if we was to have these steam tugs large enough to engage an enemy we should need double the crews to keep them clean, let alone feed them with coal!"

Miss Chumley's defence had fortified me.

"The mechanical genius of the British would overcome all difficulties, I am sure."

"Speak up, Captain," said Sir Henry. "You have as much brains as there is to be found in the service, I think."

Captain Anderson, I thought, looked a little indignant at being accused of intelligence. It was, after all, next door to *clever*!

"The real objection," he said, "if you will have an answer to a preposterous question, is this. We may stay at sea for months. A vessel propelled by steam would consume her coal as she moved. Since the possible length of a ship is limited by the possible length of timber suitable for her construction she can never move more than a distance fixed by the amount of coal she can carry in her hull. Then secondly, if she is to be a warship, a paddle wheel on either side will reduce her broadside, that is, the weight of metal she is able to throw. And thirdly, during an engagement, if a single ball should strike the flimsy members of her paddle wheel she will be rendered uncontrollable."

"We are answered, Mr Talbot," said Miss Chumley. "We are beaten from the field."

Oh, the sweetness of that "we"!

"For my part, I could not understand you, Captain Anderson," said Lady Somerset, "for I declare I was the greatest addle-pate in the schoolroom."

"Nothing," said Miss Chumley, the corners of her mouth rising and a delicious dimple appearing in what (with my exposure to Tarpaulin) I was about to call her *starboard cheek*, "positively nothing is so becoming in a young person as a proper degree of ignorance."

But after her last remark, Lady Somerset gave a significant glance at the other two ladies so that we three gentlemen rose at once. The ladies departed and Sir Henry showed us *where to go*. So there I was, an exile from paradise, standing by Captain Anderson and relieving nature into Lord Byron's "dark blue ocean". I found my deprivation from that upturned mouth insupportable and—oh, Lord, how I do go on! It was what I had always thought a myth, a stage convention, love at first sight, the *coup de foudre*, a fairy tale—but as she said, some people believe them! It may be so. Yes, it may be so.

I hastened back to the stateroom and brandy. The ladies had not appeared and I had a dreadful fear that we had seen the last of them. I talked inanely but remained since the other two gentlemen did. They were deep in Tarpaulin. I heard about our possibly drawn gudgeons, about *Alcyone*'s sweet run aft, about topmasts and a drunken lieutenant whose negligence enabled Sir Henry to turn a handsome compliment, since it was a fortunate circumstance which had enabled him to overtake us. Both gentlemen agreed that if we found a capful of wind during the day neither looked forward to people giving grudging service for being cheated of their fun. I found that Captain Anderson, though approached by a deputation, had refused to splice the main brace even though the news had been so tremendous. He would only do so at anchor, for two doses of rum in one day was the quickest way to indiscipline. So it went on. I was almost in despair when at last the ladies came back. The stateroom of a frigate naturally enough has to serve as both dining- and drawing-room. It was surely by Lady Somerset's contrivance that I found myself— against all protocol—seated *again* by Miss Chumley in what I would have called a window seat, since it was under the great stern window of the ship, but is probably called something quite different—a stern thwart perhaps, but what does it matter? God bless Lady Somerset!

My talk I fear was wild. It was not the brandy. It was not entirely the endless time I seemed to have been without sleep. It was the most tragic of all in- toxications, the most ridiculous, the sweetest.

"Miss Chumley, I beg the allemande of you—and the quadrille—and the round dance—and the cotil- lion—"

"Which shall I choose?"

"All if you please! I cannot bear—"

"It would be improper, sir. You must know that surely!"

"Then I am an advocate of impropriety. We shall dance the allemande round the mainmast and the cotillion from one end of the waist to the other and the—"

"Mr Talbot! A poor helpless young person such as I—"

"Come! You are about as helpless as *Alcyone*! I have no doubt your path is strewn with more conquests than Sir Henry's. You have added me to the list."

"I am not so hardhearted. I will release you. Nor—"

"Nor what then?"

"Peace has been declared, sir. Let us share it."

"You will not be so cruel as to let me go!"

"The wind will do so. Oh, how I fear a recurrence of that dreadful motion! Believe me, sir, *mal de mer* is so disgusting and so infinitely lowering that a young person ceases even to care how unbecoming her situation is!"

"We may prevail on them yet."

"Orders are terrible things, sir. Even when I was utterly prostrated Sir Henry would not roll up a single one of our sails to ease the motion, for all Lady Somerset begged him. You see the close limits of that power you credited me with."

"Had you begged him yourself—"

"I was then a miserable object, hoping only for death. Though come to think of it when we heard we were being drawn inexorably towards your vessel and did not know if you was an enemy or a friend, I found the imminent prospect of the death I had longed for quite, quite terrifying!"

"Dare I whisper, Miss Chumley? I put a brave face on things—but so did I myself!"

We laughed together.

"I honour you for the admission, sir, and will not betray you!"

"Was Lady Somerset not disconcerted too?"

Miss Chumley leaned her dark ringlets close to me and spoke behind her fan.

"Only becomingly so, Mr Talbot. I believe she was in hope she was about to meet a Corsair!"

I laughed aloud.

"And then to find what sailors call 'our miserable load of rotten timber' sitting there with her ports agape and mostly toothless!"

"Mr Talbot!"

"Well after all! But we are determined, are we not? I may take your hand for as many and perhaps rather more than the number of dances thought proper?"

"If I am seized by the wrist, Mr Talbot, what can I do but submit? The fault will be yours."

"I will be brazen."

There was a pause. It was then that I made my one desperate attempt to deepen this airy conversation towards something of more worth. But even as I drew a breath to make my outrageous confessions—*ma'am, I have been struck by a thunderbolt*—I saw how fixed Lady Somerset's smile had become. Captain Anderson rose to his feet. With a positive collapse of the heart I understood that our visit was—*must*—be over. I cannot tell now how I got from that enchanted palace, went to my hutch, immediately thinking and with a lump in my throat—how comical!—of who was speaking to her at that very moment and—but what am I about? I am no poet, whose *job* I now see is to ease men over these moments. "The World Well Lost" or "All for Love"! Such indeed was my sudden and overwhelming passion. I had a sharp feeling of panic at the thought of my appearance, felt my head where there was indeed a disagreeable hardness of clotted blood lying among the hairs of my scalp so that my only thought was how thoroughly this "young person" must have been disgusted. She was all politeness and— but I was clean-shaven, still clean-shaven, and my clothing was—oh, poor fool, poor Edmund, what a fall, no, what a climb—no, not either, but what a translation was there! I felt I should suffer, did suffer already, yet would not have changed places with any other man in the world unless perhaps there might be some man, some other man—*Alcyone* was full of them! Oh, God!

And I had not discovered Anderson's attitude to duelling!

(8)

Thus it was. A fire burned the exhaustion out of me and supplied with its unseen flames a temporary resource of strength which kept me, though fallen on my bunk with—but my store of language had not been assembled for what I now felt had befallen me, a man of such superior intellects, of common sense! Oh, I was, I am, fallen so deeply and generously in love! It was excitement but it was fear too—fear of treading in a new world for which my character was by no means suited or adequate, a chancy, gambler's world—she bound for India, I for the Antipodes— my career—that advantageous alliance with—

Edmund Talbot lay fully clothed on his bunk, desiring nothing so much, able to think of nothing so much, burning for nothing so much as a parson's penniless daughter!

At length I remembered and called for Wheeler, louder and louder till he came.

"Devil take it, man, you stink of rum!"

"Just spliced the main brace, sir. And I was owed some sippers."

"Captain Anderson—"

"Sir Henry persuaded him, sir. A real gentleman Sir Henry is."

"Very well. I require all my gear taken across and put in the cabin Mr Colley used."

"I can't do that, sir!"

"What do you mean 'can't do it'?"

"I haven't an order, sir!"

"I am giving you an order."

"Captain Anderson—"

"I have just been with him. He raised no objection, so you need not."

Wheeler began to grumble but I cut him off.

"Come to think of it you can lay out my evening clothes here before you do anything else."

Knee-breeches, pumps, stockings, tails—the man needed little guidance and it was soon done. I changed my clothes, then went across to Colley's cabin. What was stranger than I had imagined was to find myself in a cabin on the starboard side of the vessel—the right-hand side looking forward towards the sharp end! It was a mirror image of the one I had just vacated and to be there after all these weeks was like suddenly finding oneself left-handed! There was much noise from forrard and indeed noise of one sort or another from most parts of the vessel. Where I was at the back end of the ship there was noise too, from some of the cabins, voices raised and laughter. There had been, there still was what I was told later was called ship-visiting. The penalties for a similar activity on the part of the people were severe, for the same activity if carried out by them was known as "breaking ship". But we had had such an exchange of passengers and two sets of junior officers from wardroom to wardroom and gunroom to gunroom the air of this end of the ship was far livelier than it had been in Sir Henry's stateroom.

There came a knock at the door.

"*Entrez!*"

It was Summers wearing his accustomed shabby uniform suit and a worried expression.

"Mr Talbot, what is this?"

"Why are you not dressed for the ball, man?"

He brushed my question aside.

"Your change of cabin!"

"Oh that. We may well have Miss Chumley aboard."

"Edmund! This is impossible!"

"I am a little abroad in my wits, Charles. May we not leave it for a while?"

"You have had some hard knocks, but Colley's cabin—"

"I could not think of asking Miss Chumley to use a bunk in which the poor devil willed himself to death!"

Summers shook his head. He was not smiling.

"But do you not see—"

"Oh fudge, man! Why are you not dressed for dancing?"

Summers went pink under his tan.

"I shall not attend the ball."

"Methodist!"

"As I once told you, I have never learned to dance, Mr Talbot," he said stiffly. "Quadrilles, allemandes, valses have not come in my way. Do you not remember that I was promoted from the lower deck?"

"The sailors dance!"

"Not as you do."

"Still bitter, Charles?"

"Every now and then. But I have volunteered to

keep the watch during the hours of the ball—if it gets
under weigh, that is."

"Fate could not be so brutal as to prevent it."

"I shall spend the time pacing the quarterdeck and
meditating the suddenly changed future before us."

"The peace. Changed? No, Mr Summers. I have
studied history as much as I may. There will be no
change. The only thing to be learnt from history is
that nobody learns from history!"

"Who said that?"

"I did. Doubtless it has been said by others, will be
said again—and with as little effect."

"You are a cynic."

"Oh, I? If you only knew, dear Charles—I am
excited, and"—the words "in love" trembled on my
lips, but some remaining trace of reserve in my character kept me from uttering them—"in a state of slight
intoxication owing partly to a small amount of brandy
and the fact that I have not slept for several years, I
believe!"

"The blows on your head—"

"Self-inflicted wounds."

"*Alcyone* carries a surgeon."

"Not a word, Charles! He would keep me from the
ball, a prospect not to be entertained for an instant!"

Summers nodded and withdrew. I could hear from
the noises around me that the hour of the "entertainment" had come. I shot my lace cuffs and settled a
ruffle that had been sadly crushed in its long stowage.
I opened the door of my new *hutch* and joined the
throng which was now making its way from our lobby

up the stairs whence we were to watch the entertainment offered us by the people. It was quite extraordinary to see Miss Granham sweep past me in blue
and Mrs Brocklebank in green and Miss Zenobia in
all the colours of the rainbow! But my amusement at
seeing such a festive gathering was nothing to my
utter amazement when we issued into the waist! To
begin with, dusk had become a night even darker than
usual because of the humid mist which still enclosed
us. Islanded in this night was a space. Our space, our
whole world was now so brilliantly illuminated that
instead of being a minute speck in the midst of
infinite extents it had enlarged to become the vastest
of arenas. The sailors had hung lanterns everywhere,
some of them with coloured glasses so that our streets
and squares were not only lighter than by day but
prismatical. There was much bunting. There were
garlands, swags, crowns and sceptres of flowers far too
large to be natural. Stir, as it were, into that the
brilliance of our ladies, the glitter of uniform and the
sawing, blowing and banging of Sir Henry's band
which was now dispensing jollity from some con-
cealed cavern in the front end of our vessel! The
ladies and officers of *Alcyone* had now emerged into
their square and were coming in procession up the
street that had formerly been a gangway to *our* larger
square at the entrance to which young Mr Taylor, all
dressed up, was doing the pretty and far too attentive
to the ladies for one of his tender years! Indeed, I had
to step forward and detach Miss Chumley from him,
as he seemed inclined to detain her. I did so with much

firmness, fended off a couple of lieutenants and set
her without more ado on Captain Anderson's left with
myself on her other side. If the ship's people called me
"Lord Talbot" in jest I might as well take advantage
of my reputation! I did all this with the determination
and success which I hope would have attended our
own boarding party, had it been put to the test. Lady
Somerset was on Anderson's right.

Sir Henry rose, and the whole assembly, both fore
and aft, rose with him. The band struck up and "God
Save the King" was rendered with much solemnity.
That being concluded, we were about to sit down
again when a fellow stood forth and gave us "Rule
Britannia" which all echoed lustily and with much joy.
Indeed, at the conclusion the huzzahs for His Majesty
the King, for the French King, for the Prince Regent,
for the Emperor of Russia, then coming nearer home,
for Sir Henry and his lady, for Captain Anderson—
why God bless my soul, I believe had not Sir Henry
said a few well-chosen words of thanks we would have
gone on huzzahing all night! However, we were seated
at last and the evening entertainment began. A fellow
stood forward and gave a *loyal address* in what he
thought was verse—the most one-legged set of coup-
lets ever composed, I swear.

> *Sir Henry Somerset and Captain Anderson*
> *Now that most battles is over and done*
> *With many losses of life and horrible wrecks*
> *We ask leave to come forward, toe the line, and pay*
>   *our respects.*

My immediate feeling was one of pity and embarrassment for the man. However, looking back, I have to admit that Miss Chumley's quiet but positively schoolgirlish giggle had little of sympathy in it. The man could read and was conning paper. That was the extraordinary thing about him. He was small and wizened. Every now and then his bald head would gleam at us in the light from the lanterns. He had several papers and I began to understand that this address was a corporate effort. He had not thought, or perhaps had not enough paper, or had no previous experience to impress on him the importance of a fair copy! He was forced, therefore, to look from one paper to another, then get at a third which he held upside down and so was compelled to look up at it under his arm and address us in that position. One of his contributors had a stale poetical vocabulary, so at one moment we were in the high style and the French had

> *. . . ploughed in vain*
> *The foamy billows of the bounding main.*

Then in a line or two we were back with

> *. . . now we have done all these*
> *There is nothing between us and home but the*
> *damned Yankees—*

I leaned towards her and was about to comment on the embarrassment it all caused me when she whispered behind her fan that she had not heard anything so diverting since the bishop's address at her confirmation! I was overcome with delight at this evidence of wit in the enchanting creature and was about to confide that she had bound me more firmly than before when I was interrupted by a roar of laughter from the fo'castle—

"What did he say, Miss Chumley?"

"Something about 'Billy Rogers'. Who is he?"

I was deeply shocked but of course did not allow her to see it.

"He is one of our sailors."

But no sooner had I turned back to the performance when I heard that

Mr Prettiman and his lady have put up the banns
In order to get a party of little Republicans—

This was sailing near the wind with a vengeance! But I am sorry to say that the laughter of the ship's people was mixed with a great deal of unlooked-for applause. It did, however, disconcert the social philosopher who looked down and blushed as did, for once in her life, his redoubtable bride-to-be. I began to understand that this was to be a period of licensed fooling and listened with mild amusement to references to Mr Brocklebank and even contrived to look indifferent (oh, what a roar there was from the fo'-castle!) when the man said of the wind that it

Roared loud enough to wake the dead
Or loud as "Lord Talbot" when 'e 'it 'is 'ead.

But all was turned the other side out and a private sun shone on me and on Miss Chumley when she said severely—

"That was most unkind!"

"You are all consideration, my—"

Oh, I could not even use the simple, the gentle familiarity of "my dear" with this smiling girl I had known since God drew out that first rib from Adam!

"Miss Chumley."

So the address went on. He wound to a peroration which was concerned neither with loyalty nor duty but *food*! Was there ever anything at all as much like the *art of sinking*? The main suggestion was that we should now make for a port in South America where we might take in fresh meat and green vegetables. I had not myself noticed any great deficiency in our diet and was about to remark on this to my fair companion when I heard:

> *We find*
> *That the vittals we have on board caused so much*
> *wind*
> *That it is strange the ship is so still and steady*
> *And has not been blowed to Sydney Cove already.*

Sir Henry shouted with laughter at this and made some jocular sound in Anderson's direction. Little Mr Tommy Taylor laughed so much he fell off his seat. To my astonishment this was the end of the address. The man gave a kind of curtsey to us, then made his way back into the crowd of emigrants and sailors who thronged the fo'castle and the *stairs* up to it. He received much applause from them and there was some chanting of "Fresh food! Fresh food!" but it died away. Now the orator's place on the deck was taken by, of all people, Mrs East! She had evidently recovered if not completely from her miscarriage, at least sufficiently to allow her to walk; but she was painfully thin and there were still the shadows like a wasting disease in her cheeks.

"That is Mrs East."

"You know her, sir?"

"I know of her. She has been mortally sick. A—she has been near to death, poor creature."

Mrs East began to sing!

The effect was extraordinary. An absolute stillness descended on the city, there was not a movement, not a sound. She stood, clad in the simplest of dresses, her hands clasped before her; and that stance made her seem childlike—an appearance which was enhanced by her physical emaciation. The song rose from her mouth. She was accompanied by no instrument. Her unaided voice silenced or kept silent a whole crowd of sailors warmed with drink. It was a strange song—strange and simple! I had never heard it before. It was called "Bonnie at Morn" and it was simple as a hedge rose yet it haunts me still—oh, not for her, not for Mrs East, not for anything but itself, I think—as the sounds of the boatswain's call haunted me after the funeral of poor Colley. I was confused in my head, of course, I had forgotten what it was to sleep—yet like the boatswain's call it changed everything. It admitted us—it admitted *me* to halls, caverns, open spaces, new palaces of feeling—how foolish and impossible! Those tears which I had been able to restrain at my introduction to a new life now fell. I could not help it. They were neither tears of

sorrow nor of joy. They were tears—and I do not
know how this is possible—they were tears of *understanding*! When the song ended there was still silence,
as if people heard some echo and were loath to believe
that it had died away. Then there was a kind of grunt
that led to prolonged and I am sure heartfelt applause.
Miss Chumley shut her fan, allowed it to hang from
her little finger by the ring at one end and laid her
palms together three times.

"She sings well, Mr Talbot, does she not?"

"Oh yes."

"Our singing master, you know, would have wished
more tremolo and of course a more practised presen-
tation."

"Yes. I suppose so."

"Why, sir—you—"

"Forgive me, Miss Chumley. Remember I have
been hit over the head and am not entirely—"

"It is I who should ask forgiveness! I applaud your
sensibility. The song was indeed touching, well sung
and in tune. A piece of nature! There! Does that go
any way towards contenting you?"

"Anything you say contents me."

"You must recover slowly, sir, from such an injury!
You are not to be exposed all at once to the pro-
founder human emotions. See! They are about to
dance a hornpipe, I believe. So I may talk without
fear of interrupting the music. Do you know, sir, I
once had to compose an essay on the subject of Art
and Nature? Now would you believe it? Though I
fear young persons are sadly docile—or should I say

dutiful?—yet while the others were positively eloquent in their defence or advocacy of Nature—for it is fashionable nowadays to believe in Nature, you know—I discovered to my astonishment that I preferred Art! It was the moment at which I became an adult. For you see I believe I was the only young person in the school who saw that orphans are the victims of Nature and that Art is their resource and hope. I was dealt with very severely, I can tell you."

"They had not the heart!"

"Oh indeed!"

"I am recovered, Miss Chumley, and can only apologize once more."

"I am *so* happy to hear it! Indeed, sir, I sacrificed myself on your behalf in a reference to my unfortunate essay. Lady Somerset must never be allowed to know that I have said a word against Nature. It would shock her deeply. She is persuaded that India is a natural paradise. I believe she may be disappointed."

"And you?"

"Oh, I? What I expect is nothing to the purpose. Young persons are like ships, Mr Talbot. They do not decide their fate nor their destination."

"I am grieved to hear you say so."

"Oh, something may be done! Come, sir, I will not have you grieving!"

"What are we to do?"

"Why, enjoy the entertainment and the ball and the, the company! I cannot speak more plainly."

The hornpipe was much less expert than the one we see commonly danced in theatres. It was replaced by Morris Dancers! They were eight men in the usual smocks and straw hats. They carried wooden swords which they wove into a ring and held up for our languid applause. They also had the Hobby Horse! He committed as many improprieties as he could and chased the young women. He then circled forward to where the ladies sat but was told sharply enough to go off and return whence he came. He did so, but by some simple mechanism erected his tail in a way which would have earned John Coachman his discharge on the spot! Sir Henry then stood up and thanked the people for their entertainment and wished them joy of the peace. His band now took up a new station and our quadrille commenced. The people did not take Sir Henry's hint but crowded every vantage point with a good enough humour. I might here set down the conversation which ensued between Miss Chumley and me. But it was sufficiently banal, I think. Despite what is written in novels it is difficult to dance and talk when you have got out of the way of such a social activity. Having little help from me, Miss Chumley was silent and we moved together with a feeling of such community it was perhaps more satisfying than speech.

Nevertheless I was soon a little disturbed. Deverel, though under open arrest and forbidden drink, had most unadvisedly joined the company. Since the officers were not wearing swords there was nothing to distinguish him from the other gentlemen and he might have enjoyed the ball without being noticed. But it was plain to me, at least, that he had been drinking; and now, when glasses of wine and spirits were borne round, he took a glass and despite the captain's express prohibition boldly tossed it off. He then claimed Miss Chumley for the next dance which I had begged—without any inclination but with what I hope was a well-feigned eagerness—from Lady Somerset. What with my endeavours to recollect the pattern of the dance and the lady's practised conversation I was able only to give a glance now and then at how Deverel was conducting himself. He was, I saw, if not encroaching, at the very least ingratiating. Lady Somerset gave it as her opinion that the allemande with its steps and circling movement was a more natural dance—by which she meant I believe more according to *Nature*—than the formal quadrille. Deverel made play with Marion's hand, oh God. Lady Somerset commended the energies of our men who had so sanded the deck it was quite, quite the equal to a ballroom. Deverel made a positive *advance* to his partner! I missed two steps.

"No, no! The right foot, sir!"

Somehow we got back into time. I begged Lady Somerset to allow her protégée to exchange into our ship—there was room—to do otherwise was to inflict such suffering on a delicate person— But Lady Somerset ceased to sway and showed unexpected and what I now see to have been a clear-sighted common sense.

"Come, Mr Talbot. We know who is suffering and who will continue to!"

"I refuse to allow circumstances to thwart me!"

"A proper sentiment in a young man, sir. Why this

is the stuff of poetry and here am I, a devotee of the
muses, forced to be the one all poets deride!"

"No, ma'am!"

"Oh yes. If you were yourself, Mr Talbot, and not
suffering from the effect of your injuries you would
see it as I do. Marion is in my care. She must remain
in *Alcyone*. Of course she must. Daylight will bring
you to your, your—"

She said no more and we danced for a while in
silence. It seemed to me that Miss Chumley was finding Deverel positively impertinent. There was nothing
I could do. However—

"If the mountain will not come to Mahomet—"

The dance ended, for which I was heartily thankful
and for the fact that Miss Chumley hardly allowed
Deverel to see her back to her seat but frankly walked
away from him. After returning Lady Somerset to her
husband I went to Miss Chumley, only to find
Deverel slumped by her in my chair.

"Ha, Mr Deverel—my chair, I think!"

"Edmund Lord Talbot. Congratulations on your
elevation, my boy. That makes you the highest rank
in the Atlantic and is one in the eye for Rumble-guts
and Windbag!"

Miss Chumley, who was not yet *quite* seated,
quickly begged that we might take the air, for, said
she, fanning herself busily, the atmosphere was insupportable to one so lately arrived from England.
I offered her my arm and we went up to the rail of the
quarterdeck where there was relief from the crowded
company at least. I would wish to fill in the back-

ground to our dialogue with all the scenery of a tropic
night—stars, an inky sea streaked and spotted with
phosphorescence, but alas! Chance had wasted all that
beauty in using it as a kind of backdrop for the trifling
with Miss Brocklebank of which I was now ashamed
and which I now felt, ridiculous as it must appear,
had soiled me! I felt in need of a tub so that, did she
but know, this young and delicate creature would not
endure the merest touch of my hand! Who was now
the Methodist? The scene in reality was more suited
to my awareness of my new condition. It was a close
mist, rendered foetid by the sojourn in one place of two
crowded ships! We faced each other by the rail. I
looked down at her, she looked up at me. The fan
moved more and more slowly. Her lips moved and
she made the shape of words without saying them. It
was more than flesh and blood could endure.

"Miss Chumley, I will find some way—we must
not part! Do you not feel, do you not understand? I
offer you—oh, what do I offer you? Yes, the ruin of
my career, the devotion of a lifetime, the—"

But she had half turned away from me. She looked
down into the waist, then immediately swung round
and faced the other way, breathing quickly. I glanced
down. Deverel lowered the glass he had raised in her
direction, then staggered three steps sideways to end
by putting out his left hand and supporting himself
against the mast. He crossed his left leg over his right
one, snatched a drink from a tray Phillips was carrying past, lifted the glass with what I can only call an
air of bravado and drank directly to Captain Anderson!

Now it is to be remembered that this transaction took place in full view of all the people of the two ships— the whole population of our town! I saw Captain Anderson's head sink as he leaned forward in his chair and knew, though he was facing away from us, that he had lowered the upper part of his face and projected that minatory jaw beneath it! The next dance had not yet begun so there was no music. I heard and everyone else heard each harsh word that he said.

"Mr Deverel, you were placed under open arrest and forbidden drink. Return at once to your quarters and stay there!"

I have never seen so furious a gaze in a face as that with which Deverel received this order. He lifted his glass not as if to drink but as if to dash it at Anderson— but some glimmer of common sense must have prevented him, for instead he turned aside and hurled it into the scuppers.

"By Christ, Anderson!"

Cumbershum got to him and had him by the shoulder.

"Be quiet, you fool! Say nothing!"

He shook Deverel impatiently and half-led, half-dragged him away. They disappeared into the lobby under the poop. There was a great burst of talking and laughter. Then the music struck up.

"Miss Chumley, let us stay where we are!"

"I must not disappoint your Mr Taylor."

"Little Tommy Taylor? Good God, the impertinent scamp! I will have his ears for this—and see! There he goes, led off by our Mr Askew by one of those same ears for some misdemeanour or other! You have lost a partner, ma'am, so we may stay where we are in the lee of the poop until the dance after this when I claim again. Do you resist?"

"I am your prisoner."

"Would it were so! But you are merciful and lend an ear to my heartfelt prayer."

Below us, Sir Henry was standing up and Captain Anderson.

"I beg the favour of a few words, Sir Henry. The quarterdeck?"

The two captains came up the ladder to the quarterdeck. Miss Chumley murmured to me.

"Should we not return?"

I laid my finger on my lips. The gentlemen passed and climbed up the second stairs. They began to march back and forth so that as they approached the rail their voices were clear, then faded as they turned away again.

"—is one of *the* Deverels, is he not? Unfortunate!"

Then after a turn—

"No, no, Anderson. There is no time for a court-martial. You know I am under express orders."

And again—

"—hope you may find some way on such an occasion to reduce the charge to one on which you are empowered to award your own punishment—the young fool! And a Deverel too! No, no, Anderson. It is your ship and your man. I heard nothing, you understand, and was deep in conversation with Prettiman's fiancée, a most superior woman."

Miss Chumley whispered again.

"I do believe we should return, Mr Talbot!"

"We are plainly to be seen by at least half of our little world, Miss Chumley, and—good God, what are they about?"

It was the ship's people on the fo'castle. They were performing their own quadrille! It was, to put it baldly, a parody of ours! It was quite horridly skilful. I do not believe the people themselves knew what cleverly satirical dogs they were! They could not, of course, perform the actual figures but by moving about in a more-than-stately manner, by curtseying and bowing they accomplished much. That young fellow in a sail-cloth skirt who swooned, positively swooned past anyone he met, could be no one but Lady Helen! There was also a stocky old man with one of the "ship's boys" sitting on his shoulders. Together they reached to a considerable height and the rest of the company deferred to them ridiculously. There was much noise, laughter and clapping so that the music of the dance of which young Mr Taylor had been deprived was hardly to be heard. Miss Chumley observed the dance on the fo'castle with sparkling eyes.

"Oh, how happy they are, how gay! If only I—"

She said nothing for a while but I waited and at last she spoke, shaking her head.

"You would not understand, sir."

"Teach me."

Once more she shook her head.

Now Sir Henry and Captain Anderson descended from the quarterdeck and resumed their places of honour at the side of the dance.

"We should return too, sir."

"A moment! I—"

"I beg you will say no more. Believe me, sir, I understand our situation even more clearly than you do! Say no more!"

"I cannot leave you with as little mark of favour as might be accorded to any man in either ship!"

"It is the cotillion!"

So we did descend and took our places for this last dance. As we did so the ship's bells rang out, the boatswain's calls, and after that, the voices of authority now speaking in unison.

"D'you hear there? D'you hear there? Pipe down! Pipe down!"

It was remarkable with what docility (for all their parodies and double issue of rum) the people disappeared into their own places. Only Sir Henry's band and a few of the emigrants, Mrs East among them, stayed to watch our final entertainment. We said little or nothing though the dance, as everyone knows, is designed for conversation. For me, it was only just bearable.

At last it ended, or as I might say—since it was less a pleasure than a grief—at last the thing was done. Some of the passengers said their farewells to Captain Anderson and left, the officers of *Alcyone* too. Sir Henry *collected* his lady and looked round. But Lady Somerset bore him away firmly to the gangway. Lanterns were going out everywhere in both ships. Captain Anderson, now a shadowy figure, stood by the mainmast, contemplated what had but now been a ballroom as if to see in what way it had been injured.

Miss Chumley moved towards the gangway. I dared to take her by the wrist.

"I repeat, I cannot let you go tonight without more than such a mark of favour as might have been bestowed on any gentleman in either ship! Stay if only for a moment—"

"I am Cinderella, you know, and must run back—"

"Say rather in your fairy coach."

"Oh, it would turn to a pumpkin!"

From the deck of *Alcyone* came the dulcet voice of Lady Somerset.

"Marion dear!"

"Then say you do not regard me as little as these other gentlemen—"

She turned to me and I saw how her eyes shone in the gloom; and the whisper reached me, as heartfelt as a whisper can be.

"Oh—no indeed!"

She was gone.

(9)

My tears came again. Good God, I was a leaky vessel,
used to keep my waters to myself but now cracked
from top to bottom! I stood, my feet rooted to the
deck, but this time by happiness not fear. Will there
ever be a moment for me to match it? I do not think so.
Unless— Captain Anderson turned, grunted me a
"Good night, Talbot," and was about to ascend the
stairs when Deverel emerged, or rather staggered, from
below them. He carried a paper in his hand, came towards Anderson, then stood in front of him. He thrust
the paper into the captain's face.

"Resign   commission—private   gentlemen—issue
formal challenge—"

"Turn in, Deverel! You are drunk!"

Now there ensued the most extraordinary scene in
that semi-darkness which only the distant lights from
the great stern lantern modified. For as Deverel endeavoured to make the captain take the paper the captain retreated. It became a chase, a ludicrous but
deadly parody of "Touch" or "Blindman's Buff", for
the captain dodged round the mainmast and Deverel
chased him. Not convinced that the captain did this
to avoid being struck—possibly a capital offence—
Deverel shouted "Coward! Coward!" and continued to
pursue. Now Summers and Mr Askew with Mr Gibbs
behind them came running. One of them cannoned
into the captain so that Deverel, following close behind, reached him at last. I could not see if the

collision was intentional but certainly Deverel thought
it was and cried out in triumph, to disappear almost
instantly beneath a heap of the other officers. The
captain leaned against the mainmast. He was breathing
heavily.

"Mr Summers."

Summers's voice came, muffled, from the flailing
heap.

"Sir."

"Put him in irons."

At that there was a positively animal howl from
Deverel and the heap convulsed. The howling went on
except when it was interrupted as Deverel sank his
teeth into Mr Gibbs who took up the howling and
cursing in his place. The group of struggling men
moved away towards the shelter of the aftercastle, then
disappeared. Shocked, I saw a shadowy Sir Henry
climb to *Alcyone*'s quarterdeck. He seemed to be peering across at our ship. But he said nothing.

Young Mr Willis came running in his shirt, then
disappeared forward. Captain Anderson stood by the
folded paper that lay on the deck. He was breathing
heavily and quickly. He spoke to me.

"I did not receive it, Mr Talbot. Pray be a witness to
that."

"Receive in what sense, Captain Anderson?"

"I did not agree to take it. I made no move to take it."

I said nothing. Young Mr Willis returned. One of
the older seamen came behind him with something
clanking in his hand.

"What the devil?"

"It is the blacksmith," said Captain Anderson with his usual abruptness. "He is needed to restrain the prisoner."

"Good God! Good God!"

Summers came running.

"Sir, he is motionless. He is collapsed. Do you think—"

I could *feel* the captain lowering at him.

"Carry out my orders, Mr Summers. Since you are so tender you shall have them confirmed later in writing."

"Aye aye, sir. Thank you, sir."

"Now that paper on the deck. It is material evidence. Observe I do not touch it. Kindly pick it up and take charge of it. You will be required to produce it later."

"Aye aye, sir."

"Mr Talbot, you have noted everything?"

I said nothing.

"Mr Talbot!"

What was best for poor Deverel? My head, no longer concerned with anything but the overwhelming absence of Marion Chumley, my love, my saint, had no place left in it for the severities of the law nor for calculation!

"I do not wish to interfere in a service matter."

Captain Anderson uttered that double cachinnation which the novelist is accustomed to denote inadequately by the letters "Ha! Ha!" But in this case they are more than inadequate, they are misleading. For they conveyed, if anything, his opinion of me and my

actions in a less than flattering manner. It was nothing
so cheery as laughter. It might be what the Old Testa-
ment credits the war horse with when it utters a like
sound "in the midst of the battle". He was expressing
his opinion of me in a way which could not be committed to paper and produced in evidence. It was clear
that his opinion was unflattering. But subduing everything in me was my enchantment, my overthrow, sweet
as it had been, and my need to get away and lie in that
sweetness until at last after how many days and years
I slept.

It made me angry.

"Devil take it, what do you expect of me? I am as
aware as you are of the circumstances and their im-
plications—"

"I do not think so, sir."

"It is possible that everything said in these moments
may be produced in evidence. I will *not* be hasty!"

Captain Anderson lowered up at me in the gloom.
Then with an abrupt nod he turned away and marched
up to the quarterdeck. I held my head. Somewhere
below us there sounded the hideous blows of a hammer
on iron. I went to the gangway where even now a
marine stood at one end and a soldier at the other. I
retraced my steps and tiptoed up to the quarterdeck,
then leaned on the rail to see if I could judge the exact
spot behind the wooden wall where Marion might be
trying to sleep. Sir Henry came across the deck.

"Sir Henry!"

"That was the devil of a row! Is all well now?"

"Sir Henry, I must speak with you!"

"Oh, Lord! Well, never let it be said a Somerset was less than obliging to a FitzHenry. Come aboard, my boy—no, not here, devil take it! Do you want to fall in the drink? There, by the gangway!"

I made my way round and he met me at the break of *Alcyone*'s poop.

"Now then, it's about little Marion, is it not? A charming girl but if you wish to correspond, my dear boy, you must get permission from Lady Somerset—"

"No, no, Sir Henry, it is more than that—"

"Good God! The little minx!"

"She is all sweetness, sir. I beg you will let me take passage in *Alcyone*."

"Good God! Have you—"

"I am Mahomet."

"Good God! You've been drinking, curse it, that's what it is!"

"No, sir! I wish to take passage—"

"Your career, my boy, your godfather, your mother, devil take it, what is all this about?"

"I—"

But what was I? Where was I?

"I'd do most things to oblige you, lad, but this is beyond anything!"

"I beg you, sir!"

"Of course, I was forgetting. You've had a rare clout over the head, my boy! Now come along!"

"Let me go!"

"Lend us a hand here!"

I do not know even now how Charles Summers appeared and Cumbershum. The soldier at the gangway must have helped. All I remember clearly as they forced me back was thinking that if Marion heard what went on she would never forgive me—and then I was being pushed into my bunk, with Wheeler pulling my pumps and unmentionables off. There was the pungent odour of the paregoric.

It seems probable that without Colley's natural ability in the art of description there is no way in which I can convey the confusion of what happened. Nor do I know at what point I became delirious nor, what is stranger and more awful to contemplate, at what point previously I had become delirious! I am told that the surgeon, called out of his bunk, did indeed come across to our ship and examine me, though I have no recollection of it. Perhaps then it was a young man in the grips of a real, physical fever induced by triple blows who dreamed of a meal in *Alcyone* and all that followed thereon? But no. I have been assured these things happened and that I conducted myself with no more than the *élan* natural in a young man until, that is, I went aboard our neighbour ship in the dark and spoke with Sir Henry. Then, as if some hold or brake had given suddenly, I became temporarily disordered in my wits. Certainly I remember—not fighting—but struggling with the group which was trying to restrain me. I remember, too, how desperately I tried to explain the absolute necessity of my transfer to *Alcyone*, a declaration of nothing but the truth, but taken by my nurses or gaolers as further proof of the derangement consequent on my wounded head! Then, while they removed my clothes I found that I could not say what I meant at all but was forced to utter a string of absurdities. I was in Colley's bunk, for when they got me to what had been mine, of course it was empty, so I was bundled across the lobby and heaved not without more danger to my head into a bunk forever reminiscent of that unhappy man. The surgeon they tell me could only advise rest and promised a complete cure at the end of it since my skull was not cracked. So, busily gabbling of what neither they nor I understood, I lay held down, while somehow they got the paregoric into me in a dose that rapidly had me singing for joy among the angels. So singing and so weeping with joy I fell at last into what we must call a healing sleep.

If to be restored to a complete understanding of one's situation is to be healed let us all, all prefer sickness. I did swim now and then up towards consciousness; or since the effect of the opiate was to elevate me towards some seventh heaven, let us say that now and then I swam or dived down towards consciousness without ever getting there. I remember faces— Charles Summers as might be expected, Miss Granham, Mrs Brocklebank. I am told that I implored Miss Granham to sing. Oh, the humiliations of delirium! The sordid, the very humbling necessities of the sickroom! Nor was my cabined humiliation complete, for I was to set a positive fool's cap on it myself —though once again if I am to be blamed it is for being so physically clumsy as to do nothing but bang my head while all the other passengers were obediently contributing to our defence! Delirious or sane I must remain enraged with myself and with my fate.

Partial understanding did return. As it had departed at a bound so it came back. I was aware of movement, my head thrust against the pillow, then allowed to fall back. I lay as this happened numberless times; and then, like a blast of cold wind, the understanding was there—we were under weigh, the wind was up and the sea. These were no flat regions but waters furrowed and rolling. I remember crying out. I fell out of my bunk, scrabbled the door open on the streaming lobby. Then I was out on deck, up the stairs and climbing into the shrouds, climbing up and howling some senseless words or other.

Yes. I remember that; and yes, I have pieced the episode together in all its absurdity. The ship is making what way she can over a beam sea and with much wind. For all the wind her way is little because the stumps of masts will not allow of a full spread. Few people are on deck, thank God. But then a haggard young man, shaggy as to the hair, and bearded not a little, staggers out from under the aftercastle, his thin body plainly to be discerned beneath the nightshirt that beats against him in the wind! He crawls up the shrouds, then clings, staring forward at the empty horizon and screaming at it!

"Come back! Come back!"

They got me down. They say I did not resist but finally allowed myself to be carried like a corpse and laid once more in Colley's bunk. I remember how Summers removed the key from the lock and put it in again on the outside. After that, for a time, any visitor unlocked the door, then locked it behind him when he left. I had declined to the status of a madman and prisoner. I remember, too, how when Summers left the first time and I was alone how I lay on my back and began to weep.

(10)

No man can weep for ever. There came a time when my preoccupation with my sorrow was first mixed and then near enough swallowed up in an awareness that the movement of our ship was not such as it had been, but more nagging and restless, with moments which seemed not so much of petulance as of fierce anger. I felt too weak to understand or combat it and fell into a childish panic at the thought of being worn down and abandoned in a sinking ship. I remember at last, God help me, shouting for Charles Summers, then bawling at Wheeler when he appeared instead.

"I must see Mr Summers! Get him!"

After that there was a long interval while the ship did its best to fling me out of my bunk. At last Charles appeared. He stood in the doorway, holding it open and frowning down at me.

"Again? What is it this time, Edmund?"

The words "this time" brought me up short.

"I am sorry. I believe I have been delirious."

"That will be all, Wheeler! I am speaking to Mr Talbot. Look, Edmund, I am the ship's husband—"

"The what?"

"I am responsible for more things than you can imagine. With the greatest goodwill in the world I cannot spare more than a little time for you! Now what is it?"

"The movement. It is killing me."

"Good heavens, Edmund, you are far down. Listen.

You have been injured. *Alcyone*'s surgeon said you are
suffering from delayed concussion. Sleep and rest are
what he recommended."

"Neither is possible with the ship moving so."

"The movement cannot be helped. Will you be
easier if I explain it?"

"I might feel easier to know we aren't sinking."

He paused for a moment, then laughed.

"Well then—do you understand the mechanism of
a clock?"

"What do you take me for? A clockmaker? I know
how to wind up my repeater. That's enough."

"Come. That's more like the old Edmund."

His mouth was open to say more but he was interrupted by the sounds of a screaming fit from one of the
cabins at a distance from us. Perhaps it was the Pike
children, in a quarrel near to hysteria. Charles ignored
the screams and spoke again.

"A ship is a pendulum. The shorter a pendulum is,
the quicker its oscillation. We have lost our topmasts,
in other words we have shortened our pendulum, and
accelerated our motion. A completely dismasted ship
can have a period of roll so brief there is no living with
it, people are so flung about and sick and exhausted. I
suppose ships have been lost so."

"But not us!"

"Of course not. The most this additional movement
will do is discomfort our passengers. They do indeed
need all the comfort they can get. Some of the gentlemen are gathered in the saloon. They spoke of you and
wished you one of their number."

I sat up laboriously in my bunk.

"Accept my apologies, Mr Summers. I shall pull myself together and do what I can to cheer the other ladies and gentlemen."

Charles laughed, but amiably enough this time.

"From the depths of despair to a noble resolve in less than ten seconds! You are more mercurial than I supposed."

"Nothing like that."

"Well. The gentlemen will welcome you though you would be better advised to stay where you are like the ladies."

"I have been too long in my bunk."

Charles removed the key from the outside of the door and put it in the lock inside.

"Whatever you do, Edmund, take great care. Remember, one hand for yourself and one for the ship! In your case I advise both hands for yourself—you have been beaten about the head more than enough already."

So saying, he withdrew.

I climbed out of my bunk as cautiously as I could and inspected my face in the mirror. The sight appalled me. Not only was I heavily unshaven, my face was so thin as to be positively bony. I passed a finger over the prominent ridges of my cheeks, touched my high, but now thin nose, pushed the hair off my forehead. It is surely impossible that a skull should shrink!

I shouted for Wheeler who came with an instantaneity which showed he had been standing just outside the door. I had him help me to dress, refused his offer to shave me and then did it myself in a cupful of water which was no more than lukewarm when I started and stone-cold when I had finished. However, I contrived to perform the whole with no more than a single nick on my left cheek which in view of the ship's movement was a considerable achievement. Wheeler stood by me the while. He begged my pardon for making the suggestion but said that even if I was about to join the gentlemen in the saloon I should wear my India rubber boots there was so much water washing about. So observe me at last stumping, legs wide apart, one hand on the rail which was fastened to the outside of the passenger hutches. The ship swung me about pettishly and sheets of water slid across the darkened wood of the lobby. I knew at once it was not merely my weakness which made movement difficult. What was only tedious before was now an evil tax on strength.

Whatever talk had been among them, there was a silence for a while when I appeared. They sat round one end of the long table immediately under the stern window. Mr Bowles, the solicitor's clerk, was at the end. Oldmeadow, the young officer, sat on his left with Mr Prettiman left again. Mr Pike faced them. I reached the table at a run and collapsed on the bench next to him. Oldmeadow looked across at me down his nose. He means no hauteur by this carriage of the head. It is only natural to him because the extraordinary helmet the officers of his regiment wear has increased the angle somewhat and habituated him to it. He himself is the mildest and least warlike of men.

"I trust you are feeling more the thing, Talbot? It is good of you to join us."

"I am perfectly recovered, thank you."

That was a lie but in a good cause. Nevertheless it failed, for Mr Bowles shook his head at me.

"You do not look recovered, Mr Talbot. But then, all of us are affected."

"Oh, surely not! The movement if anything is cheering."

"Not to me. And not to the women and children."

As if to emphasize his speech, outside the great stern window the horizon sloped the other way with particular speed, then vanished downwards. The wet deck beneath lifted us up, then left us suspended as it fell. I felt sweat start out on my forehead.

"I think, gentlemen, that—"

But Bowles, whose stomach seemed indifferent to these antics, was going on.

"Now you are here, sir, you had better be co-opted at once. The motion—"

"It is due to the shortening of our masts, gentlemen. A pendulum—which is what—"

Bowles raised his hand.

"Not that motion, Mr Talbot. I refer to the motion before the committee."

"My children must be considered, Mr Talbot. And Mrs Pike, of course. But the little children, my Phoebe and my Arabella—"

I braced myself and emitted what I hope was a convincing laugh.

"Well, gentlemen, you surprise me! Britannia rules the waves, we all know, but—"

"We believe there may be a remedy."

"How? I cannot think what remedy you have found for a difficulty which is inherent in our situation! Or have you some such scheme as poor Dryden must have had in his head? I remember reading in his *Annus Mirabilis* where he describes in our seafight against the Dutch how the sailors when the masts were shot away 'raised them higher than before'."

"Mr Talbot—"

"And you know, even to a young landsman as I was then, the concept seemed the height of absurdity! I do not think that—"

Mr Prettiman shouted.

"Mr Bowles was elected chairman of this meeting, sir! Do you wish it adjourned or will you leave it?"

"Allow me, Mr Prettiman. Mr Talbot may be forgiven for supposing this is no more than a social gathering. Now, sir. We have constituted ourselves an *ad hoc* committee and come to certain conclusions. We wish to bring to the captain's notice, not so much our opinions, for it is doubtful that we have any right to them, but our deep feelings. I have the heads jotted down here. One. A prolonged continuation of the ship's movement as she endeavours to make way against the wind in her present unsteady condition constitutes a real danger to life and limb—particularly where the women and children are concerned. Two. We suppose that relief might be found by an alteration of course away from the wind and towards a South American port where the ship might be repaired and our health restored."

I shook my head.

"If such an alteration was necessary our officers would have made it."

Oldmeadow cawed into his collar in the way these fellows have when affecting to laugh.

"No, by Jove, Talbot. They may think of the ship and the people there in the front end but we may go whistle for consideration—and the Army most of all!"

"It would tediously prolong the time we spend in our voyage."

"Little Phoebe and Arabella—"

Bowles raised his hand again.

"One moment, Mr Pike. We hoped that you would agree with us, Mr Talbot. But then, does your agreement signify?"

"I beg your pardon, sir!"

"Don't misunderstand me. I mean that in the event the decision is not mine or yours but the captain's. All we plan at the moment is to make our wishes known. In fact, Mr Talbot, I must break it to you that *in absentia* you have been elected to—how shall I say—bell the cat!"

"The devil!"

"There was no one more able, Mr Talbot, we knew that—and you could take poor little Phoebe along and pull up her smock and show him the rash which I do not think is to be borne, sir, and what will happen if—"

"Mr Pike, for the love of God!"

"Or if you think it beneath you I will take her along—"

"Damn your insolence, Pike! I will take her along or

them along or anyone along! Oh, for God's sake, all of you, let me think! I have been—"

I put my head down in my wet palms. Sick to the stomach—in love with a girl gone over the reeling horizon, head split and aching inside and out—the taste in my mouth of vomit already.

Bowles spoke softly.

"It is a compliment to you, sir. We are in your hands. No one else is so likely to have influence with the captain. Your godfather—"

I shook my head and he fell silent. I thought for a while.

"You are going the wrong way about it. An approach to the captain must be your last resort. Personally, I do not agree that we should alter course. Children are liable to rashes. Why—my young brothers—we ought to endure—carry on across this wilderness until we reach our end. But you have touched my, my . . . I will try to persuade the first lieutenant that he should carry your wishes to the captain. If he will not, or if the captain refuses that first approach, then yes, I myself will go to him." At last I took my head out of my hands and blinked round at them.

"We must go with great care. The position of a passenger in a ship of war—the captain's power may well be absolute. Who would have thought when I said he was our moghool that this occasion was waiting round the corner? I will make your views known to the first lieutenant. He may even be on deck—and now—"

I stood up and bowed. I reeled to the door and took a clumsy run through the streaming lobby, got the door of the hutch open and collapsed on my bunk. When Wheeler entered, he having, I suspected, waited outside the saloon door and then my door—and was only happy it seemed within arm's length of me as if he were harnessed for my convenience—Wheeler helped me into my oilskins. I muttered a queasy dismissal and he replied that he would remain to clean the cabin and "do what he could" with the bunk. I gave little thought to his curious assiduity but slumped for a while in my canvas chair to get myself together. At last I hauled myself to my feet and opened the door as the sheet of water in the lobby splashed over the combing which is supposed to keep it out of our hutches. I went forward into the daylight of the waist, holding on where possible. There was wind on the left, a grey sky above, grey sea, dirty white foam, a wet ship drab as the skirts of a beggar woman. The water in the lobby was as nothing to the positive tides of it which made an intermittent hazard of the open deck. There were safety lines rigged everywhere. These daunted by implication rather than invited and seemed at best no more than ropes tying together the wet, belaboured box that was our ship. I saw a seaman working his way along a rope to the fo'castle. He held on with one hand while a wave washed over him as high as his waist and a torrent of foaming water fell on his head and shoulders from the fo'castle itself. I waited for a pause in our motion, then made a staggering run to the windward side of the ship and hung on to a belaying pin under the ship's rail. I opened my mouth wide and took great gulps of the wet air which at least served to quell the unease of my

stomach. I felt as strong an irritation at this latest demand on my tact and ingenuity as ever I had done when
asked by Charles Summers to do what I could for the
wretched Colley! And success, a turning aside from our
present course to redirect the ship towards the coast of
South America, would do no more for me myself than
delay my arrival in the Antipodes! It would put beyond
all possibility those faint hopes—a delay at the Cape
of Good Hope—even their ship delayed and rescued
by us as she wallowed mastless on our course—of
seeing Miss Chumley once more before the remotest
of remote futures!

I cursed aloud. As if to torment me further our ship,
struck by a seventh wave, bucked like a frightened
horse and seemed to remain without forward movement, for all her straining sails. I stared round me trying to understand what I could of our situation and I
was rendered very thoughtful by what I saw.

The last time I had watched the conduct of our ship
in such weather had been in the English Channel.
There, as if she were aware that she was under the eye
of Old England, for all the boisterousness of the sea
and sky she had seemed to take part and revel in the
friendly contest. She did so no more. Like a horse
which knows itself tired and moving further and
further away from its stable, she jibbed and went slow.
She was sullen and needed a touch of the whip—better
still, a whiff of the manger! Although her bows were
pointed up towards the wind she had next to no forward movement. The waves passed under her—or
sometimes, it seemed, over her—but she did hardly

more than heave up, then slide down into the same trough in the same place. I dared to haul myself upright and peer over the rail by me. I was rewarded by the sight of what looked like green hair swirling among foam as if those fabled and inimical sisters swam about us holding us back and pulling us down! Before I had recovered from the cold thrill of the sight the whole sea with its hair and foam rose at me, over me, drowned me, pulled at me with appalling strength so that my two hands clutched round the iron barrel of the belaying pin were no more than just enough to prevent me from being washed clean out of the ship and lost for ever.

Someone was shouting in my ear.

"This is no place for passengers! Get back while you may! Come now—make a run for it!"

It was a voice with extraordinary authority. I did run, splashing through a few inches of pouring water as the deck came momentarily up to the horizontal, then continued to swing over in the other direction. My feet slipped and I should have performed a glissade which would have smashed my bones in the opposite scuppers had not the man running beside me grabbed my arm and fairly lifted me onto the stairs leading up to the afterdecks. Here he pushed me against the rail, made sure I was attached, then stood back.

"You were nearly gone, sir. Mr Talbot, I believe."

He pulled off his sou'wester and shook out far more golden locks than a man ought to have. He was smaller than I. But then—so are most people! He smiled up at me with great cheerfulness as a volley of spray shot past us. I had an instant impression of blue eyes, pink

cheeks and ruddy lips which seemed by their delicacy
to have evaded the wildness of the weather and even
the touch of the tropic sun.

"Thank you for your assistance. To tell the truth my
strength has not yet come back. But you have the advantage of me."

"Benét, sir. Lieutenant Benét with one 'n', and an
acute accent on the second 'e'."

I was lifting my free hand to take his politely but as
I did so he raised his head and his face changed to one
of anger. His eyes seemed to sparkle as he stared forward and up into the rigging.

"Francis, you careless bugger! If I see you slip out of
the strop to save yourself trouble I'll have you at the
grating!" He turned back to me. "They are worse than
children, Mr Talbot, and will kill themselves heed-
lessly where you might well have done it through ignorance. You must allow me to conduct you to your
cabin—no, no, Mr Talbot, it is no trouble—"

"But you are employed about the ship!"

For answer he glanced up at the rigging again.

"Mr Willis! Although you are mastheaded you may
consider yourself in charge of the work there and the
men employed about it. Contrive not to lose the mainmast. Now, Mr Talbot—run for it!"

To my surprise I found myself obeying this young
man with an alacrity which even Captain Anderson
could not have produced in me. What is more I
jumped into the lobby with a sense of what a jest it
all was!

"That will be all, Wheeler. Mr Benét, pray be
seated."

"You are a sick man, sir. I am not sick in body, though perhaps in mind it is a different story. Grief fills my sails.

> *Fairest woman*
> *In form and feature really most uncommon.*

I worked that out and more of the like during the last dog. Oh, I remember now. It went

> *fairest creature lovelier than a woman*
> *In form and feature really most uncommon.*

The lines were wrenched from me. They came all in one piece.

> *Nor would I lay*
> *A feather of regret upon thy soul.*

The feather is particularly felicitous, is it not?"

A painful suspicion grabbed at my heart.

"You are from *Alcyone!*"

"Where else in this waste of water?

> *A long, long exile now must be my lot.*

Do you approve the alliteration? We shall meet again of course. But I am summoned to a conference with the first lieutenant in the hold."

He withdrew briskly. I shouted for Wheeler who as usual was near my hutch. He got me out of my oilskins.

"That will be all, Wheeler."

A young man with golden locks, fair face and weeks of access to Miss Chumley! Now I experienced all that anguish which I had thought exaggerated by poets!

(11)

I came to myself again to hear unusual noises in the hutches on my side of the lobby. They came nearer and at last, with a knock on my door, revealed themselves to have been caused by the carpenter, Mr Gibbs, who had curious leather pads strapped to his knees.

"Sorry to trouble you, sir, but I have to follow the run of the planking."

"What on earth for?"

Mr Gibbs scratched in his sandy hair. At a distance of about a yard I caught a whiff of strong drink.

"The fact is, sir—pardon!—they say she's moving a bit which is what you'd expect seeing she's so long in the tooth—"

"She's 'rendering like an old boot'."

Mr Gibbs seemed gratified by my comprehension.

"Just so, sir. Just that and nothing more. Nothing to worry the passengers. It's surprising when a gentleman like you as has been at sea no more than a dog watch knows what's what. Mr Brocklebank when I did his cabin didn't hardly understand what I was on about though he did give me a drink for my trouble—"

Mr Gibbs paused and eyed my bottle of brandy but I did not respond. He knelt down therefore and began to extract my two drawers from beneath my bunk which was not easy to do in that confined space.

"What the devil are you doing, Gibbs? Careful! Those are my shirts!"

"I won't dirty your dunnage, sir, but I just has to get my hand—ah!"

"Can't you hear me under there?"

"I got to get my hand where they're butted—"

His speech turned instantly into a kind of squeal. He backed out, put his fingers in his mouth and sucked them, rocking from side to side and moaning.

"What have you done, Gibbs?"

He went on rocking and moaning, one hand holding the other to his mouth.

"Brandy!"

"Help yourself if you must. Good God, man, you've gone sallow!"

Mr Gibbs did not trouble himself with the nicety of my tumbler. He took the bottle out of its hole in the shelf above my canvas washbasin, pulled the cork with his teeth and stuck the neck in his mouth. I believe before he took another breath he had swallowed a quarter of the bottle.

"You'll be drunk as an alderman!"

He put the bottle back in its hole, flexed his fingers and blew on them.

"After all these years to be caught that way like a 'prentice! Oh yes, she's what you might call rendering. Some might call it that, sir, and some might call it something else but it don't matter, do it?"

"Is there danger?"

"Rendering. You know, sir, being took flat aback didn't do her no good at all. Yes, she's rendering. I wouldn't really like to say what's going on in her one way and another—though when a man has stuck a spike into every piece of timber in the ship and had his nose to the planking like a dog after a bitch, why he gets her in his head—"

"Her?"

"Her whole shape more than if she was his own wife and neater than was ever drawed out in the loft. All the movement and every bolt—"

"Our ship?"

Mr Gibbs sat back on his heels.

"Our ship as ever is. And after all that, a man can do with a bleeding drink or two."

"We're in danger then!"

Mr Gibbs focused his eyes on me, frowning as if it were a great effort. He scratched again in his short, sandy hair and seemed to come to himself. His face cleared and he smiled. The smile was not convincing, however.

"Danger, Mr Talbot? Now don't you go worrying! I've knowed ships you might think was falling apart and they come home to lie up snug as if they was all seasoned timber and twenty-one shillings to the guinea. Not but what—"

He paused and sucked his fingers again.

"Go on, man. Tell me!"

Mr Gibbs smiled in my direction but vaguely.

"She's seasoned all right, sir. There isn't a bit of wood where it matters as isn't older than any man in the ship unless it might be Martin Davies, poor sod. The real danger you see, sir, is when you get a mix, like—seasoned and unseasoned. When I was only *that* high I come across a bud sticking out of a knee— must have been dead, of course, but how was I to know that? I told the chippy's mate but he took no kind of notice of it beyond giving me a clip over the earhole."

Mr Gibbs gave my depleted bottle of brandy a thoughtful look.

"I would advise against more brandy, Mr Gibbs."

"Ah well. I wasn't more than a nipper but I had nightmares about that bud. Once I woke up hollering, having fell out of the hammock and felt about in the dark for the chippy's mate—Gilbert, he was called, had me calling him Mr Gilbert—I felt about in the dark and of course I could no more than reach the underside of the hammock to give it a prod. 'What the fuck?' shouts he. 'Mr Gilbert,' I hollers, 'that there bud, it's a twig!' He leans out of his hammock and gives me a clip where he thought I was, only I wasn't. 'I'll give you twig, you bit of grommet,' he says. 'I don't like it,' I says, 'it's putting out a leaf.' He gives me a clip and that one took me fair between wind and water. 'A leaf is it now,' he says. 'You can call me when it puts out a fucking flower.'"

Mr Gibbs seemed to find the memory pleasant, for he was shaking his head and smiling.

"There was a ship once, Mr Gibbs, put out so much greenery you could hardly see it for leaves."

"You're having a little joke, sir."

"There was a vine grew out of the mast and it made everybody drunk."

"The drunk part don't surprise me at all, sir. What port was she said to come from?"

"She was a Greek ship, I think. Mythological."

"That them lot used unseasoned timber don't surprise me; but in those parts they don't hardly drink at all! You'll excuse me, I know—"

The man helped himself to another drink from the bottle.

"Well really, Mr Gibbs!"

"A nice drop, sir. I don't think I'll be in any case to work when it bites. Ah! Here it comes!"

Mr Gibbs, still sitting back on his heels, shut his eyes and swayed against the movement of the ship. There was a pause while he said nothing and my new passion returned upon me.

"Mr Benét seems a very pleasant gentleman. I imagine he might well make himself very pleasant to a lady."

"Very pleasant all round, sir, though his parents is hemmy-grease. He wrote some poetry for the entertainment, though it was so high and mighty I couldn't understand a word of it. The brandy is really biting, sir. I'd be glad if you don't let on to the first lieutenant. Yes, very pleasant Mr Benét is and, Lord, he might be the other side of the Cape and making fifteen knots and a nigger if he hadn't been so sweet on the captain's lady!"

"Doubtless he—what did you say?"

"There I go again. Never did know when enough was enough. Everybody knows, only they didn't say it above a whisper seeing he's an officer. Caught them the captain did, him on his knees and she not trying to get away very hard."

"Lady Somerset! And I, I feared that—but how was this?"

Mr Gibbs scrambled unhandily to his feet. He lurched against this table-flap at which I am writing. His face that had been sallow was now red and sweating. This together with his sandy hair made it easy to imagine a spirituous conflagration inside him! He touched his forelock in a way which I am sure is unbecoming in an officer even though he be no more than warranted. He staggered again, opened the door and went flying *downhill*, if I can so express it, half-way across the lobby. He returned backwards, thumped the next cabin, then was to be heard diminishingly as he made his way below. Wheeler, who must have been *appliqué'd* against the plywood bulkhead which formed the wall of our hutches, shut the door for me, then opened it again and announced submissively that he would replace the drawers. There seemed no room for me in my own cabin.

"Wheeler. The ladies must have found the movement of *Alcyone* insupportable."

"Yes, sir. I dare say, sir."

"Miss—Miss Chumley must have spent the whole voyage out from England in her bunk."

Wheeler said nothing. I was uncomfortably conscious of the impropriety of making such a remark to a servant. I tried again.

"Mr Benét—"

The words stuck in my throat. I could by no means move towards the subject which was the source of such delight and anguish to me! Yet surely there was someone to whom I might confess—it seemed that "confess" was the word—that I was in love and desired nothing so much as to *talk* about the Beloved Object even though I could not talk *to* her!

"Wheeler—"

The man was looking submissively at a point below

my chin. Now he lifted his eyes and seemed to examine each part of my face in turn curiously as if the face of a man was something new and strange to him.

"Very well, Wheeler. That will be all."

For a moment or two the man continued to stare into my face, then seemed to "come to" with a slight start.

"Yes, sir. Thank you, sir."

"And another thing, Wheeler. You was a lucky dog, you know. It must have been a chance in a million! It would be proper to give thanks, you know."

An extraordinary shudder shook the man from head to foot. He bent his head and got out of the door without looking at me again. Certainly there was no possibility of making a confidant of him—and somehow I could not feel that Charles Summers, so understanding in many ways, would be understanding in matters of the heart! It was Mr Benét or no one—Mr Benét who must surely know Miss Chumley—who was in love—who would sympathize—

How was I to follow him down into the hold?

Deverel! Deverel my one-time friend whom sickness and love to say nothing of circumspection and dislike had driven from my mind! Deverel in irons! I would descend looking for him and come across Mr Benét and Charles Summers as it were accidently. I would open in that privacy not just the committee's request but my opinion of it. I rebuked myself for my lack of consideration, my forgetfulness of a friend in need. Only my injuries and my "delayed concussion" could excuse it. Later, I would detach Benét from Charles and lead the conversation gently round to *Alcyone* and her ladies!

I made a lurching, zigzag progress down the ladders, rehearsing my various speeches as I went. The last time I had come that way I had been impelled, not to put too fine a point on it, by lust. Now that I was descending again through those shadowy, those heaving and creaking and dripping and trickling levels, I understood only too well the difference between that descent and this one. I felt the depth of my engagement! The penalty of a "level head", of a politic and cautious habit of mind, is that the day of our first and last passion is delayed and all the stronger for being unexpected!

Picture me then descending to the low level of the gun-room which was yet the lightest of all. Those who make themselves the snuggest in a ship are the warrant officers and here they were using more light than all the becandled passengers together. No less than three lanterns swung from the deckhead. These three—not the cut bottles which the seamen fill with tallow but heavy objects of brass—exhibited a movement which you can find nowhere but in a ship unless it might be, of all places, the ballet. They swung exactly in time and to the same angle. Or rather—this is difficult to describe, I need Colley's pen—they appeared to swing. It was the ship that moved, of course, while the lanterns by virtue of their loaded bases hung steady. It was unnatural and sickening. I looked away and found that by contrast with this brilliant illumination the corners of the gun-room were densely dark. Patches of shadow moved and changed as the lanterns performed their strange dance. As I came through the door the three presented me with their brass bottoms, then flipped back with a revealed glare of light, hovered for a moment or two, then swung back towards me again. It was enough to drive a man out of his wits, these lights dancing in a row. I had difficulty in keeping my head clear and the foul taste out of my mouth.

Mr Gibbs was nowhere to be seen. But opposite me on the other side of a fixed table sat Mr Askew, our gunner, with the ancient midshipman, Mr Davies, beside him. Mr Davies rested his wrinkled and veined hands on the table. His mouth was slightly open and he was staring at nothing. It was as if the constant inconstant lanterns with their flash then dark (huge shadows performing a similar movement over further parts of the great room) had kept him silent, and spellbound as one of M. Mesmer's subjects—kept him with an empty head, waiting for some order which might never come.

Mr Askew looked at me bleakly. He had a glass before him. He did not seem glad to see me.

"And what might you want down here, sir? He's turned in."

He jerked his head towards a particularly dark corner. A sluglike object was suspended there from the deckhead by both ends.

"Mr Deverel—"

"That there, Mr Talbot, is George Gibbs. He come down here all of a twist saying you'd made him drink brandy to which his constitution is unused. He fairly tossed down his rum and was that far gone I had to sling his hammock and heave him into it. If we see him again any time between now and the middle you can call me Lady Jane."

"I wish to visit Lieutenant Deverel."

Mr Askew eyed me closely. Then he put down his glass and took out a short clay pipe. He fumbled about under the table.

"Martin! What have you done with my prick?"

He nudged Mr Davies who rocked a little but did nothing otherwise. Mr Askew thrust his right hand into the midshipman's left pocket.

"You thieving bastard, Martin!"

He drew out a long object wrapped in canvas and proceeded to cut a slice from the end of it. He crammed the slice into the bowl of the pipe, took a piece of "slow match" from a "half-bottle" and laid the glowing end on the tobacco. He puffed out a quantity of stinking smoke so that I gagged. I became aware that I was swaying between the doorposts, one hand on each in a way which must appear positively silly.

"Kindly tell me where Lieutenant Deverel is, Mr Askew, and I will withdraw from these premises since I do not seem to be welcome in them."

Mr Askew continued to puff without saying anything. Suddenly the lights and shadows, the insane, balletic dance of the lanterns, which was a counter-image of the ship's uneasy motion in the sea, took me by the head and throat and stomach and knees.

"If you don't mind—"

I staggered forward, grabbed the table and fell onto the bench. The evil smoke curled round me and I felt the sweat start out on my brow.

"Not feeling quite the thing are you, Mr Talbot? Not quite so much the 'lord' these days?"

This was too much. I swallowed whatever was in my mouth.

"I may not be a peer, Mr Askew, but I am commissioned to serve His Majesty in ways you probably never heard of and would not understand. You will oblige me by paying my position the respect due to it from a warrant officer of the Navy, however senior."

Mr Askew continued to puff. Under the deckhead the smoke now hung, bellying as if a chimney needed cleaning. His face had turned a dusky red, but not, I think, as Mr Gibbs's had done from his potations. One puff of smoke rolled insolently near my face. When he spoke his voice was cracked and tremulous.

"It's 'ardly—hardly lovable, is it?"

"Lovable? *Lovable?*"

"The carry-on. The swaying about. The hoity-toity. Since we have got so far and there is no one to hear."

I glanced significantly at Mr Davies, still silent, still bound by the spell. Mr Askew removed his pipe and wiped the stem with a yellow and horny thumb.

"You see I liked the way you took those blows to the head and come up all set to be a hero. To do what you could, I mean. He'll be a man one day, I said to myself, if someone don't kill him. Only you don't know nothing, do you? In the entertainment when Joss read that bit about 'Lord Talbot' if you'd stood up and bowed with your hand on your heart and a smile on your face we'd have took our corn from your hand as sweet as a miller's donkey. Only you puckered up like. Oh, I know it's hard when you're young—"

"I am more than—"

"You're young, you see. There's officers and warrant officers and petty officers and seamen of this and that —captains of tops and captains of heads and the poor bloody seamen what don't know sugar from shit as they say in Pompey—"

"I will not allow this to continue in front of a witness! Make a private conversation of it, sir, and I shall know how to answer you!"

"Witness? Who? Martin? Bless you, Martin won't give trouble. Why—listen!"

He nudged the old man, then leaned sideways and spoke close to his ear.

"Sing, Martin! Good Martin!"

He paused. The lanterns danced, there were water noises and the creak and stretch of timber.

"Sing, Martin."

With a reedy, quavering voice, the old man sang: "Down to the river in the time of the day—"

It was the beginning and the end of his song. It was the endless end, over and over again.

"He's the real bottom of the barrel, isn't he? I suppose he might have rose to be a lieutenant if he'd had luck or a shove up the bum from an admiral. But it don't matter to him now, does it? Not what he was or might have become. He's had it all and gone home, sir. He don't hear us, isn't here."

"I—I don't know what to say."

"Brings a man up against it, don't it? Less trouble to stop a round shot in the guts if you ask me, though now there's no war to speak of except this Yankee sideshow there'll be a sight too many people living a sight too long if you ask me—which you have not done. But he's no trouble. Hasn't dirtied himself yet as far as I know. All right, Martin lad. Stow it."

My jaw must have dropped. I gulped my own spittle. "Does everybody—"

"Bless you, no, sir. It's living and dying in ships. He's gone home like I said. The likes of me, well we're hard as the ship's bitts never having known what it is to have parents and all that gear. But Martin, you see, he could remember his parents so he has in a manner of speaking a home to go home to, I don't really mean go home but when he's like this it's the same really."

To my own astonishment I fell into a spontaneous fit of swearing. When I had done I had my face in my hands and my elbows on the table.

"Well I never, Mr Talbot. And you living among lords even if you wasn't one of them. I've heard of being drunk as a lord but for really strong language— well there!"

"I ought to tell you, Mr Askew, that Mr Gibbs obtained strong liquor from Mr Brocklebank, then more from me without an offer on my part."

"Ah. I did wonder if he was at it again."

"As you know, Mr Askew, I have been—unwell. Now I am on my feet again I have come down to offer Mr Deverel such comfort and assistance as I may without prejudice to the 'customs of the sea service'. Where is he?"

There was a long pause while Mr Askew continued to add to the fog lying under the deckhead.

"A good question, sir. I know you've been keeping your bunk but I'm surprised you never heard seeing he was such a friend of yours."

" 'Was'? He cannot be dead!"

"I have to tell you, sir, that Mr Deverel is aboard of *Alcyone* and like as not by this time he's the other side of the Cape."

"But I thought—"

"You thought he'd put his head in a noose? It's what comes of not knowing the rules where you are, sir. I don't mean the articles of war. I mean what goes on. Ever since that lieutenant got himself hanged by that captain—I forget the names—in the West Indies it was—captains, to say nothing of their lordships, has been walking on tiptoe. So there's the rules of the service and there's what goes on in ships. It was an exchange, you see."

"Lieutenant Benét!"

"Now you see, don't you, sir?"

"It cannot be within the competence of mere captains to decide such things!"

"Mere captains? The saying is, once a ship's out of sight of land a captain can do anything he likes to you but get you in the family way. Sir Henry wouldn't want to put Mr Benét out of the ship just like that, seeing as he's a watch-keeping officer. No, sir, he arranged an exchange so nobody would have cause to complain. Very anxious to keep officers happy are their lordships. So Captain Anderson having an unhappy officer to dispose of and Sir Henry having an officer to get rid of as was too bleeding happy, we lost Dashing Jack who was very eager to go and we got Lieutenant Benét who knows far more about everything than a gentleman properly should. They say Captain Anderson can't do enough for him. It's Mr Benét's idea to bring the chronometers up one deck whatever Mr Summers thinks and damn the rating. Very popular Mr Benét is with officers, old ladies, children and midshipmen—let alone powder-burnt old horses in charge of the ship's artillery."

"Deverel! Dashing Jack Deverel! Handsome Jack!"

"Just so, sir. If you ask me, Sir Henry is out of the frying pan and into the fire."

"Ladies! He must have—oh no. Lady Somerset is a fine woman and it is true his inclination does lie that way—"

Mr Askew laughed.

"If you're thinking of Jack Deverel it's any port in a storm with him from a lord's lady to a little girl what still bowls her hoop."

"A girl! A young girl! Deverel!"

"He's a rare one is Jack."

I found I had got to my feet. A lantern was poised perilously near my head.

"So you see, sir, it isn't any use looking down here for Mr Deverel, or anywhere else unless you can swim faster than she can sail. Come to that, there's one or two of us aboard would be very glad to get news of Dashing Jack so as they might have some hope one day of being able to ask for their money back."

"Mr Benét!"

"You'll find him with Mr Summers forrard there, aft of the mainmast and the after pump. God knows what they'll do to poor George if they want advice on how much she is moving and send for the chippy. You done him proper, Mr Talbot."

"As I told you, Mr Askew, he did himself."

(12)

It was dark indeed. On my previous visit to these nether regions I had been afforded the services of young Mr Taylor as my conductor. Moreover in those days we had been gliding gently through the waters of the tropics. Now I was in a frantic ship, and feeling my way. Two yards beyond the lights of the gun-room and there might never have been in my world such things as light and direction. By the time I had gone five yards I was more thoroughly lost than I had ever been in a covert! All I knew was sound, much creaking and gritty straining, but there were sounds of water as if I were crouched on a gravel beach! I waited for a while in the hope that my eyes by habituation would adjust to the darkness and was thus only too able to listen to our predicament! Yet my assessment could not be professional and ignorance turned what had been a natural apprehension into something like terror. There were what might be called the subsidiary splashes, drips and trickles of the water in our hold but these were not the worst. There was more beyond and below these local suggestions. I put my hand in a wetness and water poured over my fingers from where I could not discover and fell where I knew not. My one hand laid hold of a wooden edge, the other, some fabric stuff. My walkway was no more than a plank wide, so I crouched and waited until the awful, cold fact that underscored our lumbering progress forced itself into my understanding. There was a rhythm down here which was not to

be heard on deck or in my cabin among the wilder
sounds of wind and sea. It was a pouring sound which
commenced at some distance—somewhere towards
the bow, for what that was worth and if I had the right
direction. I stopped in my tracks and crouched, using
ears instead of eyes. There approached me with increasing speed all the complicated sounds of a breaking wave! It passed by me yet without an increase in
the local wetness. It went on, back the way I had come,
diminishing in volume so that once more I could hear
near me the dripping and trickling of random water.
Then, as my right hand tightened instinctively on
wood to take my weight, water poured across under me
from one side of the ship to the other—and here,
returning, was the first wave, surely travelling the ship's
length! I began to claw round, fell over rope and knelt
for a moment on what might be sacking. Then there
was blessed light above me as if the deck had opened
and the sky looked in.

A voice spoke. "Who is it?"

"It is I!"

But then I could see I was looking up at the purser's
contrived office. He was standing in the opening and
had pulled the canvas aside to look down.

"You cried out. Once again, who is it?"

"It is I, Mr Jones, Edmund Talbot."

"Mr Talbot! What are you doing down here? Pray
come up."

I pulled myself over the massive knots which secured
the ladder to some even more massive crossbeam.

"You have been poorly, Mr Talbot, since we last

met. Pray take a seat. That box will do, I think. Now what can I do for you, sir? You surely have not filled the folio I was able to sell you!"

"No indeed. I was—"

"Lost?"

"Confused."

Mr Jones shook his head and smiled benignly.

"I could tell you exactly where you are in terms of the ship's construction but I believe that would not help. You have just felt or fumbled your way past the stalk of the after warping capstan."

"No, it does not help. I will get my breath back, if you please, then go on my way. I am looking for Mr—"

"Mr—?"

"Mr Summers—or Mr Benét."

Mr Jones peered at me over the half-moons of his steel spectacles. Then he took them off and laid them down on his desk.

"You will find both gentlemen through there, on this side of the pump, which is in turn on this side of the mainmast. They are in some sort of conference."

"Are they debating the question of the ship's safety?"

"They have not confided in me and I did not enquire."

"But surely you are as concerned as anyone!"

"I am insured." He shook his head and smiled, apparently in admiration—"I'm odd like that, you know."

"But however that may secure the comfort of your dependants—"

"I have no dependants, sir. You mistake my meaning. My personal safety I have put in the hands of those I take to be most useful in a crisis—powerful seamen, skilled in their trade."

"That applies to us all!"

"No, sir. Why should I concern myself with us all?"

"You cannot be so selfish and you cannot be so secure!"

"Words, Mr Talbot."

"If your security is more than imaginary we ought all to share in it!"

"That is impossible. How many of the people in this ship could lay their hands on one thousand pounds? You perhaps, sir. No one else."

"The devil!"

"You see? I have an agreement, properly signed. At least, they have made their marks. Should there be an unhappy end to the ship I am worth one thousand pounds to some of the strongest and most skilful seamen in the world. The Bank of England is no safer."

Now I did indeed laugh aloud.

"That a man of business, of affairs, should be so simple! Why, sir, in the event of a catastrophe, they—may I say we?—should preserve the lives of women and children before such as you were even considered!"

Mr Jones shook his head with what seemed like pity.

"You cannot suppose that with the ship sinking round us I should count out gold and give each man his portion? You do not understand credit, Mr Talbot. I do not have any dependants, but my seamen have. The money is there for them ashore when they get me

there, no sooner. Good heavens, Mr Talbot, the boats
we have would not hold a tenth of our people! Without some such arrangement as I am accustomed to
make, the whole of our life at sea would be no more
than a lottery!"

"I am dreaming, I think. There cannot be such—
and even reckless men such as sailors are commonly
supposed to be—they would not set your life at a
higher rate than their own!"

"My boat is up there on the boom, Mr Talbot."

"But Captain Anderson—"

Mr Jones appeared to stifle a yawn, then once more
he shook his head, and smiled as if at some remembered pleasure—his own oddness, perhaps.

"I will hold the canvas aside for a while after you
have gone down. That should give you enough light
until you see theirs."

This *congé* left me surprisingly without speech. I
tried to infuse a degree of contempt into a slight bow
as I edged past him, but cannot feel that he took any
notice. He was right in one thing. Before I had passed
into complete darkness again—and it was strange how
the light seemed to diminish the pouring sounds of our
internal wave, our tiny internal wave!—I caught the
glimmer of another light beyond what might be the
sacking-wrapped body of a coach.

"I say! I say! Hullo! Is anybody there?"

There was a pause and no sound but the glutinous
cluckings of appetite from the water within us. Then
through the intestinal wash of our wave I heard a
familiar voice.

"Who's there?"

"Charles? It is I, Edmund."

There was a brief pause, then the glimmer brightened and became a lantern held aloft by young Mr Taylor. Its light fell on coach wheels, harness, a shaft, all packed round with full sacks, against which the ship deposited me as water poured from one side of the ship to the other. I was by what looked like a hut.

"Mr Talbot, this passes everything! You must leave at once!"

"With respect, Mr Summers, is that wise? Mr Talbot is an emissary—"

"If you please, Mr Benét. I am still first lieutenant of this ship and shall remain so until their lordships see fit to declare otherwise!"

"With respect again, sir, since he bears a message from the committee—"

There was a pause while the two pale faces peered at each other. It was Charles Summers who moved first, lifting his hand in what looked like a gesture of defeat.

"Roberts, Jessop, report back to your stations for duty. Mr Taylor, leave the lantern here and report back to Mr Cumbershum. Don't forget to thank him. Now, sir; oh, for heaven's sake, Edmund, sit down! On that bale. You have been sick and are in no case to stand about when she is moving."

"I will lean against this cabin—"

"Against the magazine, you mean. Now do not, I beg of you, continue to use that box as a rest for your feet. It is the bed in which our three chronometers are kept."

"With respect, sir, kept for the time being."

"How did you know about the committee and my message—my alleged message?"

"Do you suppose such affairs can be kept secret? As it happens, you have come upon the best place in the ship for a private conversation! Your precious committee should have foregathered down here."

"With respect, sir, I will walk a step to make sure that Roberts and Jessop are not hanging about."

"Do so, Mr Benét. Well, Edmund, shall I take your message as spoken?"

"They—'we', I suppose I should say, wish to make known their *opinion* that for the sake of the women and children the ship's course should be redirected to South America."

"Have you ever heard of a null point?"

"Not as far as I can remember."

Mr Benét's face reappeared, pale in the light of the lantern.

"All clear, sir."

Charles Summers nodded.

"The sea, Edmund, which earlier peoples, savage peoples and poets such as Mr Benét, have credited with thoughts and feelings does sometimes exhibit characteristics which would still make the mistake understandable. Those who go down to the sea in ships can sometimes find themselves in a combination of circumstances which produce an appearance of malevolence! I do not refer to storms and flat calms, dangerous as they can be, but to small events and minor characteristics, to odd exceptions and unstatistical behaviours—you are listening, Mr Benét?"

"Devoutly, sir."

"—which soulless and material as they are can none the less produce a position in which men are conscious, strong, adept—and forced helplessly to watch a quiet destruction moving inexorably upon them."

We were all three silent for a while as the hold dripped and trickled around us. Below me, it seemed, the wave passed once more.

"I was not prepared for this. What are these circumstances? Is this what I am to take back to the committee?"

"Understand the circumstances first."

"I will try. But you have set my head spinning."

"The null point. The term is sometimes used of a line where two tides meet and so produce motionless water where a current might be expected. I can find no better words for our situation. *Point non plus*, perhaps? You see it's not a question of whether we will or will not stand towards South America. I suppose you mean the river Plate. We cannot proceed in that direction. What is more, we are satisfied that we cannot touch anywhere at the Cape of Good Hope. We have got ourselves too far south—"

"He, confound him, has got us too far south!"

Charles turned to Mr Benét.

"Observe, Mr Benét, that I express total disagreement with Mr Talbot's remark about our captain."

"Observed, sir."

"But ships go further south than this! Good God, how do they—why, whalers spend years in the Southern Ocean!"

"You do not understand. Are you willing to—I will not say 'to lie'—but to play down the seriousness of our situation as far as the passengers and indeed the rest of the people are concerned?"

"You had better explain."

Charles Summers sat on a bale, Mr Benét sat on what looked like a bench end, I lay against my bale and the lantern stood on the bed of chronometers and lit us all three palely.

"It goes back to—oh, as far as the ship is concerned, as far as when she was built!"

"They say of these ships, Mr Talbot, that they were built by the mile and sawn off as required!"

"Defective building is only too common in warships, Mr Talbot. Copper through-bolts are sometimes no more than a dummy head outside and a pin on the inside. It saves all the copper in between, you see, and lines someone's pocket. Commonly, of course, these things are not discovered until the ship is broken up."

Mr Benét laughed sunnily.

"Or at sea, of course, sir, when the holes begin to squirt, but this is not often reported!"

"Can men do such things? Why—it is our—"

"We do not know if this ship has such defects. They have not revealed themselves in detail. But we feel she moves too much, has spewed too much oakum to be sound in her main frame; and she is old. Now add to that, Edmund, that the wind elected to change by no less than a dozen points at the very moment when an unworthy officer, your friend Deverel, had sneaked below for strong drink and left the con to a poor creature—a midshipman—"

"Willis."

"—who will never make a seaman if he lives to be a hundred."

"Would you care to continue, Mr Benét, or shall I—? That is not the half of it, Edmund. She was taken aback, when any competent officer could have prevented it. She was wrung and might have gone over if we had not lost our topmasts. Even so the foremast moved in the step and broke it. Watch the foremast, Edmund, and you will see the hounds—the top bit of what is left—describing a small circle. We cannot use the foremast and by reason of a balance of forces which will be immediately apparent to you, we cannot as a consequence use the mizzenmast either. Now observe. The same wind which lamed us drove us back, helpless as we were, into warmer water. We idled and weed grew. That makes us even more helpless. The upshot of all is that we have no choice, you see. We can only go more or less where we are driven."

"What is going to happen? All is lost then!"

"By no means. By submission, by obedience to the forces of nature we may just outwit them."

"And the ship's people too, sir, let alone the passengers. Moreover as you know I propose we should take steps over the weed—"

"Shall I finish what I have to say, Mr Benét?"

"I beg pardon, sir."

"Very well. Now, Edmund. Have you ever seen an atlas inscribed with lines showing the advised course for a ship between one point and another?"

"No."

"You will find it curious, I think. For example a ship

bound for India would not take the direct route from the Cape across the Indian Ocean but would make a great curve taking her nearly to Australia—"

"We might come across *Alcyone* again!"

Charles smiled but shook his head.

"I am sorry, Edmund, believe me! But we shall not. They will use the wind and bend with it as we must. The course we must take from our null point takes us south again in the great Southern Ocean. There the prevailing winds will alter and blow from the west. It will blow us to Australia. So you see, by consenting to what must be we may reach our destination."

"It will be like going downhill, Mr Talbot, when you cannot go up but in any case wish to go down. We shall go downhill all the way to the Antipodes!"

"I see. No, gentlemen, I believe I really do see."

"It will be a long voyage, Edmund."

"And we may sink?"

The two officers looked at each other. Then Charles turned to me.

"I can trust you? Then yes. We may sink."

I said nothing but tried to digest this naked information into a feeling and succeeded more quickly than I had anticipated. I froze as I had done when Jack Deverel had furnished me with a cutlass. But Summers laughed a little.

"Come, Edmund! It is not today or tomorrow and may be never—with God's help!"

"And the chronometers, sir. Do not forget the chronometers!"

Charles Summers ignored the young man in a way

that persons unaccustomed to the sea service would have found offensive.

"We do not think that this information should be made widely known among the passengers and emigrants."

"But we behaved well enough when we set up a defence against what proved to be *Alcyone*!"

"That was sudden, desperate and soon over. This is a danger of a different degree. It will wear down all but the strongest spirits—as if the effect of this motion was not trial enough!"

"I agree, Charles. But this puts me in a fix. I am to report back to that idiotic committee, cannot ignore them—but now I know too much!"

"Perhaps, sir, Mr Talbot might adopt my metaphor and tell them we propose to go downhill all the way?"

Charles smiled at him pallidly in the light of the lantern.

"A degree of ignorance among the gentlemen is certainly desirable at the moment and Mr Talbot adequate to the task, I believe."

"But devil take it, what am I to say?"

"Why that we shall alter course to the south and they will feel easier—"

"I submit, sir, that Mr Talbot should mention the dragrope."

"If I say that we cannot reach either Africa or South America they will rightly fear the worst. If I say that Captain Anderson simply will not, they might well believe me and blame him for arbitrarily submitting them to this trial and real danger!"

"It is a difficulty. Perhaps the task is beyond you—oh, do not lift your chin at me in that Roman way, Edmund! I trust you to do your best but believe me that best would be a description of your own ignorance—"

"What the first lieutenant means, Mr Talbot, is that you should darken counsel a little and rely only on assuring them that all will be well and that we do the best in the circumstances. I must own the prospect of the Southern Ocean daunts me! There we shall get on with a vengeance. The reports make awesome reading. They write of seas the like of which are known nowhere else in the world. Even in a well-found ship—"

"We are rendering like an old boot."

Charles actually laughed but it was not a merry sound.

"Their lordships made do with what they could find. By the inattention of your friend Mr Deverel, we have no topmasts, substitutes no better than broomsticks, a sprung foremast and a ship that has been badly wrung."

He held out his two hands and demonstrated a wringing movement.

"Captain Anderson should have refused to command her!"

Mr Benét shook his head.

"A captain who refuses a ship will not get another."

Charles turned to him.

"Observe, Mr Benét, that I have no criticism to make of Captain Anderson. He is a fine seaman. You are fortunate, Mr Talbot, to find yourself in the hands of such an officer. If you wish to apportion blame, aim it rather at the clerks of the Admiralty who indifferently thrust you into this, this—"

"I heard Mr Talbot use the word 'hulk', sir."

"Just so, Mr Benét. Mr Talbot used the word."

"What must I do?"

"Explain that we shall turn away a little from the wind and make what speed we may to the south where we may get a steady wind on one quarter or the other."

"And the movement will be easier?"

Again the officers exchanged glances.

"The first lieutenant would agree that it will be different, Mr Talbot. He would agree you should use the word 'different'."

"Well, I am willing to do anything in this emergency. Do you wish me to keep the tone of the passenger saloon amiable and pleasant? Cheerful?"

"For heaven's sake, Mr Talbot, I can see you going round the ship with such an air of demented cheerfulness you would dreadfully disconcert the whole company!"

"What can I do? I cannot do nothing!"

"Let there be no alteration seen. Be as you were before your—injuries. The only result will be congratulations on your recovery."

"Be as I was? How was I?"

There was a pause and then suddenly Charles and Mr Benét were laughing, Charles, it seemed, with a touch of hysteria. I had never seen him so before. Tears flashed on his cheeks in the light of the lantern. Head on his knees, he reached out a hand and laid it on mine. I flinched at the unaccustomed contact so that

he snatched his hand away again and smeared the
water from his face with the back of it.

"I beg your pardon, sir. Your present mood of co-op-
eration, or perhaps I should say complicity, had made
me forget how prickly you can be. Mr Benét, how
would you suggest that Mr Talbot should conduct
himself in order that our other passengers should
detect no change in his demeanour?"

Mr Benét's grin broadened. He pushed back his
yellow hair with both hands.

"My acquaintance with the gentleman has been
short, sir, but I have heard of 'Lord Talbot'. A lofty,
not to say toplofty demeanour—"

"Well, gentlemen, I see you are determined to roast
me. Indeed it is not easy for a man of my inches to hit
off the right bearing in this world of deck beams and
squabby tars. If he goes about concealing his height
he is bent down like an ancient cripple whereas if he
stands up straight as God meant him to and lives with
his own eye level he is always cracking his skull and
stumbling over—you damned squat creatures, confound you!"

"This voyage will be the making of you, Mr Talbot.
At moments I even detect a strong streak of humanity
in you as if you was a common fellow like the rest of
us!"

"Since we are all common fellows, allow me to share
more information. There was mention made of
chronometers."

"Yes indeed. You know that the chronometers en-
able us to measure our movement east and west? Our
longitude? With the ship in such a state we are dis-

cussing the advisability of bringing them up one deck.
But—"

"The wave!"

"What wave?"

"Why the one we—she—has in her. The one I
heard as I scrambled towards you!"

"There is no wave inside her, Edmund. Before we
allowed her to reach such a state we should have the
whole crew pumping—"

"And the passengers, sir, watch and watch—"

"We should have had sails fothered over her bottom
and be busy throwing the guns overboard! That was
no wave. We have been heavily rained on. Our decks
spew oakum. Some of the rain has found its way
through the deck—for all rainwater and spray does not
run straight into the well. It will puddle at one level or
another and wash about, making for discomfort but
nothing more. It is a small matter compared with the
real danger that faces us."

"There was the corn, sir."

"We ditched a few tons of it, Mr Talbot. It was wet
and swelling. We have trouble enough without that."

"Mr Talbot could also mention the dragrope, sir.
The prospect of an increase in speed will go some way
towards making their discomfort tolerable."

I looked at Charles levelly.

"I was deceived in thinking she makes so much
water that between pumpings a wave washes to and
fro in her bilges?"

There was a long pause. Charles Summers put his
hand to his mouth, then took it away again.

"There was no wave. Your ears deceived you."

Now it was my turn to pause. Then—

"And the dragrope?"

"Mr Benét has persuaded Captain Anderson that we may use the dragrope here in the open sea to get weed off her. In that respect I do as I am ordered. After that we shall see about my own proposal to frap her hull with what cables we can spare for it. Frapping, carefully adjusted, will diminish her rendering to the seas."

"I see. An interminable period of nagging danger— the prospect of a catastrophe, perhaps. Well, so much for a career! And heigh-ho, so much for—but is there really no more to be done?"

"You could pray."

"As Colley did! I will not be bullied to my knees!"

I got to my feet. Light appeared beyond the main-mast like a dawn.

"What is that light?"

"It is the change of the watch. Men under punish-ment are come down to pump for fifteen minutes at the beginning of it."

The light brightened. The men ranged themselves at long handles projecting on either side of the mast. They began to move the handles up and down with a kind of bend-and-stretch movement.

"I thought pumps clanked."

"When they suck dry. These are lifting water."

"I must thank you, gentlemen, for taking me into your confidence. It shall not be abused."

"With your permission, sir, I will light Mr Talbot as far as the gun-room."

"You are kind, Mr Benét."

"Not at all, sir. Anything I can do for you, Mr Talbot—"

"And anything I can do for you, Mr Benét—"

Mr Benét beckoned me to follow him with much politeness.

"Lord, Mr Talbot, she is hogging like a wounded stick."

"Hogging, Mr Benét?"

"Sagging, too, sir. The one after the other. Bent up amidships, then bent down amidships."

"Like trying to break a sappy stick."

"Just so, sir. Hogged on the crest and sagged in the trough."

"I had not noticed."

"Well, you would not. You must not expect to detect the movement as excessive unless you have made a study of it. It is like the movement of the moon, sir, which you probably suppose to be a simple curve across the heavens. But it is infinitely complex. I have sometimes had the fancy that the moon is a ship with all her timbers a-creak, hogging, sagging, rolling, pitching— wrung badly and therefore not even moving all of a piece—in fact like our present old load of trouble."

"So that was why George Gibbs downed about a tumbler of my brandy and topped it off with another of rum! Following the run of the planking indeed! It is my belief he pretended to work where he knew there was drink, having got himself a thorough scare from the feel in his limbs of how the hull was working! Will he report to you?"

"To the first lieutenant, and should have done so already. I am the merest underling."

"It is not obvious. Would you care to come to my— hutch, I was about to say—and take some of whatever brandy Mr Gibbs has left us?"

"I am on duty, sir, and must return to Mr Summers. But another time *avec beaucoup de plaisir!*"

He passed a hand through his locks, clapped on his hat, held his hand at the salute as if he were about to remove it—the lanterns of the gun-room as if imbued with the "customs of the sea service" all assumed the same angle as his hand—then turned away to clamber whence we had come. Mr Askew still sat against our wooden wall. He looked at me under his brows.

"I heard you let on to the officer about George Gibbs. George won't be happy about that."

I answered him as shortly as I have ever spoken, for the movement seemed to have increased.

"That's not all he'll be unhappy about!"

I made my way up the ladders which seemed so imbued with the spirit of the sea rather than the service, they had not so much to be climbed as wrestled with. The movement had indeed increased but I soon grasped the reason. Where we had held our conference in the bowels of the ship, we had sat round the chronometers which would be kept at the point of least movement. Now I was moving away from that point and subject to the wildness of wind, water and wood, being in my proper person by no means as precious an object as these delicately fashioned clocks! By the time I had reached my hutch my calves were aching and were only the most noticeable weakness in a body grown suddenly wearied by the stresses of the motion and of sickness and of a mind belaboured with too much event. As I approached the door I heard a sudden scrambling noise from inside. I flung open the door.

"Wheeler! What the devil? You are haunting me!"

"I was just cleaning, sir—"

"For the third time today? When I want you I'll call for you!"

"Sir—"

He paused, then spoke in what I can only call his other voice, a voice with a curious trace of some other society in it, other places and customs.

"I'm in hell, sir."

I sat down in my canvas chair.

"What is all this?"

Wheeler, unlike the other servants in the ship, had commonly a submissive not to say ingratiating attitude. He had never before raised his eyes to stare directly into mine but he did so now.

"Good God, man, have you seen a ghost? No! Don't answer!"

All at once the pendulum's movement against which I had been fighting, so far from the still centre by the chronometers, overcame me. I fairly threw myself at the bucket under my canvas bowl and vomited into it. For a time after that, as every sufferer from the condition will know, I was not aware of my surroundings more than that they nauseated me. At last I lay face down in my bunk and wished for death. Wheeler must have taken my bucket away. I know he came back with it and know that he stayed. I think he was urging me to try the effect of the paregoric and I must suppose that at some point I gave way and allowed the dose with its usual magical effect. I believe that Wheeler spent all the time I was unconscious sitting in my chair, for I have a dreamy memory of him there. The first time I swam up from the swathing visions of the opiate I saw him there. He was slumped sideways in the chair, his head resting on the edge of my bunk, in an attitude of complete exhaustion.

(13)

Later still I came to myself with something of a headache and a foul taste in my mouth. Wheeler was still
in my cabin but standing up. I muttered at him but
he did not go. I sat up and found that I could deal
more or less with the movement of the ship.

"I think, Wheeler, you had better explain yourself.
But not now. Hot water, if you please. Get me out a
clean shirt—what are you waiting for?"

He licked his lips. The ship lurched in a daunting
interruption to the relentless movement of the pendulum. Wheeler reeled. He would have fallen had he
not grabbed the edge of my bunk.

"What's the matter with you, man?"

"Sorry, sir. A clean shirt, sir. This drawer—here,
sir. But the hot water—"

"Well?"

"The fires is damped down, sir. I doubt that water
would come more than warm."

"Coffee, too. Hot."

His eyes had focused far away. Whatever it was he
imagined, it would seem he did not like it.

"Wheeler!"

"Sir. I might ask Hawkins to put a pot on in the
captain's galley."

"Very well."

What a world a ship is! A universe! This was the
first time in our whole voyage that I had considered
the simple fact that hot water, to say nothing of a

hot meal, implies a fire; and a fire implies, oh, fire-brick, metal, what have you, some sort of chimney or flue! All these weeks the crew had gone about their business in the knowledge of which I was innocent! Only today, or was it yesterday, parts of the ship had come into my view for the first time—and now and then almost upside down as in a telescope!—the chronometers in their beds, the magazine, pumps aft of the main and forrard of the main—I who had determined once long ago to become master of "the sea affair"! I was irritated with myself for allowing Wheeler to give me the paregoric, as a man might be irritated who has forsworn liquor and now finds himself suffering from the effects of a debauch. I felt that I needed cleaning! There in a ship which might be the death of me, I felt soiled by real dirt, by paregoric, by my inability to shape circumstances—and all because of the distant vision of Marion Chumley! We might sink; but my mind returned upon Marion Chumley!

Wheeler came back but empty-handed.

"What is it now?"

"The captain's fire is out, sir."

"What the devil—I mean, why is it out?"

"Seeing we're likely to be at sea longer than expected, the captain said to put the fire out and save fuel for the ship's galley, sir."

"Captain Anderson? Doing without fire for the sake of the passengers?"

"For the crew, Hawkins said, sir."

"I never would have thought it!"

"Captain Anderson is a good captain, sir, nobody denies it."

"You are going to say that his bark is worse than his bite."

"No, sir. His bite is a deal worse than his bark and that's bad enough. So no drink, sir. I came to tell you. I've asked Bates to get some from the ship's galley but it won't be more than lukewarm."

He withdrew but I am sure went no further off than the lobby. I sat in my chair and waited in a confusion of head and circumstances. There was my dirt, inside and out. There was the movement of the ship, the pendulum which if it did not still nauseate me was a wearisome trial, minute by minute. There was Dashing Jack Deverel now loose where I so desperately longed to be, in that other ship, that beautiful, wild creature—

There was a strange feeling in my naked feet. It was true, good God, the planking was alive! There was a creeping and almost muscular movement! It was a realization even more disconcerting than the brutally uneven movement of the whole ship as the waves passed under her.

Wheeler came in and presented me with a mug of coffee. It was hardly lukewarm but I drank it. He poured a little water into my canvas bowl and I abandoned the coffee in my haste to wash myself. Carried away by a veritable passion for cleanness I scrubbed myself all over in water that soon became at once dirty and stone-cold—as if by so doing I could get rid not merely of my soiling of one sort and another but of the ship's dirt and of the ship's confused and

daunting circumstances. As I wrapped the clean apron
and tail of my shirt between my naked legs I felt more
nearly myself than I had done since first a "starter"
struck me over the back and head. I dressed, then
opened this book and looked briefly through what I
had written there. I even took the parcel containing an
account of the first part of our voyage from the drawer,
and weighed it in my hands, debating whether I
should open it and read critically all I had written.
But the prospect of repacking it daunted me.

Oh, that self-confident young man who had come
aboard, serenely determined to learn everything and
control everything! In prospect he had treated this
awful expedition, this adventure, as resembling that
in a stagecoach, its end as surely to be predicted as
that between London and Bath! He was to reach
Sydney Cove moving at an even pace over a level sea
in some masterpiece of naval construction. But the
war had ended, the ship had proved to be rotten as an
old apple, Deverel and Willis between them had
allowed the apple—the ship—the coach—to lose a
wheel, *Alcyone* had overhauled him and struck him
with lightning so that he now knew the pangs of
passion, of separation, of jealousy—

"Deverel! Handsome Jack!"

After some time, I do not know how long, I came
to myself like a diver returning to the surface. I stared
into my small mirror at a too much altered face. I
thought to myself then, as I inspected the wan and
haggard visage there, that my godfather would be at
once amused and condemnatory of me. Edmund in

love with the wrong girl—with the impossible girl—
why, the old *cynic* would have preferred me to attempt
Lady Somerset! Then, on top of that, Edmund quite
likely sinking in the wrong ship—

As if the wrong ship knew that I had insulted her,
the planking under my feet fairly bounced.

"Surely—"

I stopped. I said silently to myself that there was
something I did not understand behind this half-
uttered "surely" which had escaped my lips without
my volition. It was not so much a thought as a feeling
that "I" ought to be able to do something about "it"
and that if "I" could not, then "somebody" ought to
be able to! Believe it or not, my thoughts began to
centre on our glum captain! And after all, a committee, however *ad hoc*, had wanted me to interview him!
I had obeyed my own instructions and seen Charles
Summers, now I would obey theirs! I shouted for
Wheeler who opened the door almost before the word
was out. He huddled and strapped me into my oilskins. I stepped in my rubber boots through the door,
and the whole ship slid away. I stumped, tilted like a
seaman towards the waist. I do not know if it was my
imagination or not but I thought I heard someone
sobbing in the last of the hutches on my side of the
lobby. I stood in the waist, holding on to the break of
the poop. Our ship was indeed quicker in her roll. Her
movement was a constant fret, with now and then a
jerk in it which seemed like impatience or furious
anger rather. Rain and spray flying horizontally over
the windward rail stung my face like birdshot. The

ship heaved at each wave as if she might get forward
but then came upright in much the same place as
before. The sails, rain and spray streaming from the
clew, spread as they were on the mainmast alone and
huge, now seemed a pitiful response to the wind's
impulsion. Yet despite all this wild weather there was
much activity with ropes of various sizes on the
fo'castle. They were trying, it seemed, to perform
some operation with cables, though I was quite unable
to understand what it was. They seemed to spend
quite a deal of their time under water and I was glad
to be a passenger and not an officer, let alone a seaman. I turned and began to climb towards the poop.
Above and aft of the wheel with its two glistening
quartermasters, partly visible over the forrard rail of
his deck, stood Captain Anderson. He wore a shabby
oilskin and sou'wester and as one indifferent to a
capful of water was staring moodily into the eye of
the wind. I was working my careful way round the
men at the wheel when the captain noticed me. He
smiled! It was a dreadful sight, a momentary glimpse
of a few teeth, as if someone had thrown a yellow
pebble into his glumness. I opened my mouth but he
was already turning away. I followed, riskily running
up the ladder to detain him, but by the time I had
reached the deck he had *nipped* down his private companionway and disappeared. The message was plain.
Keep off! Yet he had smiled at me, however briefly
and artificially, a thing not known before.

As in a dream, I imagined yellow hair, a fresh complexion, and heard the voice of Mr Benét say: *I
submit, sir, in this difficulty you should habitually*

*greet the passengers with cheerfulness. Once they feel
the captain himself has cause for concern they will be
no end of trouble!*

Would he dare? Oh yes, I believe a young officer
who would "attempt" handsome Lady Somerset while
her husband was no more than walking his rounds
must be bold to the point of foolhardiness!

Our little sailing master, Mr Smiles, had the watch.
Now that the captain had gone below he moved over
from the starboard side and stood facing the wind.

"Well, Mr Smiles, I am recovered as you see and
would not be anywhere else for one thousand pounds!"

Mr Smiles examined my face in a distant way as
if it had been at the horizon. His eyes were red-
rimmed from the spray. He lifted one finger to his
lips as if to command silence.

"What do you mean, Mr Smiles? A thousand
pounds, I said. I tell you what, sir. After I had suffered
a few bangs on the head I thought I must be out of
my wits; but down below there is a real madman who
thinks in all this salt turmoil that he can buy safety!"

Mr Smiles took his finger from his lips.

"There are ships, Mr Talbot, in which every man
Jack is mad save one."

"To tell you the truth I am coming to believe that
all men who choose this awful waste as an habitation
and profession must be mad so you may well be right!
How she rolls—devil take it, I spend my time clamber-
ing like an ape from one handhold to another. I marvel
you can so keep your feet and treat the movement
with such indifference."

The sailing master did not reply. He returned to

watch the sea. He seemed to be inspecting what could
be seen of that vastly furrowed prospect as if he were
choosing a path over it. It came to me that my conversation with the man was not just a casual infringe-
ment of the captain's Standing Orders but a positive
shattering of them. Perhaps that was why the man
had laid his finger to his lips! Times and the weather
had changed! But I did not wish to make our position
any more complicated than it was. I nodded to Mr
Smiles and made my way down to the lobby again,
having had enough of the freshness of the open air.

I saw Wheeler slide into my hutch. I could not bear
more to do with the man and used the rails on the
walls of the hutches to get myself to the saloon. But
the committee was not there, only little Mr Pike. I
am sorry to say that I collapsed on the bench below
the stern window and stayed so with my head on the
table.

"You are sick as the rest of them, Mr Talbot."

I grunted in reply. The man went on.

"I should not have thought it of you, Mr Talbot.
But then you have been injured. I trust your head is
better. I struck my own on the lintel when the ship
rolled but it is better now. Have you seen Mr
Summers?"

"Where is the committee?"

"The movement is too much for them. Mr Prettiman has had a heavy fall. But I will go and call them
if you wish." I shook my head.

"I will wait till they are recovered enough to appear.
I believe Bowles to be a superior man. He has what
the Romans would call '*gravitas*'. I am surprised."

"You need not be, sir. He has studied law."

It was quite extraordinary how quickly little Pike was able to bore one.

"You should be resting like the others, Mr Pike."

"Oh no. I do not get flung about much, you see. As I am small and light, if I lose my footing I generally manage to scramble up. Not like poor Mr Brocklebank who dare not leave his bunk in this weather except to— You know, sir, I prefer sitting here, talking to you, rather than being with my family? That is dreadful, quite dreadful I know but after a while I simply cannot stand it no matter how anxious I am and no matter how much I love them."

"Anxious? What on earth for?"

"They do not really rest, Mr Talbot. Every now and then they play in the bed—the bunk, the upper bunk, Mr Talbot, one at each end. They play like I said but then it is tears and seems to get worse. They don't play for more than a moment but lie there— well, whining, I suppose, I had better say it though Mrs Pike does not like the word. She is not well herself, sir. What are we to do? Mrs Pike seems to believe I can do something which to tell the truth is why I am out here but I cannot. That hurts more than anything."

I recalled Charles's instructions to me.

"You should find her faith in you flattering, Mr Pike."

"Oh no."

"I must say, I would not be anywhere else for a thousand pounds!"

"Will you not call me Dicky, Mr Talbot? I know

I have not, what you said the Romans would think of
Mr Bowles—"

" '*Gravitas*.' You should not worry, sir, some people
have it, others not and are none the worse for the lack.
I have been thought to exhibit a measure of the quality
myself but it is nature, not nurture. Well, Mr Pike,
I will call you Richard if it will make you happier."

"Thank you, Mr Talbot. Do you prefer Ed or
Eddy?"

"Mr Pike, you may address me as 'Edmund' in this
emerg—in the situation which we find ourselves in.
So cheer up, man!"

"I will try, Edmund. But the children do not seem
to get any better for all we can do."

"Now there I can give you comfort. Good God, sir,
my young brothers are for ever breaking their knees
or elbows or both—all four I should say! They get
colics, rashes, colds like puppies. It is growing up,
Mr Pike, Richard, I should say, and a damned lengthy
and painful business if you ask me!"

"They say the wind is not blowing from where it
ought to be. The movement of the ship—"

"The wind may change, man! Before we know
where we are we may find ourselves riding along as
easy as in a postchaise! Come, you know that Britannia
rules the waves! I would not be anywhere else for—"

"I am afraid that is the truth of it."

"—a thousand pounds."

"It is this sinking—"

"Now come! The officers assured me—"

"They do really seem to be sinking, a little weaker

today, then again tomorrow. Oh, Edmund, is there nothing to be done? I begged the surgeon to get us transferred to the other ship, though what we should do in India I do not know—but he would not. And that was when the weather was fine."

"A foul wind cannot last forever. When we get into the Southern Ocean—"

"But the ship is not getting along, is it?"

"She will get there little by little. The seamen will operate the dragrope and take off our weed and increase our speed. Oh—I should not have said— You see? We have nothing to worry about, sir, nothing at all."

"And another thing. Edmund, I cannot help feeling that the ship is lower in the water. I do not mention my suspicions to Mrs Pike but only this morning I caught her eye—and I knew, Edmund! She was thinking the same thing!"

I laughed aloud, not a little relieved at finding there was some positive comfort I could give the poor, irritating fellow.

"What a man you are, Pike! I confess that when I was feeling sick and particularly *low* I imagined the ship was too! But today the sailors have pumped no more than they did when she was anchored at Spithead!"

"I do know that, Edmund, and everything you say is true. But Bates says she has more water in her."

"Would it interest you to know that the first lieutenant told me himself that they pump no more than they did? She has more water in her because of the rain and spray. It lies about where the pumps cannot get at it—annoying but not in any way dangerous! Be warned—it sounds worse than it is because of our movement. Down below if you are not experienced you would mistake the sound of rainwater washing about for a positive wave rolling from one end of the ship to the other!"

"The first lieutenant would tell you that, wouldn't he? I mean he would wish to keep everyone calm so as to avoid trouble. But it is good of you to talk so to me, Edmund, and I believe you partly and I will tell Mrs Pike, making as much of it as I can."

"I think before you return to your hutch—cabin, I mean, good God, man, you're not a rabbit, are you? Well—I had better give you a good stiff drink."

"Oh no, Edmund. Like I told you it burns my throat and makes me go silly. Edmund, I have even prayed but nothing happened. I keep thinking about 'Suffer little children'. It doesn't do them any good being young and small, does it? I mean they are the less able to defend themselves. Like you said the other day when we thought the other ship might be French, they are too young for the French. But I can't keep out of my head that they aren't too young for Our Lord, Edmund, and if they slip through our hands in this devilish place, this desert, I couldn't leave them to sink, not here; I should jump in after them—"

"Pike! Pull yourself together! Richard! I said Richard! Stop blubbering, man! Anyone would think you was a girl, curse it!"

"Administering comfort, Mr Talbot?"

I got clumsily to my feet. It was Miss Granham.

She had one hand out before her and the other holding her skirts up away from the streaming floor. I stumbled round the table but she got to the one nearest the door and sank on to the bench. A shift of the vessel fairly tossed me towards the other side and I sat opposite her.

"Miss Granham, you really should not! A lady— where is Mr Prettiman? He should—"

Miss Granham spoke in a weary voice.

"He is sick and I am sick. But he has had a fall. A severe one."

"What can I do? Shall I visit him?"

Mr Pike sniggered through his tears.

"Edmund visiting the sick!"

"It is comic, I admit, sir. But then anything comic in our situation is a gain."

The man came round the end of the aftermost table and huddled himself on my bench. As if she was as irritated with him as I was, the ship shrugged, the saw-toothed horizon took up a crazy angle in the stern window and little Pike shot along the bench and collided with me. He muttered an apology and backed off. Miss Granham looked at him compassionately.

"Do they improve, Mr Pike?"

"They are no better. Will you go to them?"

"Later, Mr Pike. I believe you should ask Mrs Pike to invite me. I make every allowance for her natural distress—but really!"

"She is very sorry indeed, Miss Granham, and so much regrets her unfortunate outburst. She said so. I beg you!"

Miss Granham sighed.

"I will do what I can but later. Now Mr Prettiman is injured—"

"I will tell her so. And what you said, Edmund."

Pike got more or less to his feet. He was like a man balancing on the slope of a roof and he waited till the roof changed its infernal mind and sloped the other way. He went reeling through the door and contrived to get it shut behind him. Miss Granham was leaning back. Both hands grasped the edge of the table. Her eyes were shut and either tears or perspiration ran in drops down her cheeks.

"I had hoped to ask for a little warm water but the truth is my voice is so weak—"

"That is readily remedied, ma'am, for you may borrow mine. Bates! Bates! Where are you, man? Come out of that damned cuddy—I beg your pardon, not you, Bates, you, ma'am—we want hot water and at once."

"There isn't any."

"Say 'sir' when you speak to me!"

"Like Wheeler told you, sir, there isn't any."

"We'll see about that! Wheeler! Wheeler! Wheeler, I said! Oh, there you are. What do you mean by it, giving a gentleman hot water without telling him that the ladies were in need of it?"

"Miss Granham is not on my side of the lobby, sir."

"Well neither am I now I've changed over!"

"Yes, sir, but, sir—"

"Hot water, Wheeler, and quick about it! If necessary, light the damned fire again and tell whomsoever should be told it was at my, my—"

"You are more than kind, Mr Talbot, but please!"

"Be easy, ma'am. Bring it to Miss Granham's cabin, Wheeler."

"Even hot water, the touch of it in one's mouth, the warming suffusion. I never thought in the days when I was so particular over the making of a pot of tea that I should come to value hot water without it!"

"No tea—good God, ma'am, I am the veriest, the most absolute, the outside edge of enough, the most thoughtless—"

The deck was momentarily level. I leapt to my feet, ran through the lobby to my hutch, fell on my knees and scrabbled at my bottom drawer, fished out the packet and ran back to Miss Granham before the deck had a chance to change its mind. It was, if not an elegant, at least a very nimble feat and I was pleased to have outwitted our soaked old wooden box for once and avoided doing myself a mischief.

"Here, ma'am, with my apologies."

"Tea!"

"I had it stowed away the first day we came aboard and to tell you the truth have not had much cause to remember it since then. I only hope the air of this savage ocean may not have ruined it entirely. I have seen you ladies in calmer weather clustered round the teapot and the, what is it, 'the cup that cheers but not inebriates—' "

"I cannot take it."

"Miss Granham, for heaven's sake!"

Miss Granham's head was turned away. She held out the scrap of paper she had removed from beneath the string. I recognized the familiar writing. "For 'The Little Duke' from 'old Dobbie' with love, in the hope he will drink nothing stronger."

"Oh, Lord, ma'am, good God. I mean—believe me—what a fool! She might at least have folded the paper, curse it—and here am I swearing like a trooper. I beg your pardon, really, ma'am, I do not care for tea and only drink it out of politeness. Why, Miss Dobson would be most angry if she thought—a disciplinarian I can tell you! She would stand me in the corner for an hour by the clock if she thought that—I suppose here I should find myself mastheaded by her if we have a masthead which in fact I suppose we do since young Willis spends so much time up there. She is a dear friend as you can imagine but perhaps too much addicted to the sentimental school—"

"Mr Talbot."

"—only a fanatic would have a small boy taught to read out of *Sir Charles Grandison*! She thought, I suppose, that such a perfect exemplar of Christian behaviour would do me good but I assure you, ma'am, that tale, if tale it be in all those volumes, has marked me for life!"

I thought for a moment that Miss Granham was trying to stop herself from laughing. But it was worse than that. Her face was contorted with effort, yet despite that the tears fairly burst from her eyes. They were of the "boo-hoo" variety. It is the first and possibly last time I have seen a lady grit her teeth! But still the tears flowed. I do not know how to convey my astonishment not to say my embarrassment. She began to beat on the table with her fist.

"I will not! I will not allow myself—"

Her bonnet, her very shoulders shook. Never have I seen such an evident conflict in a lady!

"Oh, God! Oh, I say, ma'am! You really must not— I did not mean that I was forced to read the whole of *Sir Charles Grandison*! Then you might well pity me! I doubt the great Panjandrum himself read it all! Did he not say that he had never read a book to the end? I will lay my horse to a shilling that he was thinking of Richardson—"

Miss Granham began to laugh. It was hysteria, I suppose, for which of course the accepted remedy is a smartly smacked face. But the truth is I did not dare.

"I believe, ma'am, you should allow me to escort you to your hutch—cabin, I would say—"

"What a fool!"

"Not really—but she hoped to bring me along in the style of Sir Charles but failed as you see. Wheeler will bring you the water. Allow me. A lady is naturally less able to counteract the movement of a vessel and even her garments must render the attempt additionally difficult, not to say dangerous. Permit me, ma'am."

She was docile. I gave her my arm but that was clearly not enough. I took her hand therefore; but before we had got fairly into the lobby the frantic movement of the vessel forced me to put my right arm round her narrow waist and I was holding her up.

An unexpected fact became apparent with stunning force. Between thirty and forty years she might carry in her reticule but she was a woman! More than that and not to put too fine a point on it, Miss Granham was not wearing stays! There was no doubt about it.

Good God, her waist, her bosom was that of a young
woman! It put the final touch to my embarrassment
and I was most anxious to have done with her as soon
as possible. But it was not to be. That other female,
jealous, I suppose a poet would say, of this newly
revealed femininity, suddenly savaged us as a hound
will savage a fox. The first movement sent me spinning
across the lobby so that I was forced to use all my
strength and an agility I did not know I possessed in
keeping my—I should say "our"—feet. The next
movement set us instantly on the slope of a mountain
and in a mountain stream at that. I grabbed at one
of the handrails to prevent us from falling towards
what was at least temporarily down. We swung out.
We fell, because the handrail came with us and,
awful to relate, the whole bulkhead, or wall, in this
instant of thin ply, came with us too. As we approached
the wooden drum of the mizzen I contrived to turn so
that my shoulder struck it and Miss Granham did not.
The whole of the buff-coloured sheet—the plywood—
now impeded us. Forced to let go of the handrail and
forced by the countermotion to dance like a clown
carrying a puppet I sped towards the open, the violated cabin. We were in it just long enough to see
that an old lady lay there, her grey hair matted with
sweat, her mouth open, her eyes in their sunken and
discoloured sockets staring at us with terror! I cannot
think how I contrived to bow and mutter an apology
before the ship swept us away. I got a handhold on
the rails at the opposite side of the lobby without
knowing what process had taken us there and worked

along it until I could deliver Miss Granham safely to
her door.

"Allow me, ma'am. It was a seventh wave I believe.
I must apologize for—you are quite safe now. Allow
me, ma'am."

I managed to usher her into her cabin and shut
the door with great thankfulness. I made my way to
my own hutch, keeping my eyes averted from the
violated cabin which, I now realized with almost as
much terror as she, contained none other than my
onetime inamorata, Zenobia Brocklebank!

I pass over the grumbling from the sailors when
they were ordered to mend the bulkhead at once, the
shrieks from Zenobia until she was hidden again, the
soul-destroying hammering which was necessary before the business was done. I got myself back to the
saloon in a rage and a determination not to be defeated by the ship and the weather. I yelled for the
servant and ordered food and drink. It came and
proved to be salt beef but pickles to go with it and
ale to wash it down. Never believe the complaints of
seamen about their food! To a man with all his teeth
in his head this proved to be a feast for a king, however much I had to wrestle with it! Admittedly, once
the plate got away from me and I saved the beef, to
say nothing of a mess of pickles with my right hand!
What is more, I licked that hand clean with positive
gusto. I cannot tell how it came about but the absurd
passage with Miss Granham restored me to a state of
cheerfulness which I believe is natural to me and
which *mal de mer* had temporarily defeated! When

I thought of Miss Chumley with a throb of longing, even that transformed itself into a determination to conquer all! This was more than recovery. It was enhancement! Once back into my hutch, I dared adventures of balance to get into a nightshirt and nightcap, got into my bunk and determined to have a good night! Astonishingly enough, with no qualms to interrupt it, I sank almost at once into a deep sleep that neither of the aches of my body—one shoulder confoundedly tender from that damned mizzenmast—could hinder.

(14)

I woke with the faintest trace of light through my louvre and lay for a while in a state of surprise at my restoration. I supposed that I had, as they say of sickness, "turned the corner", and that my concussion had run its course. I felt full of energy and determination. I even sat, half-dressed, at this flap and wrote a whole candle's worth of record—of Mr Askew, Mr Benét, Charles, Miss Granham and Mr Gibbs! By that time there was as much daylight about as ever did reach our sordid quarters and I put out the guttering candle. The effect of my restoration was still with me; but I cannot say that when I got myself dressed and oil-skinned and went cautiously out for a breath of the open that there was much in sight to please a man now heartily tired of salt water! Too much of it flew everywhere. I looked up to discover if Captain Anderson was stumping up and down the weather-side of the quarterdeck but he was not to be seen. Instead of that, an oil-clad figure waved to me from the forrard rail of it. A faint voice came through the wind.

"Hullo there!"

It was Lieutenant Benét.

"Why hullo! A nasty morning!"

"I will be with you directly."

Cumbershum emerged from the bowels of the ship. He grunted at me and I grunted back. It is all that is necessary with the man. He ascended to the quarter-deck and the ship's bell struck eight times. The ceremony was brief. The gentlemen made to raise their hats but wore sou'westers secured by what they call, of course, "chin stays". Their action was therefore purely symbolic, a raising of the right hand to the level of the eyebrow. The men at the wheel presented the course to the new quartermasters. Benét came down the ladder. He held the forrard rail with both hands and leaned over.

"Come up, sir."

"You are cheerful this morning, Mr Benét."

"It is an appearance perhaps."

"Separation as I am beginning to find out—"

"I understand you. Wilson! Keep your eye on the bloody luff! Well, Mr Talbot, I spent the whole watch occupied with the two lines I quoted to you and have improved them materially. *'Essential Beauty lovelier than a woman, too fair of form and feature to be human—'* Is that not a gain?"

"I am no poet."

"How do you know, sir? I am told you wept when Mrs East sang—"

"Good God! They were tears, idle tears and where in heaven or hell they came from—or what—besides, I had been cracked over the head!"

"My dear Mr Talbot. Once faced with the necessity of communicating with the most sensitive, most delicate of creatures—only poetry will make that connection. It is their language, sir. Theirs is the language of the future. Women have dawned. Once they have understood what syllables, rather than prose, should fall from those lips, women will rise in splendour like the sun!"

"You amaze me, Mr Benét."

"Prose? It is the speech of merchants to each other, sir, the language of war, commerce, husbandry."

"But poetry—"

"Prose will do for persuading men, sir. Why, only yesterday I was able to persuade the captain that a small alteration of course would be beneficial. Now had I represented in verse to the captain that he was wrong—"

"I am surprised you are still alive."

"No—no! Do you not see that our motion is easier?"

"I had thought my ability to keep my feet and in fact to be cheerful was the result of my complete recovery."

"We have come a point off the wind and the increase in our speed, however slight, compensates for the extra distance. But the absence of the Beloved Object—"

"You refer to Lady Somerset."

Lieutenant Benét took off his sou'wester and shook out the golden fleece.

"Who else?"

"I did suppose," said I, laughing, "that you might have had Another in mind—"

"There is no other!"

"In your eyes, no, but to mine—"

Lieutenant Benét shook his head, smiling kindly.

"There cannot be."

"It did occur to me that perhaps you had an opportunity of forming some opinion on the character of Miss Chumley."

"She has none."

"I beg your pardon?"

"She can have none. She is a schoolgirl, Mr Talbot."

"Miss Chumley—"

"I have no opinion of schoolgirls. It is useless to look to them for sympathy or understanding or anything. They are blown by every wind, sir. Why, my own sisters would follow any redcoat if dear Mama did not have an eye to them."

"Miss Chumley is no longer a schoolgirl!"

"She is pretty, I grant you, amiable with a trace of wit—"

"A trace!"

"Malleable—"

"Mr Benét!"

"Why—what is the matter?"

"Lieutenant Deverel is aboard *Alcyone*—he is notorious—"

"A cockerel, Mr Talbot. I did not like the man even the little I saw of him."

"Mr Askew told me, Mr Askew said that Handsome Jack—"

"At least I must thank him for allowing me to choose this melancholy exile!"

"But, Mr Benét—forgive me. Exile! You seem a happy man! Your accustomed attitude, your very facial expression—it is sunny, sir!"

Lieutenant Benét looked astonished and revolted. He put on his sou'wester again.

"You cannot be serious, Mr Talbot. I happy!"

"Forgive me!"

"Were I small-minded enough, Mr Talbot, I should

at this very moment envy your condition! You love Miss Chumley, do you not?"

"Indeed."

Mr Benét's face was wet but it was with rain or sea-spray not tears. His golden locks beat about his brow. The spyglass under his arm seemed so mechanically and professionally a part of his character that when he suddenly whipped it out and ran back up to the quarter-deck, it was as if he had extended another limb which until then had been folded in like the leg of an insect. He levelled it at the horizon. He spoke to Cumbershum and for a while the two gentlemen aimed their parallel glasses, all the while contriving to remain upright in a way I found admirable. Mr Benét shut up his glass and came back to me at the run.

"A whaler, Mr Talbot. She would avoid us even if we made signals of distress."

"But, Mr Benét—you said 'My condition'?"

"Why, the letter, sir. I was to put it into your hand but you were indisposed. I gave it to your servant."

"Wheeler!"

"No—no. The other one. You slab-sided son of a sea cook! Keep your eyes on the horizon or I'll have the skin off your back! You never reported that sail!"

This was with a roar much like Captain Anderson's but it issued from the throat of Lieutenant Benét. He had his head back and was addressing the top of what was left of our mainmast. Then he turned and spoke to me in his ordinary voice.

"The man is a half-wit. We shall talk together again, I hope."

He raised his hand in salute and then was racing
away down the ladder before I had time to return it. I
myself fairly ran to the lobby and shouted for Phillips.
He came and when I demanded the letter he struck his
head with his open palm and rebuked that organ for
being, as he said, a sieve. But I had been sick and he
had been this and that—I heard him with impatience
and finally sent him off to find the missive which he
passed some considerable time in finding. This enabled
me to anticipate what impossible treasures it might
hold! There would be a long letter from Miss Chumley,
written after the ball in a sleepless night! In a confession of attachment, franker than mine, she would have
given me her journal. It would be franker also than
mine—which had been limited by a sense of mascu-
line decorum! Here was a most affecting account of
the death of her dearest mama! A pressed flower from
the gardens of Wilton House, an endearingly inadequate sketch of her music master, that old, old man!
Oh, the optimism and phantasy of a young man in
love! The state heats every faculty like water in a sauce-
pan on a fire! But for all the time he took, Phillips
brought the missive to me too soon and it was small,
thin, expensive and so heavily scented I recognized it
at once with a downward lurch of the heart for what it
was. But then, how could I have been so foolish as to
expect anything more than a note from Mr Benét's
"most adorable of women"?

I hurried into my hutch.

"Get out, Wheeler! Get out!"

I unfolded the paper and a wave of scent took me by
the throat. I had to blink water out of my eyes.

"Lady Somerset presents her compliments to Mr Edmund FitzH. Talbot. Lady Somerset consents to a correspondence between him and Miss Cholmondeley subject to Lady Somerset's supervision. She assumes, nor would Mr Talbot wish her to do more, that the exchange of missives is one between acquaintances and may be broken off or suspended at the wish of either party."

Did the woman think I would *not* write, permission or no? But it was something—and then! Before me on the bunk lay another smaller piece of paper. It had been, for sure, folded into the larger missive. It had no scent but what it had acquired by contact with the more expensive wrapping. With a folly and ardour of which I should never have suspected myself, I pressed it, unread, to my lips. I unfolded it with trembling fingers. What man or woman whose heart has ever beaten more quickly at the sight of such a communication will not understand my joy?

A young person will remember for the rest of her life the meeting of two ships and prays that one day they may put down their ankers in the same harbour.

Foolish rapture, even to tears! I will not repeat the generous and copious and spontaneous promises that sprang unbidden to my lips at the thought of that dear, distant Vision! Those who run may read. This must be the crown of life and I would not have it otherwise!

A young person will remember for the rest of her life— She had written—perhaps in tears—there were marks too on the back of the paper. It had lain on another while that was still wet and unsanded. The words were none of them plainly to be read for they

were smudged and backwards at that. There were blots
too. It gave me a most complete and devout sense of
nearness to her. What would I have not given to kiss
the ink from her slender fingers? I seized my mirror,
angled it and peered at what had been written. The
mind had to restore a whole word from one letter and
a smudge, divine the sense with a passion rare in
scholarship! At last I made out what was surely the
first line. "*Her faults are legion and her virtues small.*"
(I made the word "virtue" to be plural myself. I did not
think that Miss Chumley would have written anything
so improper for her sex and years as a comment on a
lady's "virtue".)

> *Indeed 'twas rumoured she had none at all.*
> *When gentlemen appeared she straight begun*
> *To turn her face as sunflowers to the sun.*
> *And if—*

Here the manuscript became quite illegible. But it
was an enchanting fragment from that hand. I swear
my first opinion was that Pope himself could have done
no better than these gently satiric lines! I could hear
her very voice and see her smile! She, like Lieutenant
Benét, was an addict of poetry. Had he not said that
the Muse is the shortest way to the female heart—or
words to that effect?

I do not know if I have the boldness to describe what
now occurred. I have always, and alas rightly, thought
myself to be a prose person! Yet now and with no more
ado, but with an ear-tingling sense almost of shame I
entered those lists myself! Or tried to! It was the near-

est way to her heart and what else could I do in a ship
lost amid this waste of miles, this ocean of time, this
separation from all that makes life—tolerable I would
say, had I not now this overwhelming reason for living!
for living. I lay my hand on my heart and declare that
the very movement of the planks beneath my feet,
evidence of our slow peril, begot in me no more than
an impatience with such trivialities as stood between
me and what I desired.

But my only experience of the Muse as they would
call it was in Latin and Greek, elegiacs, fivers and sixers
as we used to say. However—I blush confoundedly at
the memory but the truth will be out—and even now I
had some confused sense that it was to you, my dear, my
clever Angel, that this journal should be written! I got
out of my oilskins, sat at my flap, kissed her missive a
few times and set out—let me make the confession—
to write an Ode to the Beloved! Oh, indeed, Mr Smiles
is right! We are all madmen! It is true—I am a witness
to it that not poetry but the attempt at poetry is a
substitute however poor for the presence of the beloved. I was above myself and saw things plainly as
from a mountain top. Whether it be Milton's God or
Shakespeare's Dark Lady and even darker Gentleman
—whether it be Lesbia or Amaryllis or devil take it,
Corydon, the Object lifts the mind to a sphere where
only the irrational in language makes any sense. So
then I, half-ashamed, with feelings of utter folly yet
real need, stared at the blank white paper as if I might
find at once relief and achievement there. I examine it
now with its poor traces of real passion—those blots

and crossings-out, those emendations, alternatives, laborious markings-down of shorts and longs, suggestions to myself or to her—these in their incompetence for those who understand were my real poetry of passion!

Candida for "whiteness". Indeed, an air of whiteness surrounded her, enhaloed her, the fit surround for an innocent girl whose beauty is known to others but not yet to herself! *Candida*, oh, nothing whiter—*Candidior lunâ*, therefore, a light to me, *mea lux*—*vector* is a passenger no, no, nothing so dusty, so drear, *puella, nympha, virgo*, is there not *nymphe* too?

So suddenly from nowhere I had my hexameter!

Candidior lunâ mea lux O vagula nymphe!

But is not *nymphe* a bride? It makes no matter. Then —*Pelle mihî nimbos et mare mulce precor*—the pentameter came all with a rush but I did not like it, there was no smoothness, all was rough and dull. *Marmora blanditiis*—better; and so:

Marmora blanditiis fac moderare tuis!

No—*moderare mihî!*

So there I had a hexameter and a pentameter, what you might call an elegiac couplet. The effort seemed temporarily to exhaust not so much my Latin as my invention. Having besought Miss Chumley to take care of the seas for me there seemed little left for her to do except—

No. I would not touch that innocent image with the furthest off intimation of physical desire!

If we should reach land; and if at some time in the future I should reread this book—if we should reread it together, oh, devoutly to be desired! Shall I believe what I now set down as the plain truth? For it was only when I sat back and relaxed the tension consequent on my poetic endeavours that I remembered Latin was not in the list of accomplishments with which Miss Chumley had favoured me! It was English or nothing, for my French was certainly not up to verse!

> *Brighter than moonlight, wandering maid,*
> *By thy charms be the white seas allayed!*

Turned into English my first efforts at the lyric seemed on the thin side. I had read much poetry in an endeavour to understand a side of life which I thought closed to me by the extreme rationality of my mind and coolness of my temperament! I had heaped other men's verses up and "struck them down below" as we Tarpaulins say, as if mere quantity of lines was anything to the purpose. Now, with my first glimmer of its real purpose and source, here I was, reduced by fate to puttying together the elements of a dead language, when only a living one had any use. The effect was plainly to be read in these Latin lines. Now indeed I understood those strictures on my tasks which I had accepted so carelessly and with no real intention of amendment—

"No no, Mr Talbot. The lines are constructed according to the rules but Propertius would never have written them!"

So much for the rules. With what a moved understanding did I now see that poetry is a matter of enchantment. It is folly but a divine folly.

O she doth teach the torches to burn bright!

That is impossible, that is nonsense, but that is what happens, is as the clear and inarticulate voice of every young fool who has been struck by lightning, had all his *previous convictions* cancelled, erased; and let us add at last in the tail of the number, Edmund Fitz-Henry Talbot, MAGISTER ARTIUM!

It was evident I had shot my poetic bolt. It was only then that I made another discovery which set me laughing like a jackass. I had asked Miss Chumley to flatten the seas for me when the poor girl was even less able to avoid *mal de mer* than I myself! She might in her turn have been more likely to address her lines to Sir Henry! I returned to her little paper and quickly knew the simple sentence by heart. I turned it over and reread the few words I had so laboriously made out there.

Another few words met my gaze. These were not of blotted ink. They had been—and as if to escape me they vanished again—they had been pressed into the page, pressed through a previous page by a lead or silver point, which was why they became visible only when the paper was held at a certain angle.

He has left the ship and I

Who had left the ship? The only people to have left the ship were Wheeler—and Benét! Was he—could he be —had he been—

Benét was personable. He was far more personable than I. He was a poet—his hair—his fair complexion —his agility—

An impressionable girl—malleable—and with no prospects but what lay in marriage!

I started to my feet. It was an infatuation! Nothing more! There was, however, and before I had abandoned and forgotten this lamentable episode, one person who might throw light on the situation. I went quickly to the waist. The clouds had lifted and Mr Benét's new course meant that the ship was labouring indeed but more regularly. The horizon was dense blue and clipped all round in little curves as by a pair of nail scissors. Mr Benét himself was now returned from his "bite to eat" and stood by the mainmast talking to a seaman. The ship seemed to be all festooned by ropes, cables, lanyards which lay mostly on the fo'castle but led down from it also. Mr Benét finished his colloquy, turned, saw me and came to the break of the quarter-deck with his usual agile run. He seemed beamingly happy.

"All goes well, Mr Talbot. Soon we shall be able to experiment with the dragrope and after that get on with Mr Summers's frapping."

"Mr Benét, I wish to speak to you on a serious matter."

"Well, sir, I am at your service."

"A schoolgirl, you said—"

"Did I? I'm sorry, Mr Talbot, but my mind is all tied up in the dragrope if you see my drift. Were we talking of my sisters?"

"No no."

"Ah—now I remember! You were asking my opinion of young Marion, were you not? She is entirely undeveloped, sir, as they all are. She is a sporty girl though, I give you that. Why, as man to man"—and here Lieutenant Benét looked round briefly then back again—"had little Marion not detained her 'uncle', as they agree she calls Sir Henry, with some plea about the conduct of the ship—she wanted sail reduced, I think—I don't mind telling you I should have been a devil of a sight nearer being detected *in flagrante delicto* than I was!"

"She knew! She understood! A criminal connection!"

"She was accustomed to keep *cave* for us."

There was what might be called a *moderate roar* from the companionway to the captain's quarters. Lieutenant Benét answered it as cheerfully and promptly as he had answered me.

"Immediately, sir!"

He raised his hand towards his forehead, gave what is fast becoming a kind of "salute to be employed at sea", then with his usual cheerful agility raced away along the sloping deck.

My own hand was lifted too. The scrap of paper with Miss Chumley's message on it escaped from my fingers. It went whirling aloft to cling shuddering in the shrouds. With a savage passion I determined to let it go—go, go! But without an order given a seaman put aside his swab, scrambled aloft as quickly as Mr Benét might have done and brought the paper back to me. I

nodded my thanks and stood there, paper in hand.
How had I made a phantom out of thin air? How had
that phantom become the most important thing in the
whole world? It was driving me, a sane and calculating
man, to acts of sheer folly—versifying—dragging un-
welcome truths out of such as Lieutenant Benét—why
(and this was a new dash of poison in the mixture) she
might well be devoted to the man himself and he not
know it in his foolish obsession with a woman old
enough to be his mother!

"Get out, Wheeler! Devil take it, man, are you to be
always under my feet?"

"Sir."

"In any case, Phillips should be serving this side of
the lobby!"

"No, sir, with respect. The first lieutenant said as
we was agreed, Phillips and me, the arrangement could
stand since you changed cabins, sir."

"You've become too devilish long-faced for me!"

I flung out of the cabin, nearly brained myself on
the mizzen and shouted for Phillips. But it was un-
necessary, for he was making a careful way along the
lobby to the saloon with a broom.

"Phillips, you may return to serving me."

The man looked round the saloon for a moment.

"Can I speak private, sir? It's where he died, sir."

"Good God, man—men must have died everywhere
in this old ship."

Phillips nodded slowly, considering.

"But then, sir, Mr Colley was a latiner."

With that he knuckled his forehead and took his

broom out of the saloon. I sat confounded. It was more and more evident that Mr Smiles was right. Here was one more madman. Wheeler made another. The truth appeared to me that I myself might well make a third. The horizon snarled at me, then disappeared. I did indeed have a mad feeling! I too was a "latiner" and perhaps it was the unappeased "larva" of Colley creeping about the ship like a filthy smell which was the "motus" of our idiotic decline into phantasy!

I shouted for Bates and got a further supply of brandy. Later still I ate yet more cold beef; and once more, as it might be a labourer eating his midday crust under a hedge, saved the meat at the cost of smeared pickles even on my unmentionables. Oldmeadow, the young Army officer, came and shared that meal with me and I remember a confused conversation we had about the *meaning of life*. He became quite disguised, poor fellow, not having as hard a head as I. When at last I helped him to his hutch we both went sprawling. I nursed a bruised elbow in my own hutch for some time ("that will be all, Wheeler") and did not object when he first assisted me into my bunk. Being, however, a little flown with drink I engaged the man in conversation, during which he elucidated the mystery of his desire to haunt my cabin. He had not informed on Billy Rogers but the people forrard thought he had. They would "do" him if he did not stay close to the gentlemen. It was a misunderstanding, of course. No, they had not thrown him overboard. He had in fact slipped, lost his footing. He was accusing no one. And did the officers think that the ship would sink? One

way and another he was fairly at a stand to know what
to do—

I am very vexed to think that elevated as I was I
did not behave with that degree of circumspection
which should be employed in dealing with all but the
most devoted and trustworthy of servants. I even
entered into a kind of bargain—he might "haunt" me,
provided he told me the true story of what had happened to Colley! He consented on the understanding
that his information should be revealed to no one so
long as he was in the ship. The information was of
such a nature that I do not propose to commit it to
this journal.

(15)

I got out early into the waist, having been roused by
the shouts from the deck.

"Fairly the fall about! Hazard the handybilly
Rogers!"

And then the answering cry came from forrard—

"Lie all down handsomely together!"

She was there plainly to be seen on our starboard
bow! *Alcyone!* She was dismasted completely, the
masts lying about her, white sails spread on the water,
the sailors hauling away and singing. The chant came
to us clear over the waters.

"Where have you been all the day, Billy Boy?"

We drew somehow alongside her. Our sailors were
miraculously dextrous in shortening sail.

"Stun the royals there!"

Sir Henry had climbed the shrouds of what was left
of their mizzen.

"Anderson, you see all this? My cursed first lieutenant has fairly fucked us. 'Bellamy,' I said to him. 'Eat
the main course or you'll have the masts off us.'"

And She was there on the deck, her arms out-
stretched! Tears of joy streamed down her cheeks! She
came towards me! We merged—

It was Miss Granham. She had no stays—I wrestled
with her but could not get away. No wonder the two
ships were laughing and I was unclothed—

. . .

CLOSE QUARTERS

It was morning and Wheeler stood by my bunk. He had a cup of coffee in his hands.

"I have got it quite warm, sir."

My head felt constricted and my stomach queasy. Wheeler had his gaze modestly lowered in a proper servantlike manner. I opened my mouth to tell him to get out and then changed my mind. He helped me to dress though I shaved myself. The motion was regular. I left him to clean the cabin and made my way to the passenger saloon. Mr Bowles was there. He apologized for the non-appearance of the committee though to tell the truth I had forgotten that such a gathering had ever been constituted. He said that Mr Prettiman was in great pain and Mr Pike preoccupied with the state of his children. I said little, but grunted merely where it seemed appropriate. I believe Mr Bowles (a man of some intelligence who will prove to be useful, I think, when we reach Sydney Cove) seemed to understand my disinclination for speech. It was from him that I discovered I had missed an interesting operation in seamanship. This was the only reason why I regret having got, not to put too fine a point on it, confoundedly drunk. However, I should have liked to follow what Lieutenant Benét had accomplished or been instrumental in accomplishing! At the time when I and Oldmeadow had been at our potations he had caused to be rigged something never rigged before! The crew had operated a "fore-and-aft dragrope". Thus they had removed weed from the "shadow of the keel". Mr Benét had proposed and invented it. My information is that it was a most elaborate affair. It

entailed a simultaneous "bowsing and binding in" of
the cable and a "fretting fore and aft" which had
necessitated a positive orchestration of the ship's company under the orders of my friend Lieutenant
Summers. This information illuminated an observation I myself had made when Oldmeadow and I were
at it in the saloon. For glancing now and then out of
the stern window I had on at least two occasions seen
a patch of dark weed (not like the green weed of our
waterline) rolling over and over in what wake we had.
It occurred to me with something like envy that if Mr
Benét continued as he had begun he would finish the
voyage in command of us!

By the time I had assimilated all this information
from Mr Bowles I was feeling more the thing but in
need of fresh air. I went oilskinned, therefore, to the
waist and then to my usual lookout by the rail of the
poop. The ship seemed still festooned with rope but
this time no more than the forepart of her. There were
gangs of seamen and contingent officers by a single
cable which was being laid out on the fo'castle and
rigged with what I suppose were called lanyards. Mention of a rope calls to one's mind the kind of thing
used to secure the cover of a hayrick or of a roof which
is being rethatched. But this I saw was of a different
nature altogether. It was of a knotted texture, curiously woven and twisted so as to present what I can
only call a "toothed" appearance. There were the lanyards at frequent intervals, each, it appeared, in the
charge of two men. The difficulty of the operation may
be gauged when I saw that it entailed threading this

cable from one side of the ship to the other but under
the bowsprit and through freeing ports on either side
of the waist. It was easy, apparently, to lower the rope
but by no means easy to draw it along and this was
what they were doing or trying to do. The ship's movement did not help them. I made my way along the
windward rail to examine the operation more closely
but Mr Benét, coming from aft, stopped and spoke
to me.

"I believe you should not be here, sir!"

"I will go back when I have satisfied my curiosity,
and let the wind blow last night's drink out of me. I
propose never to drink again."

"*Qui a bu, boira.*"

"Devil take it, Mr Benét, you speak French like a
Frog! It's un-English. But returning to the subject of
schoolgirls—"

"Oh, lord, no. I beg you, Mr Talbot. We may hope
for another couple of knots I think. Do you notice how
removing the weed from the garboard strakes has
made a difference? I say a clear knot though Mr Summers does not think so. We shall know at midday, of
course. He is cautious, is he not? Captain Anderson
agrees with me. 'A clear knot, Mr Benét,' he said. 'I
shall enter it in the log.' "

"You are to be congratulated."

"Before I leave the service and devote myself to the
pen I hope to show the Navy that intelligence is not
to be despised, sir, nor all virtue confined to senior
officers!"

"Talking of virtue—"

"I beg you will not, sir. I have suffered from a wearisome repetition of Sir Henry's opinion on that subject. My distance from him is the only consolation for my distance from Her!"

Mr Benét sighed. I continued: "Miss Chumley—"

Mr Benét interrupted me. "Have you sisters, Mr Talbot?"

"No, sir."

Mr Benét said nothing but nodded gravely as if confirming something to himself. This and the remark he had made was so cryptic that I could find nothing to say.

"And now, Mr Talbot, I believe you must return to the break of the quarterdeck. This will soon be no place for a passenger."

Charles Summers hailed from the fo'castle.

"Mr Benét! When you have concluded your conversation be good enough to return to your duties. We are waiting."

I clambered back and held on to the rail by the entry to the lobby. The scene before me was not so much entertaining as confused. It appeared that Cumbershum had the charge of one side of the fo'castle and Mr Benét of the other. Charles Summers was in overall charge. There were seamen lining the rail in that part of the ship all leaning outward and facing away from me. I had the nonsensical impression that a good number of our tarry heroes were being sick into the sea. They were, I supposed, holding the cable which would serve as a dragrope. As I took this in, Summers shouted an order.

"Let go!"

The men lining the rail stood up. Benét and Cumbershum started to shout and their parties of seamen to move rhythmically. I cannot describe what they were doing more accurately because at the time I did not understand it. Now, I think, being wise after the event, they were moving the dragrope with a sawing motion. Nothing much seemed to be happening. I turned and looked up aft. The sailing master, Mr Smiles, had the watch apparently, with young Mr Taylor as his doggie. Mr Taylor seemed more subdued than usual and this may have been because not more than a yard or two away the captain stood by the forrard rail, his hands clasped behind his back, his feet wide apart. He watched the operation on the quarterdeck in silence.

There was a sudden commotion on the fo'castle. Cumbershum's party appeared to fall in a heap and he could be heard swearing at them as they sorted themselves out. After that there was a long pause. Apparently one end of a necessary rope had been lost so the operation was to be done again from the start. Lieutenant Benét was arguing with Charles Summers who did not appear to be happy. It seemed to me that his customarily weather-beaten face was paler than usual—with anger perhaps. The fo'castle became a mess of ropes and blocks among which men did what I am persuaded they understood. It was a long wait. I turned and climbed to the quarterdeck where the captain acknowledged my salutation if not with amiability at least without an open expression of bad temper.

"Good morning, Captain. But it is no kind of good day I think! Tell me—what are the crew doing?"

For a moment or two I thought he would not answer me. But then he opened his mouth and whispered. This I found was not secrecy but phlegm consequent on his having held his morose tongue longer than the constitution of a man was designed for. He walked to the rail, spat over the side, came back and stood by me without looking at me.

"They are rigging a dragrope."

Well I knew that! But it seemed that the details of that interesting operation would have to be extracted from him one by one.

"How can you ensure that the rope clings enough to the hull? There must be many areas that are inaccessible."

Unwittingly I had opened his mouth!

"There are indeed, Mr Talbot, though the underwater part of a ship is near enough semicircular in section. But a careful officer will exercise his wits in finding a way round such difficulties. The dragrope may be held from several directions, not merely from side to side but fore and aft. Mr Benét has proposed a plan which we think will work. The use of a dragrope in the open sea and when under weigh is most unusual. Indeed I do not know how often it has been done before. But in our circumstances—Mr Benét has already succeeded in removing weed from near the keel, something I believe unique."

"You have profited by the exchange of officers."

Captain Anderson lowered at me for a moment. But then it seemed to me as if the invitation to continue talking about his favourite was irresistible.

"I believe Mr Benét is determined to have us scraped

as clean as if we was newly commissioned, Mr Talbot.
We shall have tackles 'thwart ships and fore and aft
and lifts from the yardarms. Mr Benét is a real seaman,
sir, all ropes and blocks and canvas, sir. There is no
steam about Mr Benét, sir. No chain cable or wire
rope!"

"He is certainly using enough rope at the moment.
I did not know the ship held so much."

"What a captain cannot do with good officers, rope,
canvas, spars and a willing crew cannot be done!"

"Well, Captain, I will not dispute with you. Mr
Benét is a very energetic young man and I must take
your opinion of his seamanship on trust."

The captain spoke with positive animation.

"He will go far!"

"His French at all events sounds much as they speak
it in Paris."

"That is natural, Mr Talbot. His parents are
émigrés."

"Certainly his general appearance and air are very
pleasing. Golden hair and a complexion which seems
wholly resistant to salt—he is a veritable marine
Adonis!"

The captain looked at me sternly as he tried the
word in his mouth.

"Adonis. You will excuse me now, Mr Talbot. I am
busy."

Good God, the man thought he had given me my
congé!

"Do not allow me to interrupt you, Captain Anderson. I am deeply interested to see what you do."

What Captain Anderson did was to utter a kind of

subdued snarl, turn, take a step to the forrard rail and
hold it with both hands as if he would like to pick it
up and use it as a club. He glanced up at the luff,
roared at Mr Taylor who squeaked at the quartermasters who glanced at the luff then into the binnacle,
rolled their quids as one man and moved the wheel a
"handspan" which as far as I could see affected the
ship not at all. I continued to watch the operation on
the fo'castle. It was very slow going and even the captain gave up after a time and began to stump up and
down on the larboard side of the deck, ignoring our
rolling and pitching—and I suppose our hogging and
sagging—in a way which spoke of the years he has
passed doing precisely that. It seemed to me that he
was capable, if the ship should capsize—which God
forbid—of marching moodily over the side as she
rolled, following the movement, then stumping backwards and forwards along her keel as if waiting for
Lieutenant Benét to devise some cat's cradle of ropes,
blocks, spars and canvas to bring the ship upright
again! He and his certainties were much like the
movement of the starry heavens.

Little Pike was coming up the stairways. There were
tears on his face. The wind tore them away and his
eyes replaced them. He reeled as he came, fell against
me, clutched me with both arms and wept against my
midriff. He whispered.

"Phoebe! Oh, my little Phoebe—"

"Good God! Dead?"

The captain had stopped in his tracks. Now he came
quickly across and stared down at Pike.

"Who is dead?"

"They say she is dying. Oh, my little Phoebe!"

"This is Mr Pike, Captain. Phoebe is his daughter. Pull yourself together, Pike!"

"Who says your daughter is dying, sir?"

Pike sniffed and hiccuped.

"Mrs Pike, Captain, and Miss Granham."

"Come, Pike," said I. "They are neither of them medical men, you know! I told you about my young brothers, did I not? Always in the wars and—"

"What do you expect me to do about your daughter, Mr Pike?"

Pike shook himself free from my grasp, reeled and clutched the rail.

"If you could only ease the motion, Captain! It wears them out, you see—"

Captain Anderson answered him in what for him was a kindly voice.

"It is impossible, Mr Pike. I cannot go into the reasons but you must believe me when I say that no power on earth could stop the ship's movement."

We were all three silent. Pike smeared his face with a sleeve and then slowly, drearily *drooped* away below.

It was then that the idea came to me.

"Captain!"

But once more he was staring forward.

"Captain! Captain! Nelson—"

The captain turned and with a positive hiss of breath hurried past me and disappeared down his own private and holy companionway beyond my reach!

"Devil take it!"

For the idea was good. I knew it! I clambered down the ladders after Pike, hurried to the door of their cabin—and hesitated! It was not like me to hesitate but I did. I raised my hand to knock—and then dropped it again. But this was a terrible crisis for the little girl! I opened the door stealthily.

Her sister lay at one end of the bunk, propped up on granite pillows. She was picking at the face of a rag doll and she looked curst sullen to me. Mrs Pike and Miss Granham were bent over the other end of the bunk. I opened my mouth to explain my idea but never got a word out, for Miss Granham must have heard, or sensed something. For she turned—I had almost said turned *on me* quickly and stared in my eyes. Her face seemed stripped of flesh and her eyes were deep in their sockets.

"Go away, Mr Talbot. Do not say anything."

It was a command uttered in a stony voice which would have daunted Anderson himself. I found I had closed the door as if my arm was no longer my own. I went cautiously to the passenger saloon. Mr Pike was there under the stern window. He sniffed now and then but was calm. I remembered the only man in the ship in whom I had complete faith. I hurried away, ran perilously along the heaving deck and seized Charles Summers by the arm.

"Charles, I must speak with you—"

"Edmund! Mr Talbot!"

"The Pike child—Nelson—"

"Mr Talbot, this passes everything! Return to your cabin or I must have you conducted there!"

"Charles!"

He positively shook his arm free and pointedly began to issue orders.

I made my way back, holding on to the windward rail.

I still think my idea was good. Nelson, who was a sufferer from *mal de mer*, used to sleep in a cot which was slung like a hammock. The little girl should have had a hammock rigged for her, a doll-sized hammock, and she would have lain as snug as ever drunken Mr Gibbs did down in the gun-room! It might have given her the rest so necessary, allowed her to sleep perhaps and so gather a little strength. I had a sudden thought that if I approached Mr Benét—but he was now enmeshed in ropes and orders. However I did not return to my hutch as Charles had directed but waited once more by the break to see how the operation went. But it was slow. So at last I went to my hutch and found the inevitable Wheeler scrabbling round on the deck with a deckcloth and pretending to mop up the seawater which was immediately replaced by more from the lobby as he did so.

"Get out, Wheeler!"

I had forgotten my drunken agreement and the order had become habitual. Instead of obeying it he rose from his knees, floorcloth in hand, and came close to me.

He whispered. "She's moving more, isn't she, sir?"

"You're out of your mind, Wheeler. Now be off with you!"

"I can't drown, sir. Not again, I can't."

The man seemed calm for all the nonsense of what he spoke. I could think of nothing to say and muttered I know not what. So we stood, he continuing to stare into my face as if in longing and perhaps even in hope. But what use was "Lord Talbot"?

The ship's bell rang and there were noises from all over the ship—shouts and the thumping of booted feet, where the watch was being changed. Wheeler turned with a deep sigh and went away. To be helpless before such an evident need; and on the other hand to have an idea of real value to which no one would listen; to find our ship not so much breaking up but decomposing; and to find men, Charles Summers, Wheeler, Mr Gibbs, seeming to change as if something of the same was operating in them—whatever I had foreseen or planned in those distant days in England when I was made acquainted with the nature of my employment seemed a childish "supposing" and was all now rendered conditional on our surmounting this present peril and was likely enough to be cancelled by it! That employment itself I now saw would be conditioned by a world at once harsher and more complicated than I had anticipated.

I remembered with a kind of chill that spread over me like a change in the weather what "frapping" was. Charles Summers proposed then actually to *tie* the ship together! He would use our great cables as a last resort in an attempt to prevent her timbers from falling apart! The officers had attempted to soothe me with their assurances! They had lied in what they thought was a good cause! We *were* in deadly peril!

At last I let out my breath, mopped my forehead, then sat down at my writing-flap. After some thought, I took out this journal and leafed through it, reading here and there as if I might find in the recorded wisdom of Edmund Talbot a solution to our difficulties. Would the book one day be bound handsomely and lie on some shelf or other, my descendants' shelves, *Talbot's Journal*? But this one lacked the accidental shape of narration which Colley and fate had forced on the other volume! I had thought it might, as it were, group itself round the adventures of Jack Deverel. But at the very moment when he bid fair to occupy the centre of the stage he had escaped from it! He had exchanged clean out of this theatre and into another one where, alas, I could not follow him. Then again, this journal had been a sweet yet painful account of how young Mr Talbot had fallen in love— but the dear Object of my passion had been snatched away from me as mercilessly as you please, leaving me to dreams and Latin verses! Any furtherance of that connection, any fruition of it must look to so far in the future that I had a moment of breathless panic lest the whole connection should wear itself out and prove to be the merest flirtation in the skirts of a dinner and a ball! But as the thought came to me I dismissed it as unworthy. In the very instant of this ungenerous thought, the face and figure, the very being of that most precious Object—that Prodigy!— flashed upon the tablets of my memory and restored all to its true position. That last look she had given me and her last whispered words—oh no, she was all I

had dreamed! Yet, remembering not a poetical phantasy but a real, breathing and feeling and speaking
young lady, a young lady of much intelligence and
esprit, I could not doubt she would undertake a course
of parallel consideration as to my advisability, suit-
ability, possibility, probability—I had a fleeting vision
of myself through her eyes, now, *that young man who
was so plainly épris*, and whom she now saw back
there, left in a wallowing and dismasted vessel bound
for somewhere else! It was a desolating consideration.

Besides, Lady Somerset had said the exchange of
letters could be broken off at the wish of either party!
No one was committed.

What had I foreseen? My position at Sydney Cove,
a handsome workroom in the residency. There, I
should apply that habit of study, that methodical
approach which would make me master of any subject
however complex and new—or at least more master
than anyone else would be! Then in the social life
which surrounded His Excellency I would be careless
master of a subject, never letting it be known that
hours of devoted work had given me such assurance!
I would be a Burghley to His Excellency's Queen
Elizabeth.

(16)

It was an evident folly! I started to my feet but my hutch was not designed for a man stumping to and fro to settle the turmoil of his mind. I went as quickly and nimbly as the ship would allow to the greater space of the passenger saloon. But hardly had I got the door opened when Oldmeadow, the Army officer, coming close behind, shared it with me. He flung himself into a seat at the windward end of the main table. He was wearing civilian clothes and looked the better for it, a young man of some breeding and sense.

"Talbot, old fellow—"

But here a stormy thump of a wave and a bounce of our stern together with a more rapid roll to starboard made him thrust with both hands at the table before him.

"The devil take the sea and the Navy together!"

I, on the contrary, had to lay hold of the other end of the table and cling to it.

"They do their best, Oldmeadow!"

"Well it's not enough, that's what I say. If I'd known how long and hard this voyage would be I'd have thrown up my commission!"

"We have to put up with it."

"That's all very well, Talbot. But you know we're sinking or going to sink or may sink—I tell you that in confidence. My men know all about it. In fact they knew all about it before I did! It's always the way, you know."

"What did you tell them?"

"What do you imagine? I told them they were soldiers and the ship was the business of the Navy and none of theirs." He gave his sudden, cawing laugh, chin drawn back. "I told them if they had to drown they'd do so with leather properly pipe-clayed and muskets clean. I also ordered Corporal Jackson if he found we were sinking to get them properly fell in and standing by for further orders."

"What good does that do?"

"Have you a better suggestion?"

"We are not supposed—Summers assures me we shall not sink."

I was about to elaborate on this when the door opened violently as usual in lumpy weather, and portly Mr Brocklebank came through, supported on one side by Mrs Brocklebank and on the other side by Phillips. They manoeuvred him to a seat half-way between me and Oldmeadow and went away. The poor man seemed to me to have lost half his substance. His fat cheeks were now pendulous as those of a certain Royal Personage though his extreme embonpoint was no longer comparable.

"Mr Brocklebank, sir! I was told you were forced to keep your bunk! May we both congratulate you on your recovery?"

"I am not recovered, Mr Talbot. It is supposed that a little movement may improve me. I am in a sad way. But so, Mrs Brocklebank tells me, is our ship. I am summoning up what little strength I have left to be on hand when we attempt the operation of the drag-rope. The artist's eye—"

"I admire your devotion to art, sir, but the ship is

not in a bad way! I have the word of the first lieutenant!
Devil take it, do you suppose I myself would be so
cheerful if we was about to sink?"

I attempted a light laugh but it was so unsuccessful
that both Oldmeadow and Mr Brocklebank laughed
heartily which in its turn made me laugh—so there
we were, the sea slanting crazily outside the stern
window, glimpses of new sun sliding over the saloon
at the ship's movement, and all laughing as if the
place were bedlam.

"Well," said Oldmeadow at last, "we soldiers are
fortunate, for we know what to do!"

"I tell you we are not going to sink!"

Brocklebank ignored me.

"I have given much thought to the situation, gentlemen. Huddled as I was in my bunk, passing days
without event, I have had ample time to consider the
future. It was a question, you see. I was able to formu-
late the great question."

I glanced at Oldmeadow to see if he thought, as I
did, that Mr Brocklebank was as usual showing the
result of extreme and habitual potations. But Oldmeadow watched him, saying nothing. The old man
went on.

"I mean, gentlemen, we know how ships are lost.
They run on the rocks. There are attempts to get
ashore, et cetera, et cetera. Or they are sunk in action.
You will have seen a dozen pictures—the battle smoke
conveniently placed, and in the foreground a smashed
stump of mast with three small figures clinging to it.
There is a ship's boat making towards them to pick
them up, with Sir Henry Somerset as a midshipman in

the stern sheets—far in the distance through an arrangement of convenient smoke HMS *Whatnot* is seen to be on fire—it has all been seen, all recorded."

"I am not sure, sir—"

"The question? It is this. How does a ship sink when it is not seen or recorded? Every year—you young gentlemen will not remember peace, but even in peacetime—ships will disappear. They do not strike on rocks or lie bilged in sand. They are not those which become hulks for prison or supply, their ribs do not decay in estuaries. They pass over a horizon and they enter a mystery, gentlemen. They become 'overdue'. No one paints a picture of the *Jean and Mary* alone in the sea, disappearing in the sea, swallowed—"

"Devil take it, Brocklebank, I said the first lieutenant—"

"Somewhere in a circle of sea not to be distinguished from any other part they come to their end—"

"Look, man, they may be taken aback as we were, overset, but not lose their topmasts and therefore sink with a gurgle, I suppose—oh, with babbling prayers and curses, shrieks and screams, shouts for help where there is none—"

"But you see, Mr Talbot, the weather may be fair, the water stealthy. It creeps on them, over them. They pump until they are exhausted and the water wins. They say the water will always win."

I reeled because I had stood up.

"Once and for all, Mr Brocklebank, we are not going to sink! You must not speak so, and if you cannot think of a way to paint the event, well I am sorry but to tell you the truth not very—"

"You mistake me, sir. I am not thinking of paint. Oh yes, there is a great, terrible picture to be painted by someone of the ship foundering somewhere, anywhere, lost with all hands, overdue, the sea and the sky and the ship—but not I, sir. Besides, what client would ask me for such a canvas? How would such an engraving sell? No, sir. It is a question not of paint but of conduct."

Oldmeadow cawed again.

"By Jove, Talbot, he's put his finger on it!"

"Mr Oldmeadow understands. My meditation has been long. How does a man drown when he sees it coming? It is a question of dignity, Mr Talbot. I must have my dignity. How must I drown? Oblige me, Mr Talbot, by calling your servant."

"Wheeler! Wheeler, I say! Damn it, Wheeler, why aren't you—ah, there you are!"

"I beg pardon, sir? You called for me."

Brocklebank answered.

"We are interested, you see, Wheeler. You're about the only man alive who has had what must have been a deuced unpleasant experience. You'd oblige us by describing—"

I interrupted him.

"Brocklebank, you can't! I don't believe the man's recovered, if he ever will!"

Wheeler was looking at each of us in turn.

"No no, Wheeler! Mr Brocklebank had not thought —I am sure he spoke in jest!"

A goose walked over Oldmeadow's grave.

"God, Talbot! It would be like asking some poor devil what happened after he was turned off!"

A strong interior convulsion seemed to shake Wheeler from head to foot.

"Describe?"

Brocklebank waved his hand expansively.

"No matter, my man. I am in a minority."

Wheeler looked at me.

"That will be all, sir?"

"I—regret this. Yes. That will be all, thank you."

Wheeler bowed in a way I had never seen before. He went away.

I turned to Brocklebank.

"I am sorry to have interrupted you, sir, but really!"

"I am still at a loss to understand you, Mr Talbot. We had what might well be a unique opportunity to understand life—and what is even more important, understand death!"

I stood up.

"I believe, Mr Brocklebank, not being a devotee of the muse, as you are, that I am quite content to wait on the event."

I went away to find Wheeler and give him the *douceur* which I thought the artist's enquiry warranted.

But Wheeler was not in the lobby nor in my hutch. I stood there, looking down at this very book where it lay open on the writing-flap. The truth is Wheeler had frightened me into a cold perspiration. Whether it was my recent foray into the realms of poetry or his strong gaze at something which existed for him alone—but it might not be his alone! I might conceivably share it with him! Images of the latter end stormed through

my mind. Mutiny—a fight for the last few places in
the boats, Mr Jones's bodyguards clubbing down the
opposition as his majesty moved calmly towards his
private insurance!

These images evidently worked on me more strongly
than I supposed, for I *came to* in the lobby. I was
holding on to the rail which was placed alongside my
door and I had not put on oilskins. I cannot remember opening the door. I simply found myself where
I was. My heart was beating as if I had run a race.

Mr Jones himself stood in the doorway which gives
on to the waist. He wore oilskins though for once they
did not seem necessary. A dense blue sea surrounded
us with white horses galloping across our course.

"Well, Mr Jones, have they taken any weed off
yet?"

"I believe so, Mr Talbot. Some have averred they
saw it go, but I cannot say I did so myself."

"I saw some weed in our wake the other day. I suppose that was owing to Mr Benét having 'cleaned the
garboard strakes in the shadow of the keel'."

"That is far too nautical for a simple shopkeeper,
sir."

"I mean his operations with the dragrope were
unexpectedly successful."

"I must approve his care of my investments."

"You own the ship as well as everything else?"

I did not attempt to keep the irritation and dislike
out of my voice. But the purser continued, placidly
enough.

"No, no. That remains to the Crown. But there is a

matter of certain goods of mine which are stowed in the hold and will spoil if the water gains on us."

"The first lieutenant—"

"Assured you that the water was not gaining. Yes, I know. But in my important and shopkeeperly way I have wondered whether the weed which Mr Benét is so anxious to scrape off the ship's hull may not in fact be keeping the water out?"

"Mr Benét—"

"He is a persuasive young gentleman. I believe, sir, that he could sell anything, did he but put his mind to it. Even damaged goods."

"They will have considered what the effect of removing the weed will be."

"I observe that the first lieutenant is co-operating in the business under protest."

"Yes. But then he is—"

I did not like to say the word. It would seem to credit Charles Summers with an almost feminine weakness. The purser turned his head on his thick neck and looked me in the eye. He spoke the words softly.

"He is?"

I said nothing. "Jealous" is a dangerous word. He returned to watching the fo'castle. I stood, not holding on now but with feet wide apart, for Mr Benét's change of course had had an even-ing effect on our movements. Together then, standing just beyond the opening to the waist, we watched the operation. The groups on either side of the ship were moving rhythmically and alternately. Then as we watched, at a shouted order both groups stood easy, the lanyards slack in their hands. I saw what the matter was. Since our rigging came down to the sides of the vessel there would come point after point at which the dragrope would have to be passed "outboard" and brought in again before the operation could continue. Such a pause the men were now enjoying and one unexpectedly prolonged, for the ship's bell rang again and there came a pipe and the cry of "Up spirits!" It was, I thought, another example of the extraordinary ossification of Noah's Service that the vital operation which might increase our speed now had to be set on one side while the crew tossed down what Colley had called "the flaming ichor!" The groups were streaming down from the fo'castle, leaving the officers, Cumbershum, Benét, Summers waiting, doubtless impatiently, by the abandoned ropes. What had the carpenter said all those weeks ago when I had first heard the word "dragrope"? *They didn't think they'd careen her what with one thing and another so they took what weed they could off her bottom with the dragrope*—and Mr Askew, the gunner—*If they took the weed off her they might take the bottom with it.*

"It is an operation for harbour."

I was a little confused to find I had spoken aloud.

"It is not a case in which they can afford to make a mistake, Mr Talbot."

"No, indeed. I propose to obtain from you a watertight and buoyant container for my manuscripts, so that they, at least, may stand some chance of reaching a reader."

That was a joke, of course, but so weak that Mr Jones nodded seriously.

We turned to watch once more. Men were climbing back to the rope. All at once I saw that Charles Summers was gesticulating at Mr Benét with a fierceness which was unwonted in him. The two gentlemen fell into an animated argument. The purser stirred, I thought, uneasily.

"Is something really wrong, do you suppose, Mr Talbot?"

All at once it came upon me that Charles Summers had been—was—my friend and it was improper in me to discuss him. I shrugged lightly, turned away and climbed the stairway to the quarterdeck. Captain Anderson was standing again by the forrard rail and staring at his ship broodingly.

"An operation for harbour, Captain?"

He glanced across at me, opened his mouth, then shut it again. I turned too. From this elevation it was possible to see more clearly the plan of what was being executed. The dragrope was not a simple unadorned cable. From regular intervals at either end subsidiary ropes were stretched or coiled on the deck. But the intricacy is beyond my seamanship or my powers of description.

"Is that really weed, sir, that great patch at the waterline?"

The captain grunted. "Some has been cut away from under her now. There will be more yet."

"And our speed will increase again?"

"So it is hoped."

"How much, Captain?"

Captain Anderson gave the sign of his displeasure

which many found so daunting. That is to say he projected his jaw and lowered the sullen mass of his face onto it.

"Oh, do not answer, Captain! It is, of course, none of my business—though come to think of it I have as great a stake in the affair as anyone!"

"Stake, sir! What stake?"

"My life."

Now the captain did look at me. But it was from deep inside and loweringly. A seventh wave, which washed the fo'castle, filled the waist and made the quarterdeck shudder. It took my attention from anything but the need to keep my feet. Was it my imagination or did the quarterdeck move in a way which was not repeated by the rest of the ship? The wind felt very cold and I regretted not having my oilskins. Nevertheless I watched a whole series of waves and rolls but could not detect that peculiarly local movement again.

"I am told she has been badly wrung."

Captain Anderson drew in his breath sibilantly. His knuckles on the rail showed dirty white. He roared. "Mr Summers!"

Charles stopped and picked up a speaking trumpet. His voice came the length of the ship with that curious, otherworldly resonance which such an instrument imparts.

"Sir?"

"What is the delay?"

"A foul lead, sir. We are trying to clear it."

" 'Trying', Mr Summers?"

" 'Trying.' "

Charles turned aside his head. He spoke briefly to Mr Benét who saluted and came racing aft. He spoke up from the waist.

"We think it is old coral, sir. Her last commission was in the West Indies. We believe it is dead coral down there which may need more than pully-haully."

" 'We,' Mr Benét?"

"Mr Summers thinks it possible. I suggested taking a lead to the forrard warping capstan but he does not want to go as far as that for a number of reasons."

"And you, Mr Benét?"

"I believe we should try a tackle to begin with."

Captain Anderson said nothing for a while. He made small chewing movements. Other than that, all that moved was his right leg—his starboard leg which flexed and straightened without, I am sure, his being aware of it. After all, my own starboard leg, and Mr Benét's—no. As Mr Benét was facing aft was it not his port leg? It depends whether, et cetera. I am so deucedly tired of this nautical rigmarole! We all flexed and straightened our appropriate legs and did so in the ship whenever we were not sitting or lying. It was a small piece of unconscious behaviour to have attached to us and no kind of compensation for the suffering surely implied in its acquirement.

Captain Anderson nodded. "Very well, Mr Benét. But—"

"Handsomely, sir?"

Captain Anderson smiled! He did! He shook his forefinger at the young man.

"Now now, Mr Benét! Wait for it! Yes. Handsomely."

"Aye aye, sir."

Good God—but this was *arch*!

Now there occurred one of those timeless pauses in a ship when men seem to do nothing but paw at ropes. Leads, it appeared, had to be rerun. Mr Summers, it seemed, was making use of a freeing port next to the break of the fo'castle and also the bitts—oh, lord! And a positive cat's cradle of ropes and blocks—there was argument. At last a party of men was mustered at the tail of a rope they were adjured to pull with a cry of "Gee up, horsies!" This producing no useful effect they were then adjured to "Walk away", then "Put your backs into it!", then "Sweat out your guts" which did indeed produce a result. There was a report like a pistol shot, I was about to say, but why not like a rope breaking? For that is what it was and they all fell down. The cat's cradle was a long time repairing. I myself went to the passenger saloon and ate some more cold beef, then came back. The cat's cradle was in place again and the men went through their motions. The lead to the dragrope stretched rigid and remained motionless.

Mr Benét cantered aft again.

"We believe we should use the capstan, sir."

Captain Anderson straightened up abruptly. He turned and began to stump up and down with his hands behind his back. Lieutenant Benét waited. Another big wave passed under us—

I was certain. Where the captain was walking away from me, his legs straddled apart, the deck had moved and moved in a way that the fo'castle had not, nor the waist either!

Now the captain came back.

"Mr Summers agrees?"

"He believes you yourself should give the order, sir."

"The man on the spot, Mr Benét. And can you not move the rope forrard?"

"I—we think that the rope has sawn its way into the coral and now cannot be moved forrard or aft."

"What does Mr Gibbs think?"

Mr Benét smiled.

"He says, 'Maybe it's coral and maybe it isn't,' sir."

"Very well. My compliments to the first lieutenant and ask him to be good enough to step up here."

Was it my imagination or had Captain Anderson shared with Lieutenant Benét some kind of reference, reminder, opinion, in the way he said "first lieutenant"? But I was versed enough now in the customs of the sea service to realize what a monstrous dereliction from duty that would be! No, it was my imagination; for Captain Anderson had lowered his face glumly again and Lieutenant Benét was cantering in his usual fashion towards the fo'castle. Summers came back quickly enough but walking. His face was expressionless. He and the captain walked away from me to the very stern of the vessel and stood there together. I heard nothing of their conversation but occasional words which flew from them like leaves on the wind. Forrard, I could see that Lieutenant Benét with the briskness I was coming to expect from him had gathered together some men from the other parties.

"Responsibility."

That word flew by. It had been said in a rather raised

tone as if Charles Summers had said it before and now was repeating it with emphasis.

How could they be certain that when they dragged off or broke off the coral that they would not break off wood with it? And that word again and in the captain's voice this time!

"Responsibility."

Gone on the wind.

Mr Summers came back. He passed me without speaking. His face was stony, but his whole demeanour that of an anxious and angry man. How we were all changed! Charles who had been so equable, now as often in the sulks as out of them; Anderson once so aloof, now said to be eating out of Mr Benét's hand; and I—? Well, I have put down, it may be, more that I might regret about Edmund Talbot.

There were now lines stretching from the dragrope itself and a master rope which gathered all the subsidiaries together and led them, not to a warping capstan below deck, but to the huge drum of the capstan on the fo'castle. Some men were putting in the capstan bars. It came to me on the cold wind that this operation carried on along there at an angle to the sea, washed with salt water and spray-shot; that this work by those ear-ringed fellows with their pigtails and quiffs was employed about my life; was something which might well see the end of that precious career towards which my godfather had impelled me!

Without much thought I abandoned my station on the quarterdeck and went down to the waist, meaning to look along the ship's side and catch if I could a

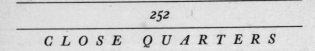

glimpse of the dragrope where it vanished under water. I do not know what impulse made me do it other than a new sense of urgency which made me want to "do something!" It was an impulse not peculiar to me. This ship resounded to rumour, scandal and nightmare as a stringed instrument resounds to the bow. Our passengers, or those of them who were at all capable of leaving their bunks, were now grouped, I might say crowded, at our entry to the waist. Bowles was there, wrapped in a greatcoat and peering forward I thought shortsightedly, his face screwed up, dark curls fluttering all over his hatless head. Mr Brocklebank of all people, our marine painter, was there, still out of his bunk, though for the first time since we had struck bad weather! But what a change! That belly which had once included his chest and seemed to descend to his knees had now contracted to a shelflike protuberance positioned between his navel and the upper part of the thigh. He and it were draped in a travelling shawl or blanket, a carriage rug perhaps which had seen far better days. His beaver was bound on his head by a length of material which passed over the crown and under his chin. I do not think I was mistaken in believing it to be a lady's stocking! The former owner of the stocking, Mrs Brocklebank, crouched under his lee. As I passed them she opened the carriage rug and huddled herself inside it against her husband and beneath his right armpit. Her pretty face was pale. No one said anything. All eyes were on the distant capstan.

And now, as if the rumour, the "buzz", had been too loud to be endured in those forrard parts of the ship where the emigrants lived as best they could, they began to issue into the waist, and then to swarm into it. There were angry shouts from the officers. Summers descended from the fo'castle and spoke with them. He gestured at the ropes. Behind me firm steps descended the stairs to the quarterdeck and poop. It was Captain Anderson, of course, and he made his majestic way forrard over the streaming deck. He spoke with Summers. He spoke with the emigrants. Like bees returning to their hive they retreated backwards into the entry to the fo'castle and the operation saw them no more. Captain Anderson picked his careful way round the cat's cradle and climbed to the fo'castle itself. He stationed himself forrard of the capstan and on our larboard side where the "foul lead" was occurring. I myself clambered to the raised rail of our larboard side, and held it, then looked over.

Colley said much of colour! I must remember the colour of things. Greyness had gone. The sky was dense blue and the sea a deeper blue over which white horses dragged their varying humps and hummocks and walls of water. The sea was covered with them to the sharp horizon, and the sun blazed down from a sky carved here and there with white and rounded clouds. The side of our ship was wasp-coloured as befits a warship, black and yellow and streaming. Certainly the first operation of the dragrope had been successful until it jammed. There was no doubt of that. A great carpet of weed floated many yards out from the side of the ship. As we rolled, the green weed along the waterline came up through the darker weed from lower down, a whole carpet of it, still attached to the ship but easy enough to cut away or be dragged away should our

forward movement increase or the dragrope be moved
further aft. The carpet was as nasty a sight I thought
as there could well be. Now and then, at the outer edge
of the carpet whole waggonloads of the pipy, bagged
and leathery stuff together with a helping of small
crabs and shellfish would detach itself and float away
in a sloth which told only too clearly that for all her
rolling, her hogging and sagging, her bucking, and her
wringing, the ship was nearly stationary in the water.
Yet the dragrope had worked and would continue to
do so. Weed had come off her hull.

Someone sighed. It was Wheeler at my elbow and
not staring into the water but into my face.

"It's true, isn't it, sir?"

I whispered back—in all that wind and spray, noise,
commotion!

"What's true, man?"

"They're taking a chance, aren't they, sir? You've
spoken to the officers, sir, haven't you?"

The man irritated me beyond bearing.

"For God's sake, Wheeler! You'll have to put up
with whatever happens like the rest of us!"

Wheeler moved away.

On the fo'castle, Mr Gibbs knuckled his forehead in
obedience before the captain and departed downwards. A detached load of weed drifted slowly by.

But Mr Brocklebank was approaching. He had
shuffled over with much caution and now took up the
position at my elbow which had been vacated by
Wheeler.

"A scene fit for your brush, Mr Brocklebank."

"Are you offering to commission me, Mr Talbot?"

"I? Good God! The idea—"

Mrs Brocklebank who had come along with her husband peeped up at me out of the carriage rug.

"If only the motion were to be easier I'm sure Mr Brocklebank—Wilmot—would be happy to paint your portrait, Mr Talbot!"

Was there ever so silly and pointless an interruption? I did not answer it but stared forrard where our fate was being decided. This will indicate how wrought on I was, and indeed how tense and anxious all we passengers were. I cannot speak for the seamen but after all they are human and had each a life to lose. Indeed my own anxiety may be judged by the fact that I preferred to ignore Mrs Brocklebank, for she was, in good weather, a pretty little thing and I had enjoyed the few moments of conversation I had ever passed with her. Indeed, in those distant days before we lost our masts—but that is irrelevant.

The purser had reappeared and stood wedged between me and Mr Brocklebank.

"They are very slow about it, Mr Talbot, the lazy dogs."

"Perhaps they do not care for the possible outcome, Mr Jones, and are putting off the evil moment."

"Debt-ridden and dissolute. What should the outcome matter to such?"

"If you prick us do we not bleed?"

"I beg your pardon, sir!"

Mr Brocklebank edged in a trifle closer.

"Mr Talbot was quoting from *The Merchant of Venice*. No, no, Mr Talbot. You do not know the lower orders as I do who have been forced to live

among them at one time and another. It is fashionable
to talk about the corruption and vice of high society.
That is nothing to the corruption and vice of low
society, sir! We should never forget that the vicious
we have always with us, as some poet or other may have
said. Even aboard here—I have been robbed, sir. Lying
on a bed of pain—"

Mrs Brocklebank emerged again.

"Now, Wilmot, we agreed to say nothing of the
matter. As far as I am concerned I am glad to see the
thing go!"

The men at the capstan began to walk around it.

"Handsomely!"

Charles Summers was leaning over the side and
watching the dragrope.

"Roundly, now!"

The men went a little faster. What ropes on the
deck had been slack now rose from it and their indi-
vidual catenaries disappeared. There came a loud
creaking and groaning from the ship or the rope or the
capstan or all of them together. I looked over the side
as the ship's side rose out of the water with all its
streaming weed, then swung down again. The dragrope was visible from the deck down to the weed. It
did not seem to be moving but water was spurting
from it. There was a sudden confusion round the capstan. Men were falling over each other. The dragrope
moved.

I have seen all this and much else which was to come
in nightmare, not once but several times, and shall do
so again. In nightmare the shape is bigger and rises

wholly awesome and dreadful. My dreaming spirit
fears as my waking spirit fears that one night the thing
will emerge, bringing with it a load of weed that only
half conceals a face. I do not know what face and do
not care to dally longer with the thought. But then,
that morning in the wind, the salt air, the rocking,
heaving ship, I saw with waking eyes down by the crazily unstable waterline something like the crown of a
head pushing up through the weed. Someone screamed
by my shoulder, a horrible, male scream. The thing
rose, a waggonload of weed festooned round and over
it. It was a head or a fist or the forearm of something
vast as Leviathan. It rolled in the weed with the ship,
lifted, sank, lifted again—

"Vast heaving!"

I know now that this was a foolish order and un-
necessary. For the men had first fallen with the sudden
movement of the dragrope, then fled from the capstan
as if their work had been unlawful. I am told that the
petty officers used their starters and that the ship was in
confusion from one end to the other. But I saw none
of that. I could not look anywhere but at this awful
creature which was rising from the unknown regions.
Its appearance cancelled the insecure "facts" of the
deep sea and seemed to illustrate instead the horribly
unknown. Impossible as this is, but with a rolling and
pitching ship the sea was where it could not be and the
thing towered black and streaming above me. Then it
slid sideways, showed a glimpse of weedy tar and
timber massive as the king tree of a tythe barn, slid
sideways and disappeared.

(17)

"Still!"

That was the captain's famous roar, late this time but to be obeyed on pain of death. It came from the waist. Somehow he had got himself there in the seconds during which I had been mesmerized by the apparition. Even we, the passengers, felt the compulsion of that roar and froze where we stood.

Captain Anderson now continued in a very loud voice.

"That was flotsam caught under the forefoot, Mr Summers."

"The dragrope had worked past the forefoot, sir. I believe that was a piece of the bilge keel."

The captain snarled.

"It was flotsam, sir! Flotsam! Do you hear?"

"Aye aye, sir."

"Come with me."

The two officers stumped towards us. Captain Anderson ignored us but continued to issue orders.

"Let the men stand by. Check in the hold."

"Aye aye, sir. Mr Cumbershum—"

And then as they went up the stairway Summers continued in an angry voice. "It was indeed the bilge keel, sir. I saw it. The fore end must be rotted and the rope able to catch under it then work along."

"No, no, Mr Summers, it was not! *And do not talk so loud!*"

I believe that in circumstances such as ours were at

that time there comes to an educated and thinking
man something as strange and perhaps in its kind as
awesome as the wooden monster itself. There is an in-
grained habit of dignity which asserts the positive
necessity of proclaiming to a world of blind force and
material something like—*I am a man. I am more than
blind nature!* At this imperative discovery or command
I found I was searching my mind for some word or
action which would make this evident.

"I suppose the keel, whether it be bilge or bottom,
may still be called 'flotsam'."

Mr Jones at my shoulder cleared his throat ineffec-
tually, then tried again. He did not turn his face towards
me but continued to watch the place where the ancient
baulk of timber had appeared and disappeared.

"How can it be flotsam, Mr Talbot? It has sunk."

I found myself nodding sagely. But as the import of
his words came home, my feet stuck to the deck as they
had done at the cannon shot, or only just now at the
captain's roar. Aware of this, I surveyed the scene before me as if searching for something—a friend perhaps. The men were standing idly but quietly now.
The emigrants were crowded back into the fo'castle,
but visible by their pale faces in the opening to it. Mr
Benét emerged from the depths below the fo'castle in
company with Mr Gibbs. They came down the deck
towards us, Mr Benét accommodating his pace to that
of his fellow. Round us the sun was bright, the billows
white and bounding as Mr Benét had bounded on
every other occasion when I had seen him moving from
one part of the ship to another. All crests in that lively

sea were exactly delineated and the horizon was taut as a rope under strain. Mr Gibbs was talking in an aggrieved tone of voice.

"What did you expect, Mr Benét, you and him? Though there's but the one through-bolt drawn that's bad enough."

"Well, plug it!"

"What do you think I was about down there? Water may come in, but not that way from now on!"

Mr Jones shifted his feet as if they too had been stuck. He cleared his throat again.

"Well, Mr Talbot. At least I have taken every precaution I can." He shook his head admiringly. "I'm odd like that, you know. My boat up there on the boom is supplied with every necessity."

"I have no boat, sir! I do not see accommodation in boats even for the children and ladies!"

Mr Jones nodded slowly, as if he, too, had noticed that lack. Then, as slowly, he shook his head.

Mr Benét came down the stairs, bounding again, and went forward in the same fashion as if he were the very personification of this bright air and wind and sea. Mr Gibbs followed him like a dull after-thought. Then at the last came Charles Summers, pale and thoughtful. I spoke to him by name as he passed but he seemed deep in some consideration and did not hear me. Nor did Mr Brocklebank who now stood between me and the way back to my hutch.

"After all it was given back to me and I am positive I put it away in the lower drawer. You have not seen it by any chance, Mr Talbot?"

But Mrs Brocklebank was shaking him by the sleeve. "Oh, let it go, Wilmot dear! I am sure I am very glad to see the back of the horrid thing!"

They walked their wet way together before me into the lobby. Mr Brocklebank was speaking with that painful clarity and emphasis which a man employs to make clear his own patience and understanding in difficult circumstances, particularly, I have noticed, when addressing his wife.

"It was *in* the *bottom drawer* under my *bed*. Bunk, I suppose I must call it, for never was bed so uncomfortable—and now it is gone. We have a thief and I shall tell Mr Summers."

Mrs Brocklebank, who all the while had been talking, prattling rather, like a kind of descant on his base, fairly thrust him through the door of their hutch and pulled it to behind them.

I made my way towards my own hutch, the one that for some time had been used by the late Reverend James Colley.

Life should serve up its feast of experience in a series of courses. We should have time to assimilate, if not digest one before we attack another. We should have a pause, not so much for contemplation as for rest. However, life does not operate in such a reasonable fashion but huddles its courses together, sometimes two, three or what seems to be the whole meal on a single dish. Thus it was with me—with us. I will try to report what happened next as accurately as I can. That grim baulk of waterlogged timber was still, I suppose, sinking towards the ooze where Colley stood on his

cannon balls when I approached my hutch—his hutch.
I see it still and try to change what happened but cannot. I saw that Wheeler was inside. I could tell it was
Wheeler though only his baldness and the two puffs of
white hair on either side of it was visible through the
louvre. Then as my mouth opened to dismiss him with
a severe injunction against his haunting of my cabin
beyond the necessity of cleaning it, his head tilted and
lifted. His eyes were shut, his expression peaceful. He
raised towards his lips a gold or brass goblet. Then his
head exploded and disappeared after or with or before,
for all I know, a flash of light. Then everything disappeared as a wave of acrid smoke burst out of the
louvre. My left eye was, or had been, struck and filled
with a wet substance.

I heard nothing. Is that not impossible? Though
others heard the explosion of the blunderbuss I who
saw it heard nothing.

I have tried again and again to put what I saw in
logical order but come always to the fact that there
was no order but only instantaneity. The brass goblet
which Wheeler held to his peaceful face was the bell
of Mr Brocklebank's blunderbuss, but realization of
that fact came to me later. What I experienced was the
peaceful face, the head bursting, the flash, the smoke
—and silence!

I staggered away from the door, fanned smoke, tried
to smear my stuck left eye open—saw at once the
colour of the mess in my hand and made a rush for the
open deck, reached the rail by Mr Jones and vomited
over it.

"Are you injured, Mr Talbot? Are you shot?"

For answer, I did no more than vomit again.

"You do not speak, Mr Talbot. Are you injured? What has happened?"

The voice of the lawyer's clerk, Mr Bowles, came to me.

"It is the steward Wheeler, Mr Jones. He has killed himself in the cabin which Mr Talbot is at present occupying."

Mr Jones's uncomprehending and calm voice answered him.

"What did he do that for, Mr Bowles? He had been rescued. He was a most fortunate man. You could say he was the object of a special providence."

My knees were loosed. I sank to the deck and voices faded far away as a wave of faintness engulfed me.

I came to lying on my back, my head supported in a lap. Someone was sponging my face with cold water. I opened the other eye and examined a dazzle of light reflected on a wooden ceiling. It was the passenger saloon and I was lying on a bench. Miss Granham's voice spoke above me!

"Poor boy. He has far more sensibility than he knows."

There was a long period of pendulum movement. I became aware that my coat had been removed, my stock undone and my shirt opened. I sat up slowly. The lap belonged to Mrs Brocklebank.

"I believe you should lie still for a while, sir."

I embarked on what would have had to be a lengthy
expression of thanks and excuse, but Miss Granham
had other ideas.

"You must lie still, sir. Celia will fetch a cushion."

I tried to get off the bench but she held me with
surprising firmness.

"Thank you, Miss Granham, but believe me I am
able to return now."

"Return, sir?"

"Why, to my hutch—cabin, I would say!"

"It would be most inadvisable. At least sit for a
while."

What I remembered more than anything was the
mess in my eye. I gulped and looked at my hand. It
had been washed but there was an indefinable tinge of
what I suppose was the remains of dried blood and
brains on it. I gulped again. It now came to me that I
was homeless! What still puzzles me is that I felt this
strange "homelessness" more than anything else and
had some difficulty in restraining my tears—tears for
the seclusion of that hutch or one like it where I had
spent such hours—what am I saying—such weeks and
months of boredom! But Zenobia now lay in the bunk
which once had been mine, and Colley's was not to be
thought of.

"I have been in a faint I suppose and for no reason!
Ladies, I do most sincerely—"

"Better, Mr Talbot?"

It was Charles Summers.

"I am quite recovered, thank you."

"He is not, Mr Summers!"

"I have questions to ask him, Miss Granham."

"No, sir!"

"Believe me, ma'am, I regret the necessity. But you must see that in a case like this the questions are official and not to be delayed. Now, Mr Talbot. Who did it?"

"Mr Summers, really!"

"Excuse me, Miss Granham. Well, sir? You heard the question. Shall I repeat it? The sooner you answer, the sooner Colley's—that is, your—cabin is able to be—tidied."

"Tidied, sir? That is landsman's talk. You should have said 'made all shipshape'."

"You see, ma'am, he is recovered. Well, Mr Talbot. As I said, 'Who did it?' "

"Good God. You know already. He did it himself!"

"You saw it happen?"

"Yes. Do not remind me!"

"Really, Mr Summers, he should be—"

"Please, Miss Granham. Only one more question. He had constituted himself your servant. He may have let fall some observation—have you any knowledge of why the wretched man did it?"

I thought for a while. But against the bloody fact my thoughts were trivial and wandering.

"No, sir. None whatever."

All at once and as it were on the rebound, the full fact of my homelessness came over me.

"Oh, God! What shall I do? Where shall I go?"

"He cannot use that cabin, Mr Summers! It is impossible!"

Charles Summers was staring down at me. With a

dreary sense of loss and a foreboding that the feeling would grow to a real pain, I perceived a look of evident dislike on his face.

"I am supposed to make special arrangements for you again, Mr Talbot. We have kept the wardroom out of bounds to passengers. We lieutenants are, after all, entitled to our own place. But the circumstances are unusual as is your position. Come with me if you are able to withstand the movement of the ship. I will find you a bunk."

"I beg you will be careful, Mr Talbot!"

Charles Summers led the way down, waiting for me now and then when the swift roll made the descent difficult. He opened the door of the wardroom and gestured me through. It was a large room with many doors leading off it, a long table and a variety of instruments and objects which I had neither the time nor the inclination to examine. The whole was lighted by what I supposed was the lowest register of our great stern windows.

"But this is big enough for every officer in the ship and you have only yourself, Cumbershum and Benét!"

He said nothing but opened one of the doors. The bunk was empty, the folded blankets lying ready on the thin mattress.

"This is for me?"

"For the time being."

"It is small."

"What did you expect, Mr Talbot? It was good enough for your friend Mr Deverel and is good enough for your new friend, Mr Benét. It is designed, sir, for a mere lieutenant, some poor man with no prospects, no hope; designed perhaps for a man thrust out of his legitimate place by a, a—"

"My dear Mr Summers!"

"Do not protest, sir. At least I may say what I choose now you have found a new friend for your patronage!"

"My what?"

"That patronage which you once promised me but have now withdrawn as is evident from the—"

"What is all this? There is some dreadful mistake! I never promised you my patronage, for I have none to bestow!"

The first lieutenant laughed briefly and angrily.

"I understand. Well, it is as good a way of ending the affair as another. So. He has everything then."

I seized the door and hung on to the handle as a roll promised to throw me across the wardroom.

"Who has everything?"

"Mr Benét."

"You are talking in riddles. What has Mr Benét to do with us? Where on earth did you get the idea that I had the gift of a ship or a place in my pocket?"

"Do you not remember? Or is it more convenient for you to forget?"

"I think you had better explain. What have I said which promised you anything?"

"Since you have forgotten the words it would shame me to repeat them."

"Once and for all, before my brain bursts—no, not that!—once and for all will you not tell me what you think I have said?"

"It was in your old cabin when we were concerned with Colley. I said, 'I have no patron.' You answered immediately, 'Do not be so certain, Mr Summers!' Those were your very words! Deny it if you choose!"

"But that was not an offer of patronage! It was an expression of esteem, of my sincerely proffered friendship! I am as far beneath the possibility of exercising patronage as I thought you was above it!"

"Say no more. I have mistaken us both. I will wish you good day."

"Mr Summers! Come back!"

There was a long pause.

"To what end, sir?"

"You compel me—we are down among embarrassments. And the ship may sink, good God! Are we not laughable? But enough of that. The journal which I kept for my godfather and which you suppose to contain nothing but a description of our good captain's injustice—you may read it if you choose. It will lie before my godfather, a nobleman of much influence in our country's affairs. He will read every page. Take it away, sir, slit the canvas, read every word. I—you will find there a positive hymn in your praise. There can hardly be a page on which your name, your conduct and character is not set down in terms of admiration and dare I say—esteem and—affection. That was all I could do for you and it is what I have done."

There was now an even longer pause. I believe we did not look at one another. When at last his voice answered me, it was hoarse.

"Well, now you know better, Mr Talbot. I am not worthy of your admiration or regard."

"Do not say so!"

We were facing each other, each, as usual, with one leg straight, the other bending and stretching. Despite or perhaps *because* of the high seriousness of our exchange I could not but be aware of a certain comedy in the situation. But it was no time for pointing this out. Mr Summers was speaking. His voice vibrated with emotion.

"I have no family, Mr Talbot, and I do not believe myself inclined to marriage. Yet my attachments are deep and strong. Men, like cables, have each their breaking strain. To lose my place in your regard, to see a younger man, one with all the advantages which were denied me, achieve on every level what I could never hope for—"

"Wait, wait! If you were only aware of my meanness, my attempts at manipulation, let alone a self-esteem which I now perceive to be—I cannot explain myself. Measured against you I am a paltry fellow, that is the fact of the matter! But I would be honoured above all things if you would agree to continue my friend."

He took a sudden step forward.

"It is more than I could hope for or deserve. Oh, do not look so distressed, sir! These clouds will pass. You have been sorely tried of late on several counts and I am much to blame in adding to your cares."

"I am learning too much, that is the fact of the matter. Men and women—I beg you will not laugh but I had proposed myself a political and detached observation of the nature of both, yet in my association with you and her too and with poor Wheeler—these tears are involuntary and the result of my repeated blows to the head. I beg you will disregard them. Good God, a man of—"

"*How* old are you?"

When I repeated the figure, he cried out.

"No more than that?"

"Why so astonished? How old did you think I was?"

"Older. Much older."

The forbidding distance in his face disappeared, to be replaced by quite another expression. Hesitantly I held out my hand; and like the generous-hearted Englishman that he is, he seized it with both his own in a thrilling and manly grip.

"Edmund!"

"My dear fellow!"

Still conscious as I was of a certain comical element in our situation, it was a moment at which reserve was no longer possible and I returned the pressure.

Postscriptum

I must record here in this same folio an explanation and apology for the abrupt ending of my journal. A possible reader—a dear reader—might tease himself or herself endlessly in pursuit of that explanation without ever coming to the right one. The reason for my abandoning my pen was in a sense trivial and even vexing, yet at the same time the cause of much hilarity. Now I am safely ashore and have got back my landlegs I have begun to suspect—though it may seem unkind to say so—that our hilarity was a kind of madness throughout the ship as if the sailing master, Mr Smiles, had been right!

Briefly then.

While I and my dear friend Charles Summers were ridding ourselves of a foolish misunderstanding Cumbershum came off watch. I myself was not witness to what followed, for the suicide of poor Wheeler before my very eyes came to work on me strongly and I was forced to retire to the hutch Charles had found for me and lay there for a long time shuddering as if the blunderbuss had wounded me in addition to killing Wheeler. But I was given an exact account of what occurred.

Cumbershum was buttonholed in his descent by Mr Jones, the purser. Mr Jones, increasingly concerned for his property in the ship, begged for a few moments of Mr Cumbershum's time. Later Mr Cumbershum related the interview to Charles Summers and the other officers with every evidence of enjoyment.

"Mr Cumbershum, I beg of you. Will the ship sink?"

As luck would have it, Cumbershum was one of the most heavily endebted officers. He shouted with laughter.

"Yes, the bloody ship will sink, you yellow-bellied bastard, and death pays all debts!"

The result was not what Cumbershum expected. Mr Jones, in the grip of his ruling passion, hurried away, then returned with a handful of IOUs for which he demanded payment on the spot. Cumbershum refused, suggesting a use for the papers which I do not feel called on to particularize. The effect of this refusal was to throw the man into a kind of subdued panic. He hurried about the ship, heedless of her movement which sometimes put him in peril of drowning as if his own safety were the last thing in the world he was considering. In another man it would have been folly or heroism or both. He tried to call in his IOUs throughout the whole ship and met everywhere with a refusal sometimes even blunter than Cumbershum's. I believe nothing, neither the arrival of King Neptune when we crossed the line, nor the entertainment given when we and *Alcyone* lay side by side, caused such general and on the whole beneficial amusement. For a while we were indeed a "happy ship"!

By the time I had recovered from my strange disability or sickness, whatever it was, it was my turn to be approached. Mr Jones presented me with an inflated account for candles and paregoric. I was inspired! I reduced the man to stillness and silence when I replied that I did not owe him anything. I owed money to

Wheeler who was dead. I was prepared to pay
Wheeler's heirs and assigns in due course.

After much anxious expostulation on his part Mr
Jones recalled our previous conversation.

"At least, Mr Talbot, you will pay me for the container you spoke of!"

"Container?"

"For your journal—to float it off!"

"Ah, I remember. But why should I pay you? Is not
an IOU sufficient?"

The man gave a kind of whinny.

"No cash, Mr Talbot, no container!"

I thought for a moment. As the reader may recollect,
it was true I had asked for something in which to put
my writings and commit them to the waves but the
suggestion had been made more than half in jest. It
was typical of Mr Jones to remember the remark, take
it seriously and determine to profit therefrom. A way
opened before me of revenging Humanity on In-
humanity!

"Very well, Mr Jones. I will buy a container from
you—on one condition. That you find room for it in
your boat!"

There now ensued a passionate argument. At last
Mr Jones agreed to carry the thing ashore and see it
forwarded to the appropriate address. The first container he produced he called a pipkin. When I saw how
small it was and that it was made of pottery I would
have none of it.

"Suppose you and your boat are dashed on the rocks,
sir. Why you might burst like a dead sheep in the sun
and the pipkin with you!"

Mr Jones's complexion took on a greenish hue. He would sell me a firkin.

"And what is a firkin?"

"A small wooden cask, sir."

"Very well."

The firkin when it came proved to be a barrel that had held eight gallons of some liquid or other.

"What the devil, man! This would go near to holding me myself!"

The price was exorbitant. I reduced it by more than half, using, I am compelled to say, some of that "hoity-toity" which had so displeased Mr Askew.

"And now, Mr Jones, you will swear to take this firkin ashore with you and forward it to the right address, remembering that at this solemn moment we are both near that eternal judgement which awaits all men— Good God!"

I must own that this last ejaculation was out of my part however much it was in character. The fact is, years of religious lessons, thousands of church services and the whole mighty engine of the Church rose up behind me and I found it come near to clouting me over the head like a flailing sheet. I did indeed experience a touch of that judgement I had mentioned so frivolously and I did not like it.

"Swear."

Mr Jones, touched possibly by the same feelings, answered tremulously,

"I swear."

Devil take it, this was Hamlet and I felt downright uneasy! I could not but feel that the ghost of Colley was roaming the ship. Well—we were in mortal danger, and the mind plays tricks.

"And Mr Jones, if we should survive you will buy the cask back for what I gave for it—I'm odd like that, you know!"

Now it has to be added that if the ship was in a perilous state and I in a strange one, her company were in even stranger case. As if Mr Jones and Cumbershum between them had released among us something until then bound in and confined, the happiness of our "happy ship" changed in quality and became what I can only call a communal hysteria. Nor was it woman-ish as the word suggests. At its worst and most severe it could be typified as a kind of uncontrollable laughter at the most trivial of causes. At its best it was a pecu-liarly British sense of fun, of play. There was a little coldness in it, a contempt for life, even a touch of savagery. It came to me that at its best it might be something like that humour said to prevail among the victims of the French Terror before their martyrdom. At its worst it had something of the blasphemy, wild humour, debauchery and fury which sometimes erupts in Newgate Gaol when the wretches confined there hear the last confirmation of their fate. I suppose, too, there were men and women who prayed. For by now there was not a man, woman or child who did not know in what a sad case we stood. The dragrope took off more weed and the business was finished but I do not believe many of the passengers or emigrants took much notice. By now we all saw too clearly.

So much, then, for the efforts at concealing the state

of the ship from all but the naval officers! I thought my own joke was now over, but the truth is it got out of hand. Mr Gilland, the cooper, asking nothing for the service, loosened the bands of the firkin and knocked out the head. I placed the journal intended for my godfather inside and this same folio with it. But I had not realized how widely all was known. Good God, hardly a passenger or an emigrant but wished to have some message included, some small package, some object, a ring, a bauble, a book—a journal!—something, anything which whatever it was would seem by its survival to prolong a vestige of life. This is how people are, but if I had not had the experience I would never have believed it. Indeed so general was the demand for space in my firkin that Charles Summers was driven to protest, though amiably enough.

"My dear Edmund! You have so many clients that Webber who ought to be looking after the rest of the wardroom has become little more than your doorman!"

"What am I to do? The thing has become a bore and thoroughly out of hand."

"You are now the most popular man in the ship."

"If anything were needed to convince me of the volatility of the common people—"

"Speaking for us common people—"

"Charles, I will have no more of this modesty! I shall live to see you an admiral yet!"

"I will have it piped through the ship that papers may be brought to Mr Talbot but only during the first dog. The thing will die off in a day or two."

He went off to continue his preparations for the "frapping".

There was I, then, sitting like Matthew at the seat of custom for two hours a day. I do seriously believe that during one short period and before I had dressed him down, Webber was actually charging admission! Like the ghost of Colley, the spirit of Mr Jones was abroad. Nevertheless the great majority of those who came were simple souls. They divided sharply into two groups. There were those who giggled and hoped to share the jest against Mr Jones. There were those who were only too sadly in earnest. The white line which had been drawn across the deck at the mainmast was now, it seemed, washed clean away. I was to find this more than a simple fact—it was indeed a metaphor of our condition! But more of that at a later date. Suffice it to say my visitors were many and various. It might be a poor emigrant, his hat in one hand, his paper in the other, or a sniggering tar holding out an inch of his own queue or pigtail with the hope that I was "making the bugger sweat, sir". Indeed my cask soon began to resemble the "bran tub" which we children used to enjoy at Christmas. God knows, in that ship we could have done with any enjoyment we could get!

I must say also that among the other frivolities which rose so preposterously from our danger was a series of catch phrases. A part of watch ordered by a petty officer to pick up a rope or the like would reply as one man—"Aye aye. We're odd like that, you know!" There was even one occasion—and here I must implore the ladies, for after all poetry is their proper speech and prose means nothing to them—I must ask them to avert their eyes from the following paragraphs.

Mr Taylor appeared noisily with even more than his

usual high spirits. He could not stop laughing until I shook him. Knowing Mr Taylor I was prepared to hear of some monstrous piece of misfortune which had befallen someone and which seemed to him the height of comedy—but no. When at last I got him quiet and he had recovered from my shaking I demanded to know the worst.

"It's a riddle, you see, sir!"

"A riddle?"

"Yes, sir! What—" but having got that far humour was too much for him and he had to be shaken again.

"Now then, my lad, finish what you have to say before I throw you overboard."

"Sir. The riddle is: 'What makes the ship roll so?'"

"Well, what makes the ship roll so?"

We had another convulsion before he got out the answer.

"Lord Talbot's firkin!"

I dropped the boy and returned to my hutch. If the result of peril was to lower the ship to that level, I thought, she has no need to sink but has done so already.

After I had sat for a dog watch without a "client" I asked for Mr Gilland, the cooper, and summoned Mr Jones. When they were together before me I had Mr Gilland replace the lid and put back the bands. They were, I said, witness to the security of the container. I had the bung left open though the rest of the cask was sealed. I explained to Mr Jones that I might want to insert some dying wish or prayer when we were foundering and before he himself left the vessel. I must confess the joke had become tedious. It

even turned sour when I contemplated all that remained of Edmund Talbot bouncing round the Southern Ocean in circumstances where its chances of
reaching the desired destination would be small beyond
computation! More than that, I found myself suddenly
deprived of my journals and with nothing to write or
do except endure the antics and threat of our increasingly unseaworthy vessel.

The reader will have grasped that I, at least, survived
the voyage. But like any possible reader, when I reread
what I had written, the abrupt end of my journal—call
it "book two"—troubled me and does so now. Indeed,
to call it a journal is to stretch the term unduly. An
attentive reader may well be able to identify the widely
separated occasions on which I tried to describe what
had happened during a period of days and so bring the
thing up to date. I was often writing of the past when
much was happening at the moment. A considerable
length of time separates the ending of my journal
proper and this *postscriptum*. I have been tempted to
avoid the problem of the too abrupt ending by continuing the journal retrospectively so to speak, pretending
to have written it in the ship. But the distance in time
is too great. The attempt would be disingenuous. More
—it would be plain dishonest. Worse than that if it
were possible the attempt would be detected, for the
style—I flatter myself I have a style, however thread-
bare—would change. Immediacy would be lost. When
I reread "book one"—in the *next* volume you will find
out when and why that was!—I found it had gained a
great deal by the inclusion of Colley's affecting if
unfinished letter. For though the poor fellow may not

have been much of a priest there was a touch of genius
in his vivid and fluent use of his native tongue: whereas
"book two" must rely on my own unaided efforts except where I report the actual words of other people. It
is true, however, that what I now think to have been
an ingenuous opening of my heart to the page is not
without a force which I did not suspect until I came to
read it much later. But to return to the head of this
paragraph. To add this *postscriptum* seemed the most
reasonable solution to my difficulty.

Yet a properer and lengthier description of the remainder of our voyage still remains desirable. In my
memory the voyage is a single thing, with a beginning,
a middle and an end. Our further adventures were no
less and perhaps more arduous than the preceding
ones. Honesty compels me to promise a plain narrative
at some later date which will see the voyage ended and
which narrative shall be my "book three". I cannot
pretend to Colley's talent and hope that the strange-
ness and hazard of the events will compensate for the
plainness of the writing.

There is another consideration. I am in half a mind
to publish! Perhaps then these words may be read not
just by those dear to me but by a far wider audience.
The desire of print has grown on me. What began at
my godfather's behest proceeded by my own growing
inclination and I now find myself no more or less than
a common writer with all the ambitions if not all the
failings of that breed. I put this very point to Mr
Brocklebank during the highest days of our hilarity,
confessing that I felt myself insufficiently dissolute for

the profession, to which he replied in his voice rotten as a medlar—"My dear sir! Continue to drink as you do and you will carry all before you!" I need hardly say he was deeply in his cups on that occasion as on so many others. But may it not be that a man of breeding, education and intelligence will lend the profession a little of the dignity our hack-writers have taken from it?

Failings? I admit to ambitions. To be printed is the smallest of them! Come, my dear reader, who has ever written without the desire to communicate? We assume a reader of our words even when we use them to deny his existence. I will go further. Who has ever written extensively without finding himself lured little by little into the desire to captivate an audience? There is in me, as in all writers, what Milton called "that last infirmity of noble mind", the desire for a name more widely known, admiration more generously given, for a greater measure of interest in the author's character and person on the part of the Sex. So though I have sometimes said and often thought that I wrote only for myself I have more often wondered *to whom* I was writing—my Lady Mother, or Another, or an old school friend, his face remembered, his name forgotten. I have also found myself envisaging with gusto the three splendid volumes of *Talbot's Voyage* or *The Ends of the Earth!* All this then to apologize to a conjectural audience which may have been startled by the abruptly ended journal of "book two" but may be mollified and excited as much as I can contrive by this "puff" for a third volume!